18·06·07

SWAMP FE

Memories of Jakaka'.

Happy Birthday,
          dear Margaret.

Love Joyce and Jocku

SWAMP FEVER
A Golden Bay Memoir

Gerard Hindmarsh

CRAIG
POTTON
PUBLISHING

First published in 2006 by Craig Potton Publishing
98 Vickerman Street, PO Box 555, Nelson, New Zealand
www.craigpotton.co.nz

© Gerard Hindmarsh

ISBN 10: 1-877333-61-1
ISBN 13: 978-1-877333-61-3

Edited by Mike Bradstock
Printed by Astra Print, Wellington, New Zealand

The author has asserted his moral rights in the work.

CONTENTS

This book is dedicated to the memory of
Cole William Chick
1986–2006

You came into our family's life for such a short time.
But we will remember you forever

ACKNOWLEDGMENTS

There are so many people in Golden Bay to whom I am thankful for sharing their personal tales, both serious and hilarious. Hearing them brought home what a lucky man I am, to be involved long term with such a clan of richly spirited friends. If you think you recognise someone, you're probably bang on. I've only changed a few names, specifically where they relate to incidents of an illegal nature. I do appreciate the fact that my past and present associates have, unlike me, nothing to gain from airing their dirty linen.

I am grateful for the written sources from which I have gleaned bits here and there to fill in gaps, including *A Hard Won Freedom, Alternative Communities in New Zealand* by Tim Jones and Ian Baker, which so articulately brought back for me the *zeitgeist* of the early 1970s with all its untamed drifts and feelings. *Nga Uruora, The Groves of Life* by Geoff Park, made me realise how limited my ecological and historical perspectives were on Whanganui Inlet. I have used the names Whanganui Inlet, Westhaven, West Whanganui and Westhaven Inlet more or less interchangeably for the harbour lying immediately south of Cape Farewell, because these names are all in common use.

To Len and Ruth Leov, who lived at Greville Harbour; I will always be in awe of your two decades of tenacity and determination to drain the great Greville Swamp of D'Urville Island. Special thanks also to their son, Fred Leov, for sharing their story. I first became aware of that account in Olive Baldwin's *Story of New Zealand's French Pass and d'Urville Island (Book 3)*.

It was wonderful to stumble across Elizabeth Caldwell's nineteenth century account of her fascinating life at Tukurua in *The Adventures of Pioneer Women in New Zealand* by Sarah Ell.

To all the news and feature reporters of the *Nelson Evening Mail* and *The Dominion*, especially Paul Bensemann; your coverage during the 1980s dope-growing era provided a most wonderful source of information. My collection of clippings at the time certainly paid off on this subject.

Finally, thanks to my editor, Mike Bradstock, for putting me right in more than a few places; and to my publisher, Robbie Burton, for encouraging me to throw caution to the wind and tell it exactly the way it happened.

INTRODUCTION

Everyone has a favourite place, some special, almost magical space that seems to resonate with them and provide shelter and nurture. More often than not, it's somewhere in nature. Some prefer being perched atop a high mountain where they can feel the cool crisp air upon their faces and look expansively all around. Others cite a wild West Coast beach, where their bare feet can bask in the last lick and spume of a mighty ocean wave attenuated against the shore. Some like a quiet bush-clad valley, while the seriously stressed-out brigade usually visualise themselves participating in seven tight days of vacation freedom, doing little more than lying under coconut palms along the white sand and turquoise waters of the tropics.

None of these places is a favourite of mine. At the age of almost 50, I have come to the point where I will cheerfully confess that my natural place is standing fair and square in a good swamp. I purposely do not use the word 'wetland' here. That is a modern word invented by the ecologically correct to categorise everything from bogs to mires, fens to flushes, marshes to seeps. Just give me a good old swamp and I will feel quite at home. Where I can feel the sticky mud oozing between my toes; where I can appreciate the faint stench of sulphur rising up to my nostrils and watch the slow flow of tannin-discoloured waters; where I can creep slowly among the strange plants and animals that take refuge there; where I can strain to hear the almost-inaudible drone of the mosquito, the soft single *click* of a distant fernbird. Call me mad, but this is the type of place that I'm nurtured by and that makes me feel whole again. Unencumbered. Primal. Receptive enough to be overwhelmed by these subtle displays of nature.

Really, this should all be no surprise. It's even in my surname, Hindmarsh, which can be traced all the way back to a humble man named John, around AD 1066 when William the Conqueror ordered his subjects to come up with surnames. This particular John, my earliest-known forebear, could not draw on his primary occupation for a name, like Miller, Cooper, or Baker. He had to use a name based on his place of residence, and living tucked in be-*hind* the common *marsh* of Northumberland town, he became John Hindmarsh. It was conveniently his name and address in one.

Forty-three generations later, my journalist father proudly considered it his duty to remind me of this fact, but with a hidden appendage of advice that he delivered to all my siblings as well: never ever give any Hindmarsh child a first name beginning with B. Anyone called B. Hindmarsh would be teased mercilessly at school. I got the message early: know your roots for sure, but be careful associating the family name with primal swamps, especially bum ones.

So you can imagine how horrified I was then when 'Bumswamp' took off as my nickname at school. I nipped it in the bud with a few well-directed blows to selected perpetrators' noses, exactly as my otherwise gentle mother had advised. Never hurt 'God's poor defenceless creatures' such as the birds and insects which did us no harm, she had always said. But when it came to defending yourself from those who sought to subjugate, including name-calling bullies, then the rules went out the window.

I was amazed how easy it had been to silence them. Soon after my arrival at school on that decisive day, the ringleader bully-boy began calling me 'Bumswamp'. Next thing he was on his knees, nursing a bloody nose, never to utter the B word ever again – not to my ears, anyway. I had to bend over and get three cuts of the strap for it from a bottom-loving Marist brother, but it was a small price to pay. Victory or not, however, I knew from that moment on that I could never escape the fact that I was descended from an Old English marsh dweller. Perhaps it was for no other reason that I made the conscious decision at age 19 to settle beside a swamp, just as that ancestor of mine found himself 43 generations before.

CHAPTER 1

THE NEST

It was a defining moment for me. The shocking realisation that in all my life to date, I had been nothing less than a brute. Here before us was the living proof. Cleverly secreted in a bowl of tufted rushes and surrounded by dense tanglefern: the finely woven nest of a fernbird. Three hours of meticulous searching had left ornithologist Graeme Elliott and myself both seriously scratched by scrub and muddied well above our knees, but finally we had found it. Using both his hands Graeme parted the vegetation as we craned our necks to look inside the nest, deeper but little bigger than an eggcup. Neatly arranged within, and partly obscured by a necklace of tiny feathers, were three speckled, pinkish eggs, each no bigger than the nail of my index finger.

'What a find!' Graeme whispered excitedly. 'Hardly anyone gets to see a fernbird nest. Incubation for these birds is only twelve-and-a-half days and they nest only in dense swampland. There's just not many left around here, because all the coastal swamps in Golden Bay have been drained. Yours is one of the last.'

In the scrub beside us, the concerted, concerned *click, click, click* of the parent birds indicated they were closing in on us, the intruders.

'We'd better go,' said Graeme. 'If we disturb them too long, they might abandon the nest.' I gazed at the little eggs for the last time, unable to conjure up in my mind anything but the image of the bright orange 12-tonne Hitachi digger which I had booked to drain my swamp, and which was scheduled to start early the next morning. This was in January 1978. It was then that I knew that in all my 21 years, I had been nothing less than a brute.

Over a late-evening barbecue and a few drinks back at my home that night, Graeme told me all about the thesis on fernbirds he was doing at Canterbury University, and in the process gave me a crash-course in swamp biodiversity. 'Swamps like yours are just full of life,' he told me passionately. 'Probably a hundred times the number of species you'd expect to find in an equivalent area of grass, and more even than in rainforest.'

I was already a keen back-to-the-land homesteader, not to mention an avid deershooter and tramper of the backblocks, but I had never heard anyone talk about ecology like this before. It resonated immediately with me, as though I had been waiting years for such a revelation. After Graeme left on his trail-bike that evening, I sat out on my little deck, looking out over Golden Bay, and watched a perfectly full porcelain moon rise out of the shimmering water, and four times a minute, the flicker of Farewell Spit lighthouse just off to the left. It was quarter past eleven, too late to ring anyone, but still I picked up the phone and dialed the number scrawled under the next day's date on my calendar.

'Colin, sorry to wake you, mate,' I said to the groggy digger driver. 'I'm cancelling your digger tomorrow.'

He didn't care: he had months of work booked ahead. 'Whatever ... but once this dry spell breaks, mate, you'll never get another chance like this.'

'Yeah, I know, it's just that ... well ...' I thought about telling him about the dainty fernbird nest but decided against it. He was the sort of guy who called a drink a beer, a kahikatea a 'kaik', and a pukeko a 'bukaki'. 'Guess I just changed my mind,' was the best I could come up with.

So began my love affair with the swamp. There was no point babbling about my new infatuation to anyone. My father's advice still applied: don't advertise, someone might get the wrong idea. This was one affair that had to remain totally clandestine, for the time being anyway.

Everything I heard and read at the time reinforced that too. I was already working as a heavy-haulage driver for Solly's Freight, whose depot was up the valley at Rockville. The name of this rural locale was derived from its spectacular limestone rock formations, the best example being the so-called Devil's Boots, on the track to the Aorere goldfields. I have to confess the name Rockville always made me think of Bedrock, the town in *The Flintstones*, even if it was nothing like it. Rockville might have had a few quarries worked by men with old-as-dinosaur machinery, but mostly it was populated by a close-knit pack of cow-cockies. The Rock-villains, I called them.

Working at Solly's Freight, I got the Rock-villains' clover-and-ryegrass mentality pushed in my face like stale custard pie every week. But they were not alone in wanting to turn 'useless jelly-dirt' into profitable grazing land. Back in the 1970s, hardly anyone in the whole country could be expected to appreciate a swamp. Everyone hated them, except for a handful of ecology-orientated scientists and emerging 'greenie' environmentalists, all considered by the general populace to be half crazy.

Draining 'useless' swamps for pasture was seen as a good, even noble thing to do. What agrarian reader in New Zealand could have missed all the celebration about the Kongahu? This huge sprawling basin just south of Karamea had once been one of the largest swamps in the country. Vast and twisting, it was 1200 hectares of flax, raupo and rushes – after its original canopy of tall kahikatea trees got cut down first. Looking down onto it from vantage points in the Karamea Forest, it was all big brush, swathes of colour stretching as far as the eye could see. So it got drained too, and was hailed in 1978 as the ultimate victory for government-funded regional development.

The *New Zealand Farmer* ran a big story headlined 'How the Mighty Kongahu got Conquered'. It was a piece of triumphalist journalism describing the incredible five-year effort that had gone into draining one of the country's last great lowland swamps. Halfway down the second column, the writer got in a passing scoff: 'A 2.5 acre reserve around a side creek, where it is speculated that some species of whitebait return every year to breed, has been reserved to keep a handful of "outsider" environmental activists happy.'

An impressive photo showed a gargantuan digger at work, rafted upon huge pontoons to keep it from sinking out of sight, its giant arm gouging deep into the swirling mud. The caption said it all: 'After a century of attempts, the great wasteland that was once the Kongahu has finally been reclaimed.'

Everyone was in on these development ventures. Nearby, the New Zealand Forest Service had just napalmed a vast area of pristine rainforest in the Oparara Basin so it could plant the incongruous patches of largely unmillable exotic trees that exist there today. This action, ostensibly to create a few extra jobs (which it didn't), succeeded in securing a few local votes but prompted rabid criticism nationwide.

Ironically, it was the Kongahu story that I had followed with greater interest. Not, at the time, out of any environmental concern, but because maybe I could learn a trick or two. Before Graeme Elliott had come along, I too had wanted to 'conquer' my big bog and turn it into pasture. It was part of my plan to become a self-sufficient homesteader.

This urge had not come overnight, but it did come early. Although I was born and raised a city boy, in Berhampore, Wellington, both my mother's brothers, Tony and Les Moleta, were highly successful market gardeners at Opiki, along the Manawatu River, where we would often visit on weekends. I always felt at home on their sprawling spud paddocks interspersed with lush-growing grass as far as the eye could see. I cannot recall reaching any of their boundaries: to me as a kid, their lands seemed to stretch forever. Like much of the Horowhenua, this plain had been reclaimed from swamp forest, burnt off and deeply drained during the late 19th and early 20th centuries. But it was all still consolidating: every year my uncles had to pull out more of the stumps that erupted like big pimples throughout their paddocks. They used wheeled and crawler tractors, and explosives to loosen the largest. Piled up, the stumps made tremendous bonfires that would then smoulder for weeks.

I loved running from one paddock to the next, swinging on the wooden gates, calling their racehorses then chasing them off to see them fling turfs high into the air with their hooves as they galloped away. Exploring the woolshed, I would let the sweet, fetid smell overtake me before breaking free to jump the long lines of ditches. Although completely flat, that former swamp country, still sinking, oozed magic for me.

Then, at age 15, I had another formative experience, or a 'life prompt' as psychologists call it. My older brother John took me to stay with his friends in Nelson, who were living in an abandoned Catholic convent boarding school once called Sunnybank, but which they had renamed Garindale, at Whakapuaka, just out of town. This property fascinated me: its rabbit warren of weatherboard buildings, the old chapel, ablution blocks with overkill numbers of stained handbasins and showers, its paint-peeling corridors and classrooms, and the long block of cubicle quarters.

The place was occupied by an extended family collectively called the Dromgools. Chris and Jacq Dromgool had two pre-school children of their own, but these humanitarian-minded folks had, with the assistance of Catholic Social Services, added eight stray boys to their flock. The idea was to offer these delinquent or 'at-risk' boys the experience of living in a stable home for the first time in their lives. This was good in theory, but you can't expect a leopard to change its spots, especially a teenage one. Every day the well-meaning Dromgools seemed to become embroiled in some new drama. The day before I arrived, one of their charges, 12-year-old William, had escaped to Wellington by air. He had marched confidently into the NAC office on the corner of Trafalgar and Halifax Streets, clutching to his chest a big glass jar of coins taken from piggybanks in houses he'd ripped off just that morning biking into town. But as he neared the counter, William tripped on the mat, spewing the coins everywhere. The staff rushed to help him pick up his booty, then unsuspectingly sold him a window seat ticket for the next flight out. He enjoyed a week of freedom, before being spotted walking down a Lower Hutt street by a former teacher who threw him in the back seat and arranged for him to be sent back to Nelson.

This was my initiation into a truly 'alternative' family. It was the first time I had ever heard that word used to describe a lifestyle, to mean that they were different from the rest of society. In a sense, what I witnessed was communal living, but with only one set of parents. The Dromgools could have opted for the relatively easy life of bringing up their two children on their own, but they had made a conscious choice to extend themselves in a creative and compassionate way. As I thought about it, I saw that by comparison, the nuclear family was exclusive and possessive, not to mention subject to domination and submission.

Suddenly I was experiencing an alternative family that expected co-operative effort, and not without reward either. The Dromgools were running their 20-hectare church estate as a highly productive farmlet, producing virtually all their food. Two house cows, three pigs, ten sheep, a gaggle of geese and a henhouse full of fowls not only all appeared to thrive under their care, but supplied a spectacular bounty of fresh produce as well. From bacon to freshly clotted jersey cream, hand-ground cereals to bright yellow-yoked free-range eggs, beef jerky to organic chicken meats – every breakfast, lunch and dinner table was full of the fruits of the land. Everyone was expected to help, and in doing so to stay out of trouble, even if it didn't always work out that way!

In that marvellous week, the hard-working, well-meaning if long-suffering Dromgools introduced me to land husbandry concepts like growing potatoes under a mulch of straw, companion cropping, and simple complementary feed-management practices like giving the skim milk from the cows to the pigs and food scraps to the chooks. Nothing was wasted. Everything was so basic that it needed minimal explanation to make good sense to me. I left there thinking this was how I wanted to live: simply, and without the stresses of city life.

Returning to school after that holiday, I continued to get excellent grades, but simply could not stand the confinement. Halfway through the sixth form I couldn't put up with it any longer, and walked out of a particularly boring assembly at St Patrick's College, headed directly for the corrugated iron perimeter fence and risked my balls jumping over the jagged top edge to freedom. Even several priests screaming, 'Hindmarsh! Come back NOW!' could not stop me.

Within a month I had a job as a cartographic cadet for the Lands and Survey Department, seconded to the Department of Scientific and Industrial Research. My elderly relations all rang to compliment me on securing a position in the Public Service, insinuating that I had been lucky to secure a 'job for life'. Initially I found the work stimulating, but being desk-bound soon got to me, even if our department had been chosen to trial the new system of working flexible hours known as glide time. This we immediately learned to fudge, so that on paper we were accumulating so much 'time in lieu' that we could take two days off a fortnight. Then, of course we also had paid sick leave, fifteen days a year that we treated as additional annual leave and planned into our itineraries.

'Maybe you should take the day off?' Chief Cartographer Francis Tindall suggested one day to one of his draughtsmen who had had a heavy night out drinking and was looking greener by the hour. 'No thanks,' the young man replied, 'I don't want to waste any of my sick leave.'

Unlike the majority of other well-behaved civil servants, certain individuals in our division really pushed the limits. One man used the job as a front for his pirate music-taping business, running multiple tape decks on his desk and using the darkroom to manufacture labels. Another openly made car-tyre sandals on his desk. Some routinely germinated dope seeds on the windowsills. We all had lots of fun, but overall the place reeked of unattained dreams. I could not help noticing that all the older members of the office had big fat bottoms from sitting on their draughting stools so much, and that most of them expressed frustrated regrets, wondering what kind of a better life they could have had. Suddenly my 'job for life' seemed nothing short of a life sentence.

For three years I put up with working on the third floor of the appropriately named Cubewell House (it really was like a big box!) on Kent Terrace in downtown Wellington. Then in 1976, at age 19, I began seriously looking for a piece of suitable rural land. I was not alone in my thinking either. Clare, my girlfriend, who worked as a technician for the Dairy Board, was also eager to strike for freedom, not to mention several of my workmates. In fact, four of the 20-odd staff in my office would eventually end up opting for the homesteading life in Golden Bay.

Finding the land we wanted was a mission. We spent months of lunchtimes in the Wellington Public Library reading-room checking out properties for sale in all the daily newspapers. Land was still dirt cheap in many provinces around rural New Zealand. Any time a bargain caught my eye I would follow it up later at work by checking it on a map. I had not randomly chosen cartography as a career. Ever since I was a young boy, my father had noticed that I was good with maps, and encouraged me to have as much contact with them as I could. He even taught me how to fold them back together properly (something surprisingly few people ever learn to do). I grew up regarding maps not just as simple tools with a language expressed in two dimensions, but as objects with a life of their own, like the land itself, and worthy of great respect. Good maps could speak to me; in fact they still do. For me they have always been the first line of information-gathering about a place – ahead of *Encyclopedia Britannica* or *Longmans' Larousse*.

So it was natural that the first thing I should do after spotting in *The Dominion* a small three-line advertisement, 'For sale, 14 acres in Golden Bay,' was to race back to work and dig out the appropriate map. The asking price of $7,800 was cheap compared with other sections nearby, but I soon saw why when I looked at the 1:15,840 (four inches to the mile) topographic map of the area. Snaking right up through the middle of the property was an unmistakable swathe of swamp symbols, sandwiched between the contour lines that swept around both sides of a steep gully.

Swampland is marked on maps by a patch of little symbols, blue tufts of vegetation and dashed horizontal blue lines, which have always inspired in me that strong and exciting sense of *terra incognita*. Those symbols imply Indiana Jones territory: unexplored and unknown. A swathe of swamp symbols on a map conjures up to me a warning: Do not enter unprepared. Here be dragons. Ancient mapmakers used to embellish the unexplored interiors of continents with such warnings. But today the world is all discovered, although until recently there was still the occasional small blank patch marked 'Obscured by clouds' on a few maps, even in New Zealand.

You may think me a little affected in saying this, but I know I am not alone. In their subconscious at least, map aficionados appreciate the significance of borders: the way they confine, define, and challenge. Avner Falk, an Israeli clinical psychologist who studied the relationship between maps and the mind, regards borders on a map not just as lines on a bit of paper, but rather as powerful psychological metaphors. 'The crossing of that border, even if it's just in the mind, symbolizes transgressing against moral commands or trespassing into forbidden territory.' This is a view that truly resonates with me and others who love poring over maps: they bring out the inner explorer in us.

The NZMS 252 topographic map I looked at that day gave me heaps of other clues too as to the nature of what I immediately suspected could be my future home. Like the pale green shading of cut-over or secondary bush on both sides of the swamp, and the single word 'pakihi' in 6-point type overlaid on open land nearby. Pakihi is land with an impervious ironpan layer below the surface, meaning it drains poorly and is sour and infertile. I began to visualise the landscape features of those 14 acres. First and foremost, I saw a snaking swamp surrounded by scrubby hills, with a flat-topped knoll looking down upon the impoverished soils of its drier parts. Along one side, a little creek trickled through a ribbon of bush that came out of the vast Northwest Nelson Forest Park. It was exactly what I wanted.

Without hesitation, I took the next day off work, drove my Hillman Avenger on to the 5.20 am Picton ferry, and made the four-and-a-half-hour drive to Takaka in time to meet the real estate agent by 1 pm. Within a few hours I had my offer accepted and typed up, and was able to drive back to Picton just in time for the 10.20 pm ferry back to Wellington. Quite a day! Standing on the knoll overlooking that swamp and out to sea had filled me with a sublime feeling of coming home. I had seen it all before of course, *déjà vu*, resonating out of that map.

My older brother John accompanied me on this trip, and later confessed his reason was to talk me out of it on behalf of my family, who thought a move to the backblocks was not wise. I had listened to his arguments all morning, but once I saw the land my mind was made up. I just had to get him to stop arguing, so after eating a banana for lunch, I held up the empty skin and said to him, 'John! I'll tell you what: let's let the banana decide. I'll throw this empty banana skin up in the air. If it lands inside-skin-up, I'll buy the land. If it lands inside-skin-down, I won't.' He thought about this for a few seconds, then to my amazement agreed.

I threw the banana. It landed inside-skin-up, meaning I could buy the land. The deal was done. I felt victorious at having settled the argument so easily. Years later though, I confessed to him that I had always noticed that a banana skin tends to land inside-skin-up when tossed high. I think the weight of the stalked end pulls it down so that it usually lands that way. Also I confessed to him that if it had landed outside-up, I would have bought the land anyway. We still laugh about that 'banana oracle'.

And so it was that in 1976, at the age of 19, I threw in my career as a draughtsman and put my entire $2,000 savings down as a deposit on 5.6 hectares of pakihi scrubland and swamp at Tukurua, in Golden Bay.

CHAPTER 2

DROPPING OUT

The next morning, on arriving back at work in Wellington, I handed in my resignation, and Clare did the same the following day. She hadn't even seen the property, just the black-and-white photos I had developed and printed off on my father's old enlarger on the night I returned. But she was as keen as me, in fact ecstatic to be escaping the city too. In two months' time we would be living in Golden Bay; that gave us enough time to tie up all our loose ends, pack up and, last but not least, get married – a move mainly designed to keep our families happy and perhaps legitimise what seemed to many at the time rather a drastic action for a young couple.

Eagerly we threw out everything that we thought would be of no use in our new life, and packed up the rest on the back of my Series 2A Land Rover pickup. On went a bunch of second-hand tools, nails, old window frames, an old treadle sewing machine, preserving jars, a coal range scored from my farming relatives in Opiki, a big roll of copper wire, a few sea-worn posts beachcombed along the Makara coast, a Tilley lamp, a small drum of kerosene, an oak barrel, three alloy cream cans from a scrap-metal dealer, and an assortment of books and manuals about homesteading. On top of all this, some beams of timber straddled the oversized load. Looking back, it was all crazy stuff. The deckhands on the inter-island ferry *Aramoana* pointed and laughed outrageously at us as we drove up the rear ramp for the one-way journey to a new life in our new home. But we didn't care: we had so much to look forward to.

Our first view together of Golden Bay unfolded as we rounded the hairpin bend just over the summit of the Takaka Hill. That gloriously welcoming scene of the Kahurangi Mountains sliding into a sublime sea has been enjoyed by generations of motorists, and is also the subject of Colin McCahon's iconic painting *Night and Day*. Golden Bay got its name from the precious metal that precipitated New Zealand's first gold rush, on the Aorere River in 1857, but today it is synonymous with the long, lazy swerve of golden-sand beaches that arch around to Farewell Spit.

For the first few weeks on our land at Tukurua, we lived in a little two-person tent atop the knoll. Stunted manuka trees protected us from the westerly winds, but not from the rain, which came down in buckets. Golden Bay's annual rainfall is about three times that of Wellington. It felt so raw, waking up to the throaty roar of a swollen creek on one side and a gushing swamp on the other. Atop our little knoll, we felt as though we were stranded upon a desert island.

Our presence was greeted with delight by the dedicated band of at least 14 resident weka, or woodhen, an inquisitive species of flightless rail. They would emerge from their little tunnels and tracks in the tanglefern, with a stealthy gait and inquisitive demeanour, always on the lookout for something to steal, particularly anything shiny that they could drag back to their nests. It was impossible to leave anything out: they would even have a go at purloining fairly large objects like shoes or gumboots. All night they would utter their shrill, far-carrying whistle, *coo – eet*, repeated many times. When one started up, all the others in the vicinity would take up the cry until their cascade of sound seemed to be echoing all around the hills. They were never far away though, at night continually pulling at the guy ropes or the opening of our tent. An early European settler in Golden Bay wrote: 'The peculiarity of these birds was their spirit of comradeship. They seemed to look upon man as a harmless and very curious animal.'

As naïve 19-year-olds we had counted on leaving behind all the drop-in annoyances of civilisation like Jehovah's Witnesses and insurance salesmen, the latter in particular drawn to the capital's civil servants like flies to carrion. But to our surprise, both species of human pest turned up during the first week after we arrived. First came the pious husband-and-wife team who spotted our tent from the highway and trudged up the 300-metre muddy track carved by our Land Rover, only to get short shrift. A few days later, the macho insurance man insisted on driving right up to our tent, ripping his exhaust off on a giant boulder in the process. Later, I found both his mudflaps in the mud as well.

It was with some relief that we finished building our 9 by 16 foot weatherboard, weather-proof and weka-proof cabin, complete with the coal range we installed all by ourselves, and moved in. All my lighter tools – rules, pencils, pliers, even the measuring tape – had been stolen by weka during the three weeks the job took. I would be on one side busy building, and they would all be on the other side dragging stuff away. The whole building cost us exactly $960, and that included two new redwood windows and a door that I got a joinery shop in Motueka to knock up.

Our new home felt like luxury, even if the amenities were basic. For months we relied on water from the creek, fetched in hand-drawn buckets twice a day. We had no toilet, not even a long-drop, simply because the pakihi ground was so hard, and the thought of digging any sort of deep hole all the way through the ironpan put me off. If you have to know, whenever we wanted to 'go', we just took the spade from by the door and headed off in any random direction, way out into the scrub. At night it could be as scary as hell. Neither of us had a job, but we felt like millionaires – lifestyle ones, that is: without the money.

We soon found out that in fact our cabin didn't quite stop the weka. They became bolder and bolder, jumping up on to the step if we left the door even slightly ajar, then sneaking in to steal anything that took their fancy. It was as if they were waiting around for us to go out. We ended up playing games with them, leaving the door open and hiding outside to see how long it took them to cotton on to the fact we were gone – invariably only a few minutes. They always entered like stealthy rogues, their little degenerate wing stubs hard back against their bodies making them look as though they had their hands in their pockets. It was always fun to catch these avian criminals in the act. A quick shout or slap of hands would send them in an abrupt 180-degree turn with a flurry of scratching feet on the polished wooden floor before bursting out the door to freedom. I realise now their nocturnal calls were a warning, possibly the last echoes of the flightless rail. However much I cursed them at the time, we missed them terribly when they started disappearing a decade later.

At first, many of the locals treated us with extreme suspicion. Trev along the road was quick to remind me of two Golden Bay 'rules': 'Ya can't call yerself a local till ya been here 25 years. And never ever pay more than two-fifty ($250) an acre for par-kee.'

I could come to terms with the first rule – after all, I had youth on my side – but my still-teenaged mind refused to comprehend his second piece of advice. I had paid just over $500 an acre, more than twice Trev's recommended retail price. But I knew he was referring to the big expanses of undeveloped pakihi terraces, each around a thousand hectares in total, which started just inland of Collingwood and stretched all the way to the Quartz Ranges, which in more primeval times had all been covered in healthy bog forest. Our 14 acres was just a fraction of the usual block-size being offered for sale in Golden Bay, so I figured I couldn't expect such a low price per unit of area. And I still had Wellington in my head, where a miniscule building section was fetching around twice the price I had paid for a hundred times as much land. It seemed too silly for words, and location did not enter into it.

We had made the purchase subject to the provision that I could get a building permit, something that everyone from the real estate agent to the vendor farmer to the clerk at the local council reckoned in a rural zone would be just a routine shift of paperwork. But it didn't go off without a hitch. Almost immediately we received a formal letter of objection from the Ministry of Works and Development, stating they were, as a precedent, objecting to our application. I could not believe what I was reading: 'There is a grave danger, if the present trend continues, of sporadic urban development occurring on a wide scale in Golden Bay County...'

They seemed to be particularly concerned about our location, off State Highway 60 between Takaka and Collingwood: 'The use of the motor vehicle should be recognised particularly where a State Highway is concerned. A proliferation of residences along it will compromise the safe and efficient operation of it as a carrier of arterial traffic.' It was crazy! Where was all this traffic supposed to be going if no one was allowed to live here? And ironically, the letter of objection finished by stating that the population forecast for Golden Bay was abysmal. This backwater of scant meaningful employment was going to shrink even further, from the current 3,000 to under 2,000 by the year 1996, 20 years into the future. How short-sighted and lacking in heart those planners were, basing their models on economic and industrial growth predictions that took no account whatsoever of city-dwellers in search of the good life.

So, all het-up and ready to declare my teenage independence from local bureaucracy, I flew down from Wellington and turned up at the council hearing, where I was at once intimidated by the world of men in suits. Five sworn-in councillors, whom I found out later were just two local Trevs, a couple of Wallys and a Harry, lined the bench, all looking as though they'd come straight out of a Fred Dagg skit.

I didn't find out any of their names at the time, because no one introduced me, so I resorted to remembering them by their defining features. One had a pointy nose, another was bald; one was fat, the next looked like he'd escaped from an old folks' home and might expire any second, while the last wore an obvious toupée.

Opposing me was a man in a particularly flash European-tailored suit, who introduced himself by his full name and somehow added B.Sc., Dip. T.P. to identify himself as a suitably qualified planning officer with the Ministry of Works and Development, based in Wellington.

A big bible was produced, which the male clerk asked me to swear upon. I gave my evidence first, a rambling dissertation about my small-farming plans. Then the man in the flash suit gave his arguments, of which I did not understand a word. First he quoted Section 28C of the Town and Country Planning Act, then Section 28C 3A and so on, until he finished exactly 38 minutes later. But there was one fundamental flaw in this man's argument: he had got the location of our property wrong. Instead he mistakenly described our turnoff as a dangerous spot, an old mill road on a sharp blind bend in the highway. Our actual driveway, some 300 metres further south, had in fact excellent visibility in all directions.

The moment I realised his mistake I wanted to burst into song and play my trump card. Politely I restrained myself and waited for him to finish before I stood up. Surely the council would realise the man from the Ministry had got it all wrong. But before I could get even one word out, I was rudely ordered to sit down.

'You've had your say, sonny,' snapped the councillor with the pointy nose. 'I've just got two questions.'

Number one was directed at me: 'Did you buy this land from Tommy Bennett?'

'Yes,' I replied.

He then turned to his bald-headed fellow councillor with his second question: 'Isn't this purchase dependent on us granting a building permit?'

'Yes,' came the answer.

'Isn't Tommy building a new cowshed, Trev?'

'Yeah, Wally – that's why he subdivided off this bit of rubbish.'

'Think we've heard enough,' said Chairman Harry, banging down his big matai gavel so hard it nearly split the old rimu table. 'You'll both hear from us in due course.'

Three weeks later I got a letter granting me my permit! What the decision was based on, I realised, had nothing at all to do with me or any legal arguments that the man from the Ministry could muster. It was about a bunch of farmers elected as part-time councillors being affronted that a swish man from Wellington had turned up and tried to interfere with the sale of Tommy's useless section. Farmers already had enough interference without another bureaucrat adding to it. The local old boys' network certainly worked in my favour that day.

Suddenly we had overcome the last obstacle to becoming 'alternative lifestylers' like several thousand other individuals around the country at that time who shared the same sentiments and bought cheap 'wasteland'. These people tended to be concentrated into loose clusters in Northland, Coromandel, Westland, Nelson, and for some reason unknown to me at the time, some areas around Christchurch. Most notable was 'Gricklegrass' out at Oxford, which flourished in association with its parent Chippenham community situated in the city itself.

Well documented now, the 'dropouts' making up this nationwide drift were typically described as being in their early twenties, often well educated, idealists, pacifists, individualists, creative, long-haired and resistant to the pressures of social conformity. If they hadn't actually participated in anti-war and civil-rights protests, then as teenagers they would have at least been very aware of them, and that they belonged to a social system that kept creating more problems.

There were alternatives to the suburban-dwelling nuclear family and consumption-orientated permanent employment systems, and for many around this time, homesteading emerged as a viable option. Not the only one though. Many so-called dropouts opted out primarily to become painters and potters, basket and rugmakers, flower or garlic growers, organic farmers, practising pacifists, tree-planters, even possumers. Land was still cheap, or in the case of the ohu communities set up on unoccupied Crown land, available at token leasehold rates from Norman Kirk's benevolent Labour government. The minimum size of an ohu group was eight people, and disused schools, in particular around the North Island, became fair game. All you had to do was apply to the Director-General of Lands in Wellington – and be a New Zealander, a condition they added after refugee hippies started applying from overseas.

Like all new property owners, we enjoyed exploring our land, going off on little forays of investigation to this corner and that. While Clare most enjoyed the more upland part of our property, I came to know every part of our swamp, a snaking primeval bog half a kilometre long and up to 150 metres wide, which had its soggy beginnings in the rain-soaked hinterland of the Northwest Nelson Forest Park (now Kahurangi National Park).

What distinguishes a swamp from, say, an inferior marsh or bog, is the presence of standing or exposed water. In the month I arrived, Tuku-rua Swamp was 10 centimetres deep throughout, flowing imperceptibly through what looked from a distance like a near-impenetrable lushness of flax, ferns and rushes, with the odd cabbage tree protruding like a tuft of unkempt hair. The water half-filled the 1.2-metre-wide culvert where it left my place and flowed under the highway.

People prefer to look at swamps (if they take any notice at all), rather than enter, thinking they will sink out of sight. But venturing in usually proves to be a pleasant surprise. There are usually small raised lumps of ground like stepping-stones, soft but still adequately supporting careful footfalls. Pathways suddenly appear, zig-zagging this way and that through the maze of flax bushes. Because swamp flax can grow over two metres high, it is not always possible to see where you are. The view is tantalisingly just out of reach. Whether you're 10 metres into a swamp or 200, you're in it! Far from feeling lost, when completely surrounded in this fashion I get a cosy feeling of being completely enveloped.

But a word of warning: the presence of fine *Baumea* rushes will provide some discomfort, especially if you are a man. Referred to as 'ball-spikers' by those in the swampy-know, the sharp tips of these otherwise fine and graceful rushes are just the right height to jab up the open inside legs of your shorts as you walk around.

After heavy rain, I enjoyed listening to the gentle rapids gurgling away between the flax bushes, or the soft whooshing at they cascaded down in a series of low waterfalls. But the enticing sound of rushing water was hardly ever matched by a corresponding view. Even in a flood, the swamp seemed to hide everything in its overwhelming pristine lushness. Sometimes though, I would pull back the *Blechnum* ferns to spot a tiny half-metre-long rapid, to my mind as intricate in wonder as any Grade 5 rapid.

The lushness of my swamp contrasted strongly with the vegetation that swathed the gully sides, which were scrubby and comparatively unattractive. A massive fire, purposely lit, had swept through this back country a year before our arrival. 'Mustering with matches', as the back-country farmer who was responsible had described his actions. He, of course, was only guilty of carrying on what paleoanthropologists describe as one of the defining and enduring traits of our species – that hominoids everywhere burn and cut down trees to make savannah. Swathes of dead trees on my land bore witness to where the blaze had jumped clean across the swamp in the howling westerly winds that must have fanned the flames.

No town in New Zealand ever got built without a pall of forest-fire smoke first. But in comparison to Maori, European settlers were late starters, and Golden Bay was no exception. The long-established farming families of the Aorere Valley remember how the burning off of pakihi in the area was already well advanced by the time the first white settlers showed up in Collingwood. The large tracts our Pakeha forebears burned off for farmland were mostly already second-growth. Our Eurocentric history gives us the impression we inherited a primeval landscape inhabited by a few softly-treading Maori living around the edges. In fact those edges were anything but untouched. Humans simply don't like being confined by thick, clammy, cold, overbearing and impenetrable rainforest. They can't grow things, spread out and dry out, or feel secure against the possibility of attack, when the forest is omnipresent and oppressive.

Despite all this, some remnants of bush had survived. I still recall my joy at finding a small grove of regenerating rimu, some as high as a house, tucked into a gully along my back boundary. It was my first hint of what vegetation there had once been along this section of Golden Bay's coastal zone. I took pride in regularly measuring the largest, which reached a diameter of 42 centimetres before a serious slip took out the lot. It all looked like mashed rainforest at the bottom, a horrible orange clay scar searing its way up the hill to where the runoff from an old logging road had caused it to slip away. An example of how human disruption creates more disruption.

There was plenty of that around. Just over my boundary in the forest park was a small clay-extraction operation. A Nelson-based company known then as Potters Clay Ltd had a permit to extract 500 tons a year from each of the two distinct layers of clay that lay just below the powdered silica surface. A New Zealand Geological Survey report on the deposit described the distinctly different yellow and blue layers as the highest-grade kaolin clay in the country. When it was carted to Nelson to be pugged and mixed with various additives, it yielded a porcelain clay which was much in demand. Potters all over the country bought it in 20-kilogram bags, often by the palletload.

A succession of excavations by diggers and loaders around the clay-pit had left the discarded stumps and logs littered around like bleached dinosaur bones. It was easy to identify the wood by a quick slash with a knife: most of it was yellow silver pine (*Lepidothamnus intermedius*), a slow-growing tree once prevalent throughout the ancient bog forests along the western flank of the South Island. Being the most ground-durable of all our native timbers, these trees, which rarely grow higher than 15 metres, were largely chopped down for posts, telegraph poles and railway sleepers, so few stands now survive. Another characteristic of the wood is that even when buried, it remains full of extremely inflammable resin. It was the best firewood around, even if hellishly sparky. Which is why, after every clay excavation, I would drive up and collect the clay-smothered stumps and splintered logs to cut up. Waste not, want not.

Into the rush-filled paddock alongside the highway I introduced half a dozen Romney sheep and a single Jersey house-cow which we named Betsy. Every morning and night we had a milking routine. Suddenly we had gallons of creamy milk to dispose of, so we got a pig as well. Gardening in pakihi land was not so easy, but as we introduced endless Land Rover loads of manure and seaweed it began to slowly produce all the vegetables we needed. Our dream was in some small way starting to come true, but it was obvious that to be truly self-sufficient we would need more grass. That's why I planned to turn my swamp into productive pasture: it would mean I could keep two cows instead of one.

We had no shortage of advice, not only from local farmers and other lifestylers, but from books like *Five Acres and Independence*, *The Cow Economy*, and *The Complete Book of Self-Sufficiency* by John Seymour. These essential manuals we purchased by mail order from Tapui Books, the whereabouts of which we only knew as R.D. 13C, Oamaru. Its owners, whom we also only knew as Bob and Patricia, had bought a few acres of land in North Otago and set up a mail-order bookshop. By means of a chatty newsletter, they promoted their practical books to an alternative nation, and then used their mailing list to help launch Mushroom, a quintessential back-to-the-land magazine that made you see shit in a whole new light.

In preparation for the task of getting so-called 'productivity' from my swamp, I also studied some more conventional texts, boning up on everything I could about soil texture, structure, consistency, porosity and pH. Soil was one subject about which the country libraries had plenty of books, all well leafed through. I learnt all about water movement in saturated soils, permeability interpretation, hydraulic head and hydraulic conductivity. In a little notebook I recorded outflows and determined exact falls by calculating contours, using aerial photos and topographic maps I had brought with me.

However open I was to alternative ideas, in the end pragmatism ruled and explosives became my drainage method of choice. Although I had never actually seen a drain dug through a swamp by explosives, by all accounts it could be extremely effective if done expertly. It left clean ditches and scattered the debris to kingdom come, meaning there were no annoying piles of spoil such as diggers leave behind.

Getting the explosives was easy in those days before we had the whole terrorism thing: it was just a matter of buying what you needed off a local farmer and keeping quiet about it. First I practised on an old lawnmower, blowing it sky-high, then progressed to a car at the local dump, blowing all its doors and roof off. My finale left a crater the size of a small house on an isolated beach. The fun you could have by yourself in those old days!

Then I worked out my blast plan for the swamp: a single line of charges placed in spiked holes half a metre apart in the mud right down the centre line of my proposed channel. Like an excitable boy, I pored over explosives catalogues and came up with the ideal weaponry: A.N. Gelignite '60' cut into lengths of exactly 38 mm should do the trick nicely.

My plan was to excavate a 30-metre section of ditch at a time. Once the charge line was in position I would insert the end of the safety fuse into a No. 6 detonator that I would then crimp and attach to the end of the Cordtex line with insulating tape. The safety fuse would burn at 90 seconds per metre, giving me plenty of time to retreat out of my sticky swamp. Just a few hours' work along each 30-metre section and soon it would all be done.

When the summer of intended explosions did come around, it suddenly stopped raining. It got drier and drier until even the last little muddy pools in my swamp were bone dry. Not good conditions for a swamp terrorist, because hard ground means more blast force is required to excavate. Meanwhile, farmers throughout the country took advantage of one of the driest seasons on record, and the government financial incentives which were then still available, to drain thousands of hectares of swamp. Anyone who had a piece of hitherto undrainably muddy ground was looking for a digger. Which is why Colin moved over 'The Hill' with his big 12-tonne Hitachi digger and began clocking up 18 machine hours a day ditch-digging his way around Golden Bay. Everyone wanted him yesterday, and definitely before the autumn rains started. Suddenly that 'everyone' included me – until Graeme Elliott stepped out of my bog that January morning in 1978 and introduced himself.

'Just let the fernbird come to you,' he told me on his second visit, showing me how to breathe in, at the same time flicking my tongue against the roof of my mouth, to imitate the bird's agitated challenge, a soft but sharply repeated *click, click click*. It worked like magic. First you only saw the branches move, maybe in still airs heard a faint rustle. Then, sure enough, one of the secretive but highly territorial birds would bristle with annoyance from the undergrowth, coming to within metres of us. The fernbird is not much bigger than a sparrow, with a warm brown back streaked with dark brown, and underbelly white with dark brown spots on the throat and breast, a bit like a small thrush. But what most distinguished the fernbird, to me anyway, was its tail feathers, which were spine-like owing to the disconnected barbs of the webs and the dark brown shafts. A creature created in such delicate detail.

These birds can't fly far, 50 metres being exceptional. Why this little bird was so reluctant to take to the open air was quite beyond me. If I had wings and were capable of flight I would surely soar, but the little fernbird prefers to stay hidden, moving foliage as it shuffles in search of the insects that frequent the crannies along the twigs and branches. But when it does take off, its tail feathers hang down almost vertically in flight, a most odd sight.

I would never once have picked the humble fernbird as an inspirational animal, but the more I found out about them, the more they enthralled me. I dug out and read any bird book that mentioned these tiny yet powerfully musical birds. Older books often called them matata, or by their regional names, like Takaki thrush, as they were called around Foveaux Strait. In Golden Bay, fernbirds were known as koropek.

In his reminiscences of 1860s Golden Bay, Harry Washbourn painted a dismal picture for the fernbird after the big burnoffs up the Aorere when thousands of them got burnt up in the flames: 'We thought the little koropeks were exterminated, as they were never seen or heard from for a good many years. Then we saw one in the Tukurua Valley ...' My heart jumped when I read this, realising that my swamp must always have been a refuge for the little birds! Harry continues, 'A few weeks afterwards, passing this place with a friend, I pointed out to him the bush where it had been seen and to our great pleasure we saw a pair of them. Now the country is too bare for any more firing, so they may adapt themselves to the changed circumstance and increase again.'

Fernbirds, brown creepers, whiteheads, yellowheads, grey warblers and Chatham Island warblers. In the bigger context, these little New Zealand birds are just a few of the 380 species that worldwide make up the warbler family, or Sylviidae. Most grow no bigger than 16 centimetres long, but the Australian brown songlark has been recorded at 25 centimetres. But no matter what their size, all warblers are capable of emitting the strangest of notes. Like the rarely-seen grasshopper warbler of Africa, which can throw its extraordinary whirring song like a well-accomplished ventriloquist, or the marsh warbler that can accurately mimic 80 other bird species.

The willow warbler, although just the same size as the stay-at-home fernbird, migrates 12,000 kilometres from northern Europe and Siberia to Africa. The Aldabra warbler, first found in 1967 living on Aldabra Island in the Indian Ocean, may already be extinct as it has not be seen since 1983 despite exhaustive searching by a dedicated international band of ornithologists.

Looking through bird books, I could see that physical differences between warblers could be almost imperceptible. Chiffchaffs and willow warblers look almost identical, and were first distinguished only by their different song patterns. I got to immediately recognise the fernbird call, no matter where I was on the property. It usually consisted of a low and sharp metallic note, sometimes accompanied by a single soft *click*. Rarely, I would be treated to a typically warbled song of around six metallic notes. But pairs travelling through the swamp would keep in touch, one calling *plik* and the other *choot* in such quick succession that it sounded like one bird operating in stereo. A brilliant ploy to warn and stay in immediate touch with each other, not to mention thoroughly confuse any stalking intruders as to their whereabouts.

As my understanding of the swamp's ecosystem and its inhabitants grew, new creatures began to appear that I had barely noticed before. Caught out in an open patch of low rushes, a solitary brown bittern froze absurdly just metres from me, pointing its bill skyward. The bittern is another bird of the marshes, about the size and shape of a heron but much less conspicuous. It has a skulking habit, and is well camouflaged when standing in its surveillance posture, when the eyes are able to look all around it at once. With a sudden burst of broad, rounded wings, neck tucked in, it rose, legs dangling, crying a single *cr-a-ak* in alarm as it fled into the air.

I once read that the resonating, booming call of the male bittern, made following an audible intake of air, can be heard up to five kilometres away, usually in the late evenings during July to February, which is breeding season. Most likely not one but a pair nested in my swamp, and Graeme advised me how to find them: 'Watch for them soaring and spiralling directly over their nest. On the ground, listen for a bubbling call accompanied by a distinct flute-like note as the female approaches her nest.' There was nothing this man didn't seem to know about birds.

One March morning I was excited when a white heron, or kotuku, made a guest appearance from its usual haunt in nearby Parapara Inlet. This one had recently migrated from its breeding colony near Okarito. These exquisite birds, no more than 250 in number, disperse after their summer breeding season to live, often alone, for the winter in little inlets all around New Zealand. Kotuku means 'bird of single flight', implying it was a creature to be seen perhaps once in a lifetime, and a symbol of things beautiful and rare. Which is why the Maori used to try and catch them, to pull out all their elegant plumes and incarcerate the birds in a supplejack cage so they would grow some more. I always wondered how these birds could keep so absolutely spotless, until I found out that special feathers on the heron's breast and rump crumble into a powdery substance which the bird rubs into its plumage to remove dirt and fish slime. It's as though this fussy white bird has its own built-in stain remover.

All summer and autumn Graeme Elliott continued his groundbreaking research into fernbirds around Golden Bay, working out through tedious observation that a single pair maintained a vigorously defended breeding territory of about a hectare around each nest. He could determine this by mimicking or playing tape recordings of their challenging call. Graeme would entice out opposing birds, which would then squabble among the branches until one would retreat back. The fernbird would always storm out to the edge of its territory to see the invader off, but rarely cross over, so it was possible to mark out the exact boundaries of each pair's territory. Sometimes the pair would police these boundaries together.

Drawn over an aerial photograph of my swamp, these territories looked like a well-defined subdivision plan with a narrow buffer zone between each 'section' and the next. This explained why I never saw fernbirds in groups. Their relationship was exclusively exclusive. Once established, they kept to their patch and would not tolerate any intrusion, particularly from other fernbirds, or in my case anyone imitating one.

I can still call up a fernbird in my swamp. A few minutes is all it takes to get one to come within a couple of metres, although I have to stand perfectly still. Just watch it strut from branch to branch, chest puffed out in the most offensive of postures as it appears to say, 'Get out! Leave us alone, this is my patch don't you know; go back to yours!' That I was 300 times bigger than it never seemed to enter into the argument.

CHAPTER 3

THE MUD

In rainy Golden Bay, the mud produced from the late summer rains made it impossible to get anywhere near the swamp. Even after the first few deluges of autumn, the swamp would swell, its water table rising and spreading over the base of the flaxes, out among the rushes and into the paddocks. Owing to the impermeable ironpan layer underneath, the pakihi soils became super-saturated, meaning that immediately upon being trodden on, even just once, they magically transformed with squelchy ease into a dark slosh of super-clinging mud. Some sun would dry the leached silica in white patches, but it only took another shower to turn it all into a big mess again. Even the steep banks, which you'd expect to be drier owing to the better drainage, became unwalkable bogs.

It became impossible to walk anywhere without high gumboots. In the morning, we would step down from our door straight back into them after knocking off the big balls of mud from the previous day that had encrusted around them.

I had noticed that all the New Zealand homesteading books contained sections on coping with mud. But it wasn't until I had to cope with it myself that I appreciated why. Mud was always the bane of pioneering settlers in this country, especially since it was in the swampy lowlands that they preferred to settle because they made the best farmland. 'Farmer Bill' Massey, who became the Reform Party's first prime minister in 1912, campaigned upon an ambitious roading programme aimed at 'getting the farmer out of the mud'.

For anyone who has lived with mud, the attractiveness of Massey's earliest manifesto cannot be over-emphasised. Alan Mulgan wrote in 1944, 'Mud has been a strong factor in the shaping of New Zealand life. It has tried many hearts and broken some. It has cost MPs their seats and swayed governments. It has marooned settlers in the winter, and levied a huge toll on health services.'

Truckload after truckload of gravel and 'goolies' (big rocks) went nowhere on our driveway, sinking deeply and uselessly into the mud. At times Clare despaired of our infertile soils, and her feelings intensified at the same rate as the mud accumulated. If it hadn't been for our Land Rover, we would never even have got out.

Our first baby, Joshua, was born at the little Takaka Maternity Hospital, to the barking of a huge Alsatian dog that strangely had jumped up to the open casement window of the little cottage hospital. 'Shoo that dog away will you, nurse?' said Dr Pearson calmly as he cut the cord. Ten days mother and baby stayed in that hospital, the mandatory care and total rest given every mother and new baby in those more compassionate days. Even I was given a hearty meal whenever I went in to visit.

Coming home must have been a let-down for Clare. No power in our hut and surrounded by a sea of mud. I have heard it said that 10-acre blocks provided more mental patients to this country's psychiatric hospitals than any other type of land holding, but in a strange way we were cosy. The glow of the Tilley lamp was all the light we needed; the coal range kept us warm as toast, and we listened to National Radio for entertainment, the only radio station we could get on our battery-powered 'wireless'. I listened to all the parliamentary debriefs, knew all my bird calls from listening to them at 7 am sharp, and followed story serialisations with avid interest. Most memorable for me was *The Hitch-hiker's Guide to the Galaxy* by Douglas Adams. The idea of hitching across space, Zafod Beeblebrox, the Vogons – it blew my mind, just like Pink Floyd had with their music.

If there was nothing on the radio we often took turns to read to each other, the rationale for this being that we both liked the same type of books. I recall one moonless night reading for the first time Bram Stoker's *Dracula* out loud to Clare, the growing suspense of the storyline having revved us up for three nights in succession. Just at the passage where one of the dreaded vampire bats was beating its wings at the window to get in, what I can only postulate now was a morepork attracted to the moths at our window, began fluttering madly against the glass. The timing was uncanny and it terrified us. I raced to bolt the door, fastened the windows and extinguished the kerosene lamp. I began thinking where exactly the garlic was in our pantry cupboard, and the tiny crucifix brought down for use as jewellery. I tell you, we were both so freaked that night, I am not ashamed to admit that we even used a bucket for a bedtime pee because neither of us was game to venture even one metre out into that dark night.

With time, we began to have more of a social life, especially with other newcomers to the area who were much the same age and shared our 'back to the land' mentality. In particular our baby Joshua opened doors everywhere with all the other alternative lifestylers who were contributing to the hippy baby-boom of that time. At Tukurua alone, in a valley just a kilometre long, some seven babies were born around that heady, fertile time of the late 1970s. Most weekends there was a party somewhere in one of our cabins, huts or studios. We shared our home brews, organic salads, home-killed meats and brown loaves of bread baked in the searing heat of a manuka fire in a wood range. A whole clan began to form in Golden Bay that continues inter-generationally to this day.

Confidence came with numbers. For pre-school education we collectively seized the day and inaugurated our own playgroup, which we held at the Onekaka Community Hall every Wednesday, thus 'saving' our kids from attending the rigidly structured Playcentre recently established in the community. It was the age not only of free thinking, but of knowing you could implement it as well. The Education Department was receptive to our alternative ideas and provided money, books, toys, bikes, art equipment and advice to help put our loose ideas about free play into practice.

Sometime we parents got too loose though, extending the concepts a little too far – well, for the Establishment anyway. We couldn't help but notice our kids loved playing with mud, and lots of it, so a few dads and mums got together and dug a huge pit in the pakihi lawn by the hall, and filled it to ground level with a thick slurry of dark rimu sawdust and water. I don't think that I have ever seen children having so much fun, certainly more than I'd seen them having at Playcentre. When they had had enough, we simply hosed them down. But we ended up filling the pit in after the Preschool Education Advisor saw it and went ballistic.

Back at home, the winter storms made us feel so holed up especially when thunder and lightning would rage all around the mountains. Golden Bay and Northland share the distinction of having the highest number of electrical storms in the country, with at least a dozen spectacular shows a year. Josh would crawl under the bed with our dog Sam, as we counted the seconds between the cracks of thunder and bolts of lightning, feeling apprehensive as the times shortened, meaning the storm was getting closer, then relief when the interval lengthened as the storm drew away.

I will always recall the afternoon we got hit. The intervals between the lightning and the shattering peals of thunder became shorter and shorter, rocking our little hut on the knoll. All of a sudden this enormous shockwave hit us and everything lit up outside, followed immediately by a big bang like a cannon going off in our ears. The whole hut shook and a huge blue flash shot across the room. It was all over in a second, but it took us several more to take stock of the damage, which spread across the whole inside wall where the telephone had been, leaving it all charred and streaked. Just a few days before we had been connected to the Collingwood telephone exchange, and already our new unearthed hand-cranked wall phone was acting as a conductor for several hundred thousand volts of celestial electricity into our little home.

The Post and Telegraph repairman who came to replace it told us the lightning had struck a transformer on a power pole barely a hundred metres from us, then arced down to our telephone line and raced at the speed of light straight into our hut. 'Lucky you weren't on the phone at the time,' he said as he left, 'otherwise you'd have been fried to death.'

I know modern phones are well earthed or plain cordless, but I have never used any phone during an electrical storm since.

CHAPTER 4

TRUCKING YEARS

Clare and I always looked forward to the dry spells, when we knew our property would dry out, but we knew that there was no such easy solution to making a living. Our meagre savings were running out. Our families' warning words came back to me: 'Whatever will you do down there?' For work, that was. There was little chance of ever getting work with the only really big employer in the area, the Golden Bay Cement Company, because the recruitment process there was pretty much sewn up. Thank goodness for the optimistic näiveté of youth, otherwise looking back we would never have taken the risk.

So I got a job, the only one available in the whole district at the time, as a truck driver for Solly's Freight, based at Rockville. Starting there was simply the biggest wakeup call of my working life. From my previous job of being a fair-skinned and delicate-fingered cartographic cadet working glide time, I suddenly became a real worker, smeared in diesel fuel and oil, toiling from dawn to dusk.

The first day on the job I was told to 'cart rock' and assigned a 12-ton TK Bedford truck which I was expected to load with car-sized limestone rocks from a distant quarry, then take them to a remote washed-out section of the Aorere River at Hickmott's farm. Here my mission was to dump them over a severely scoured-out section of riverbank to prevent further erosion of the productive farmland. The two or three four-ton rocks that made up my load required precision placement with the big front-end loader, and extreme care when tipping off so the truck would not simply roll over.

A Caterpillar D-4 bulldozer on the site was operated by a mountain of a man whose real name I did not find out for over a year because everyone just called him 'Animal'. His defining features included huge bulging muscles with matching bull neck, super-tight shorts, a beer gut that stretched his black singlet to bursting, and a crew-cut that matched the several days of stubble covering his face. This man looked business. No wonder hotelier Tinky at the Collingwood Tavern could always rely on him to drive down in his beat-up Land Rover at a moment's notice to break a few arms and legs when his drinkers got out of hand.

At first I could get no actual words out of Animal at all, just grunts. But slowly we warmed to each other as the day wore on. His job was to push the rocks into the riverbed with the bulldozer after we had dumped them. He carried a gallon can of diesel beside his seat and every so often would smear some of it over his bulging muscles to ward off the sandflies that descended upon him in hordes as he worked. I asked him why he used diesel for sandfly repellent. 'Nothin' else works,' he replied, deadpan. With nothing but a roll cage above him, he was a sitting target of course, and desperation had driven him to this extreme action. At least we truckies could roll up our windows whenever we got near the river.

I was expected to run with the working pack, but while my other two truckie workmates would roar and slip-slide their trucks in with relative ease, on that first day at work I somehow managed to get stuck with every load. Sometimes it would be driving in, my 10-ton load of rock helping to make me sink into the mud on a dangerous angle. Other times I would get stuck trying to get out again, the empty deck meaning I could get little grip on that muddy track. With a slight smirk on his face, Animal would take his cue, track his dozer up the bank and edge the big blade under the tail end of my deck so gently that I wouldn't even feel it. Then, gradually turning on enough deep grunty power, he would push me out with seeming ease. Despite his outward appearance, this man was nothing short of ballet on a bulldozer.

Animal's favourite trick, he told me later, was using the dozer to roll his kids up in a big carpet of earth. Sometimes he would even take the machine home on weekends just so they could enjoy this treat. His two small children, son and tom-daughter, would eagerly lie down in front of the machine, which he would then track towards them. At the last second, just when it seemed he was about to squash them flatter than roadkill, Animal would lower his blade a few inches into the ground so that the turf layer would peel up to curl over and around them, rolling them forward inside the curl which would wrap right around them two or even three times, their little heads sticking out each side. When they had had enough of this he would turn the bulldozer around and unwrap them again with his blade. He even did it once for one of their birthday parties, all the neighbourhood kids lining up two at a time for a turn.

At smoko, we all sat around on a rock each. There could be no more perfect vista than along the beautiful Aorere River, with its spectacular backdrop of weathered limestone cliffs forming the Whakamarama Range.

'Shut up you fuckin' birds! We want some peace and quiet!' one of my workmates screamed out to a particularly noisy pair of paradise ducks making their endless zonk zonk calls as they flew wide circuits over the riverbed just in front of us. Not wanting to feel left out, I joined in too, throwing a few rocks wildly at them. Anyway, I could kind of understand. All morning we had worked these smelly, smoky, noisy, diesel engines. No earmuffs back then, either: you were expected to listen to the engine all day and pick up any unfamiliar noises to pre-empt a breakdown. When we stopped for smoko and the last engine was turned off, the silence was magical. And we did not want it ruined by any stupid birds.

Animal pulled open his duffel bag to reveal a booty of 'gie gie' that he had picked just that morning while standing atop his roll cage. These elongated fruit of the kiekie (*Freycinetia banksii*), covered in masses of berries, had delicious white flesh much prized by Maori. They called them tiore, the sweetest fruit of the bush. 'Always the big bonus working in the bush in May, finding these,' Animal told me. His great-grandparents had been some of the first white settlers in the area. In fact they broke in the farm just next door, and they had learned much from local Maori about the abundant natural fruit of the Aorere Valley. As I was leaving after dumping my last load of the day, he tracked his bulldozer up alongside my cab and handed me a few more of his succulent fruit. When we ate them in our hut that night, they tasted like some sweet preserve. I told Clare all about my wonderful day, and the many new things I had experienced. Quietly I also took some pride in having survived, body and truck unscathed.

The next day was a freezing start, with a five-degree frost at inland Rockville. Some of the drivers who had started earlier had lit a truck-tyre fire in the middle of the yard to warm their hands before they headed out on their various missions. They had been thoughtful enough to throw on a few inner tubes and some diesel so it would still be going for the later starters like me who turned up at half-past seven. No matter how much they had you on, everyone in that company watched out for their workmates. I joined the circle around the blaze, trying not to breathe in the thick black pall of acrid smoke that smothered the yard and drifted out all over the surrounding countryside like a modern-day Iraqi oilfield on fire.

With blackened face and lungs, but warm hands at least, I was sent off again to 'do more rock', only to be recalled two hours later to cart a load of superphosphate out to Wyllie's airstrip, and then to transport bales of hay between two sheds on opposite sides of Golden Bay. Never had I been so exhausted after one day's work. On the third day I was assigned to work on a gravel-crusher and a jackhammer up at Solly's quarry, which left me shaking at the end of the day as though I had a severe case of Parkinson's. Every day at that work was totally different: you never really knew what you'd be doing, except to clock up a heap of hours in those heady pre-logbook days.

Like many other rural carriers, Solly's was a family freight business. It got going on 28 February 1928, when Ken Solly of Ferry Point Farm at Ferntown bought a brand-new Chevrolet Four lorry from W.J. Dick and Co. in Nelson. It was driven over the Takaka Hill by Noel Miller, who not only taught Ken to drive it but later moved to Collingwood to establish the garage which is still operated by his sons and grandsons today. Charlie Hickmott was good at carpentry, so Ken got him to build the wooden cab and tray for the brick-red lorry, which could carry exactly one cubic yard of gravel.

Ken Solly immediately began contracting out his services on that trusty truck, mainly to the Golden Bay County Council. A massive upgrading of the district's roads was in progress, and there was unlimited work. Every morning in those early days, Ken would help his wife Clarice milk their cows in the dark before setting off to work. Freight picked up so much that in 1932 they moved to Rockville and began a regular freight run to Nelson in the Chevrolet. The Solly's Freight depot is still on that same site, backdropped by a majestic remnant of swamp kahikatea. Today there is a fleet of 25 trucks, and the company is still run by Ken and Clarice's grandson and great-grandsons.

Ken was still alive when I started, a most straight-up man with words if ever I met one. On day four on the job he introduced himself by grabbing me by the beard and waving an axe in my face. 'You ain't one of those marry-are-na bastards are ya, son?' I assured him that I wasn't.

And I wasn't lying – not at that stage, anyway. 'Well, ya need to get a shave then,' he said, laughing.

Ken's grandson Merv Solly was my boss. He may not have started the company, but today he is nothing short of a living legend in the transport industry. As a sheer survivor, he rates A+. Accidents, liquidations, hard times, boom times, ulcers: he's had them all and come up trumps. I learnt a lot working for Merv; had plenty of laughs too, even if it was usually at my expense.

'You ain't much use to me around here if you don't have your heavy trailer licence,' he told me three days after I started. 'I've booked your practical test for tomorrow morning, so take "23" and get some practice. Make yourself useful and deliver this parcel while you're at it.' Because Solly's operated an entirely Bedford fleet back then, every one of the dark green trucks was referred to only by its number, in this case '23' being a long-bed articulated truck.

I headed out to Totara Avenue, the address on the little parcel sitting on the seat beside me. Behind me, the full 16-metre tray was completely empty. 'Drive right to the end – there's plenty of turning,' Merv had advised me. But what I found at the end of the single-lane road made my heart sink. There was no turnaround whatsoever! Even a Mini-Minor would have had to do a six-point turn there, and here I was driving a truck-and-tray unit. So I spent the rest of the afternoon trying to reverse my rig out along the slightly curved, one-kilometre-long road. A handful of residents came out to make sure I didn't run over their flower beds. 'Ain't ya got ya licence, sonny?' one old codger chirped, little knowing that he was right on the money. Plain embarrassing, it was!

When I finally got back to the depot, late in the afternoon, arm and neck muscles aching like hell, there was Merv waiting with a grin. 'I thought if you can back out of Totara Avenue, well you'd be ready to sit your licence in Collingwood. Nine sharp tomorrow morning; don't forget now.'

Tuesday used to be the one day the traffic cop came over to Golden Bay from Motueka. It was the one and only day every week that you could sit your licence, or get a ticket in those Ministry of Transport days. Six days a week you could drive any unwarranted, unregistered wreck around with almost total impunity, but on Tuesday watch out: the cop might just catch you. Which is why on Tuesdays, Golden Bay roads fell strangely quiet. No one's car could go fast enough to be much of a hazard, anyway. Most of them seemed to have number plates beginning with AT, dating from 1965 when blocks of black and white number plates got dished out to different regions.

Getting my heavy trailer and heavy special licences greatly expanded the range of jobs I was called upon to do. For the next couple of years I did freight and stock runs, mostly over the Takaka Hill to Nelson and back. The road over Takaka Hill (elevation 791 metres) is not the highest in New Zealand, but it is the longest hill road, 25 kilometres in length with 365 bends between Riwaka and Upper Takaka. Yes, three hundred and sixty-five: driving continually over that hill, I had plenty of time to count them as I tediously ground my fully-loaded truck and trailer up the hill in 'low, low' gear. Gutless, those early Bedfords were: 'Bastard Bedsteads' we called them, especially when they broke down. At times of crisis, our mechanic could swear like no other man I had ever met. 'The fuckin' fucker's fuckin' fucked,' was his verdict after doing a compression test on a truck with a serious engine rattle. What more could anyone add to a diagnosis like that?

Rainwater has etched Takaka Hill, the marble mountain, into a bizarre landscape of rifts, runnels and flutings – a landscape known as karst topography. Down the side road to Canaan, there is a 183-metre-deep abyss known as Harwoods Hole, the biggest hole in the country. No one had been inside it until 1957, and a member of the original descent party was killed by a falling rock while being winched back up.

No rural job can introduce you to an area quite like being a truckie. My deliveries took me down every side-road in the district and along lots of farm tracks too, not to mention meeting every farmer around. Each assignment was like a little voyage of discovery, and I always carried a selection of maps with me for that purpose. Little swamps I couldn't bear to miss were everywhere, usually tucked down low, popping into view as I would come over the crest of a hill or negotiate some bend. If time permitted I would take a few minutes to stop and turn off my engine. Get out. Observe. Every swamp was different. Some just had raupo growing out of them; others grew nothing but flax, while rushes dominated others. Some had fernbirds, which would always reveal their presence with an alerting *click*. Other swamps just seemed to be dominated by families of noisy pukekos. Some ponds were home to many noisy frogs which pulsed like creaking bellows, while others were strangely quiet.

Slowly I hooked into the overall swampy picture, connecting in my mind the way that the various combinations of flora and fauna were related to rainfall, hydrology, surrounding soil types and geology. Along the exposed western flank of Golden Bay, facing the turbulent Tasman Sea, rainfall was high and the limestone country channelled, so that the lowland valleys running down to the sea stayed true watery swamps. These were usually filled with flax, unless they were wind-scoured or debris-choked dune ponds, in which case raupo tended to dominate. In contrast, the golden sands of the beaches along the eastern side of Golden Bay were derived from a highly porous, easily-eroded parent rock called Separation Point Granite. It was not good bedrock for swamps, which is why there were so few of them there. All the stuff I had learnt as a cartographic cadet, labelling geological and soil maps back at the DSIR, certainly came in handy for understanding my new environment.

All the lowland areas of warm, moist Golden Bay had once been covered in towering forest, but less than one per cent of that area remains as tiny forest remnants on farmland today. Even just 30 years ago lush swamps still filled many of the shallow watercourses in the vast catchments of the Takaka and Aorere Rivers.

I know I'm totally biased, but compared to the others I saw, my swamp was relatively spectacular. Its colours to my eyes seemed more vibrant; it seemed to buzz with more life and was more in keeping with its surroundings, even if they were mostly just scrub.

Of course, working as a truck driver wasn't all fun and swamp-spotting. Most of the time it was dealing with tight schedules, breakdowns, holdups, stressed-out farmers, and either avoiding soft ground or getting unstuck from it. Because we were rural contractors servicing the agricultural industry, much of our work was off-road, and anything could be expected to happen in the course of a normal day.

In Nelson's old rail-freight depot, a prize bull I was delivering went berserk as we tried a truck-to-truck transfer. It pushed the two vehicles apart and jumped free. Fifteen rail workers and I chased it on foot down St Vincent Street; it must have been a hilarious sight. Finally we lassoed it on some vacant land where The Warehouse now stands, then used our combined strength to drag it all the way back up the street. Thankfully no newspaper photographer was out and about that day.

Returning from remote Te Hapu late one Friday afternoon, I managed to drop Trevor Solly's precious D-4 Caterpillar bulldozer off my truck. Trevor was Merv's workaholic dad, who I swear loved his bulldozer almost as much as his wife. I didn't mean to drop it of course: I just pulled over a fraction too far on an inside corner of the Big Hill

43

to make room for Eric Wilson who was coming home in his big white Mercedes logging truck. My truck just sank sideways into the soft ground alongside the road, settling at such a steep angle that the bulldozer just fell off in slow motion, wrenching the tray and chassis of my truck into a banana-shape in the process.

My heart sank like the *Titanic*, but worse was yet to come. Roydon, my co-worker in the area, immediately went to fetch Solly's second D-4 bulldozer so he could pull mine free. But in the urgency of the task he forgot to put the handbrake on, so this bulldozer dropped off his truck too, exactly half a kilometre from where mine lay. Two D-4s and one truck wrecked in half an hour: needless to say Trev and Merv were not happy.

I was put 'on wash' for a week after that, using a high-pressure hose to clean the shit off every truck that came into the yard. In between, I got the job of delivering the groceries to Collingwood General Store, driving a battered ute. After my week as yard dunce I was released back to duty, but not without one last reminder of my sins: 'You're coming out with me today,' said Tom. 'Trevor asked me to give you a real driving lesson.' In that big-boy world of truck driving, I felt suitably humbled.

But what I would discover on that day out would make it all worthwhile. We headed out in the company's biggest stock truck and trailer, to remote Nguroa Station on the northern side of Westhaven (Whanganui Inlet). No one had ever before taken a heavy trailer over the winding gravel track around the bluffs of the Nguroa Road, but Tom negotiated every tight turn with ease, at the same time dishing out advice about water tables, corrugations, defensive-driving tactics when meeting oncoming trucks, and all the off-road-driving tricks to keep a big rig on a gravel road.

When we came over the crest of the range and saw the Nguroa Swamp, all my concentration went out the window. Finally, I had to admit, here was a swamp that rivalled mine, even if it was just one of many swamps that had used to exist along the wild western flank of Golden Bay. Between lofty limestone outcrops, these snaking swamps had occupied virtually all of the vast valley systems. Just like the Nguroa, they would have all been primal and visually resplendent. I was particularly taken by the gully setting, and the way the lushness of the swamp twisted so gracefully out of sight.

Tom noticed my diverted attention. 'He's planning to drain that one day soon, and not before time either. Most of the farmers along here did theirs years ago.' Until that moment I had not cared about what anyone else did with their swamp. Only mine mattered to me. It was a personal and private thing, and I respected any other swamp-owner's right to do whatever they wanted on their land. After all, only months before I had come within a digger's whisker of draining mine, so I still had real empathy for those whose priority was making farmland. But on that day, looking over the Nguroa swamp, I somehow wished I could have waved some protective wand.

Next day I was back in serious driving business, starting at 5 am sharp in the dark loading 170 hefty baconers into my truck and trailer at the Collingwood Dairy Company for transport to the abattoir at Grovetown, near Blenheim. The pigs were already pretty agitated when I arrived: obviously the early wake-up call to go and get killed didn't agree with them. Sometimes when animals were calm you could stand in the crate while loading them, but if they were agitated like these pigs, it was best to climb halfway up the crate, straddling the pen partitions, to herd them in. As each pen filled tight with the animals, I would shut the internal gates with my foot, then swing around on to the next pen, until all were neatly filled. Keeping animals comfortably tight in a stock-crate is preferable to giving them lots of space, because they don't lurch around so much and get bruised on the way to the works. Farmers got less for animals delivered bruised, so as a stock-truck driver you could expect some strident feedback from cockies if you didn't deliver their stock in good order.

Taking those pigs over the Hill that morning, I could tell they were getting more agitated by the minute. By the time I hit the bottom of the other side they were all fighting like crazy, the noise reaching me in the cab as mad squealings and thudding against the metal crate. Travelling through Riwaka, one of the baconers must have finally had enough of all the antics and decided to abandon ship. He probably climbed on top of one of his mates before leaping straight over the side of the 'poop deck', the crate extension directly above my cab. Suddenly this huge pig fell directly down beside me, crashing hard against my arm which was leaning out the open window. That pig gave me such a fright as it tried to climb in on me.

Pigs can fly; or in this case, pigs can fall: very hard on the tar seal too, at 80 kph. It took me 10 seconds to bring the truck to a stop, and another five to run back to one very grazed pig, which was still gathering its wits. Before it could take off I grabbed it by one of its back legs, but

45

it was about as heavy as me so we were evenly matched. It struggled and struggled but I just hung on. Neither of us was going anywhere. Several cars stopped, their occupants pointing and laughing, but no one would get out and help me with the pig.

Finally a couple of tobacco farmers came out of the Hart farm and helped me lift the pig back into the crate. I got to the abattoir at Grovetown just outside of Blenheim with my full load of 170 pigs, including one already well-tenderised baconer.

But even worse was to come. After I unloaded them in the abattoir yards, the company's stock agent came out and looked at them. I could tell he was not happy before he spoke: 'Too heavy, all of them. I told your joker over there 170 pound max. Can tell just by looking that most of 'em are over 200. Sorry mate, ya gotta take 'em all back again. Run 'em around a bit and put 'em on half-rations. A couple of weeks should be all it takes. Bring them back then.' So I had no choice but to load them all up and go back. That day was 17 hours away from home.

Being a truckie didn't give me much of a home life, I can tell you. Josh spent much of his toddler years waking up after I'd left for work and going to bed before I came home. On weekends I would try to make up for it by taking him to the beach or just playing around the property. His favourite game was swamp hide-and-seek. There were endless places to hide in the acres of rushes and flax, but the slightest rustle would always give him away, even if it took a couple of hours.

It was around this time that Clare decided to cut the first track across the swamp, snipping away daily at the flax with hedge clippers. Slowly she snaked the path across the swamp, laying the cut vegetation down as a corduroy. One day Josh was playing along it and sank in up to his knees. She could hear him crying and ran to his aid. There he was, stuck to the spot – with a green gecko perched perfectly still on his head.

Some workdays I would take Josh in the truck with me, and he would end up sleeping for hours at a time stretched out on the passenger seat, which he fitted neatly lengthwise. I never even thought of a safety belt: only new cars had anything like that back then. We just trundled along. Josh's most exciting moment was always tipping off a load, when the truck would shudder and shake as if excited to be finally rid of its encumbrances.

Together in my work we negotiated tracks up gorges and riverbeds, and under towering limestone bluffs and ancient trees – not that the latter could be expected to last for long. Baigent & Sons were clear-felling the last remnant of rimu and kahikatea up the Turimawiwi and Anaweka Rivers, south of Whanganui Inlet. It was the last significant stand of virgin kahikatea left in the country, and one of my regular jobs was taking fuel and supplies out to the logging gang.

Early ecologist Paul Colinvaux postulated that 'all colonisation is aggression.' European go-getters with a good eye for resources swooped early upon Whanganui Inlet. Extracting wealth in the form of gold, coal, timber, flax, fish and farmed animals is a well-established tradition around these parts.

Virtually all of New Zealand's great kahikatea had been harvested by the late 1930s. But one large patch of the virgin timber remained in the wide sheltered valleys along Golden Bay's western flank. This whole area is brushed by the Westland Current, a northward-flowing surface current created by a mingling of the West Wind Drift and a current that flows south from the east coast of Australia. This massive body of comparatively warm water greatly influences the coastal climate of the west coast, making for comparatively favourable growing conditions so far south.

The Benara Timber Company was a well-established Australian company which was keen to supply the burgeoning Australian dairy industry with white pine boards, which made perfect cheese boxes because they imparted no discoloration or odour. The company leased cutting rights to the vast 48,000-hectare Taitapu Estates from the Westhaven Harbour, Land, Coal and Timber Company. Proclaimed the triumphant Benara company in its 1933 prospectus:

> This is the only place in New Zealand where there is any quantity of white pine left ... splendid stands lie within one mile of the harbour, very thick and tall, all on flat lands and valleys – all easily logged. In the opinion of experts, this is the best White Pine timber in the South Island. For five chains each side of the mill alone, there is half a million feet of standing timber ... one continuous block of White Pine, in the most wonderful condition for milling.

Systematically the big logs were all taken, largely exported to Australia for cheap packaging. The last logs came out in the mid-1970s, some still so huge that one would make an oversized load for the huge 18-wheeled logging trucks towing swiveling jinker trailers; and that's even after they'd been chainsaw-notched for the bolsters (uprights that held the logs in place) as well. For certain, it was the best 'kaik' you ever did see, or will ever again.

Those logging rights expired in 1976, exactly 100 years after the shrewd Wellington solicitor Alfred D'Barthe Brandon Junior first secured the Crown grant over that vast area from Knuckle Hill to Kahurangi Point. The government paid the last Taitapu Estates Ltd exactly $650,000 for what was still left of it in forest. Previously ecologists had only been able to identify the remnant patches of forest from the air, because the loggers would not let them in, under threat of physical harm. Staunch settlers!

It's always been like that out there, even recently. Burn off a hundred hectares of bush to get rid of a few pesky wasp nests: no problem at all. One man didn't like the way his mate, who had a house bus parked on his property, didn't get treatment for his dog who'd broken its leg after jumping out one of the bus windows. So when the owner was out, the man killed the wounded dog, then cooked it up and served it to the owner when he came home, saying it was possum stew. When the unwary man had finished the last mouthful, he was told he'd just eaten his dog, and that it served him right for not looking after it properly. The dog owner was shocked, but learnt his lesson. Summary justice, served up Whanganui Inlet style.

At least once a week I was sent to work out at Whanganui Inlet. There was no more stupendous scenery than the drive around the inlet on the Dry Road. In ideal conditions – no wind and high tide – the mountain reflections on the water were as superb as any I have ever seen. Usually I wouldn't see another soul except the odd local setting a fishing net or gathering up seagrass or some of the Pacific oysters that had recently become established around the big culverts. After talk of the proposed marine reserve started, some smart-alec put up a sign along the inlet that read:

Westhaven Human Reserve
No birds, DOC or bird brains.

Back in 1926, Jack Nicholls started up his horse-drawn coach service, dubbed the Mudflat Express, across the Inlet. 'Working the tide,' he called it. 'I never once got caught by the tide, just close to it on many occasions.' Once he had to stand on the handrails of his cart in the deep places. That was before they put in the Dry Road, which was completed with Depression labour in 1937. A little longer than the straight-across route, this first all-weather road made it possible to avoid the stretches of mud and corduroy track that previously had been the only route across. The causeways were largely built by countless wheelbarrow loads of spoil from the hand-dug cuttings that skirted the inlet. The whole road is a tribute to the team of a hundred men and their families who were recruited to work on one of the most isolated Public Works projects in the country. On the big sand peninsula at Rakopi, not far from the Clay Islands, a workers' settlement grew up almost overnight. The workers' children loved living there, with the whole benevolent inlet at their disposal. We still go camping there every year, right where they all lived. It's our pre-Christmas 'de-stressing' time. The men of that era used to bore a six-inch hole in the top end of their tool handles, fill the hole with linseed oil, seal it with a small cork and sand it smooth. As they worked, the oil would slowly percolate through the wood, preventing it from becoming brittle and keeping their hands lightly oiled to prevent blisters. Tricks like this have largely been lost in today's more mechanised age.

Just beyond the southern head of the Inlet, the road these tenacious men carved weaves inland again, before emerging at the coast where it crosses the Paturau River. Along this stretch, where Charles Heaphy in 1846 climbed to view a 'remarkable flax valley', the road makers had little choice but to skirt the massive Mangarakau Swamp, which was deemed uncrossable. It was always a treat to me, driving past that great expanse of flax, raupo and rushes. It teemed with birds, including one of the highest concentration of fernbirds in the country. No wonder they congregated here to nest: their tiny eggs would have made easy morsels for rats, stoats, weasels and ferrets on any drier ground.

The billiard-table-flat swamp is interrupted only by small islands of swamp forest that used to look as if they had been purposely laid, with zen-like precision. Anything but, of course. Given the 150-year history of gold and coal mining, logging, flax-harvesting and farming in this immediate area, it's nothing short of a miracle that the 420-hectare Mangarakau Swamp has survived. Today it's as large as all the other swamp remnants in the Tasman District put together.

For a start, it impeded access to the coast from as early as the 1860s, when gold and coal brought the first miners into this remote area of northwest Nelson. The Golden Blocks became the most isolated goldfield in the country. Walking from the southern end of the inlet, you could take the old 'Maori Trail' through the Te Hapu bluffs to reach the coast, but if you had a horse and cart there was little option but to take it down the fine-gravelled bed of the Paturau River. The river was relatively easy going, but first you had to get past the swamp by sidling around under the towering limestone cliffs, a route that was always extremely boggy. So in 1907, Collingwood County Council workers were sent in to dig a large central ditch through the swamp, which is today crossed by a narrow concrete road bridge simply signposted 'Mangarakau Swamp Drain'.

However, the long-anticipated ditch – really more like a ravine – had little effect on the water table. Perhaps owing to a unique set of hydrological factors including high recharge capacity and the high water-retention of deep peat soil, the great Mangarakau Swamp simply failed to dry out. Mercifully, it would continue to defy a myriad of later attempts to drain and farm it, almost until it was finally bought by the Native Forest Restoration Trust in 2001.

But if the swamp settlers failed to drain it, they still managed to do a good job of clearing much of the swamp's original vegetation – kahikatea and pukatea swamp forest, interspersed with flax, all of which were valuable. A sawmill was established in 1909 to process timber from the swamp and surrounding lands until 1920, and then it was opened again from 1932 to 1968. Vestiges of old wooden tramlines can still be seen along the old logging road beside the swamp, along with sawmill relics and a huge chunk of matai trunk which testifies to the grandeur of the former forest.

During the 1950s, Mangarakau was a lively settlement with its own rugby and cricket teams, store and post office, library service, swimming pool and community hall. Every able-bodied man was employed at the mill, the coal mine, or working on the road. Families supplemented their income by growing vegetables, hunting deer and pigs, fishing for crayfish, paua, eels and whitebait, and gathering blackberries and the banana passionfruit that used to grow all along the bluffs.

But disaster struck this area on 17 January 1958 when a gas explosion in the mine just at the end of the tiny town killed four men – Maxwell Barrett, Bernie Pitalls, George King and Max Anderson – on their first day back after the summer holidays. The town's fifth miner, young Alan Hart, was seriously gassed when he went down to help. It was a bitter blow to the tiny isolated community, losing half its men in one cruel blow.

Today the houses, shops and post office of the once-thriving settlement have gone, along with all the extractive industries. While I was working for Solly's, I helped cart several of the solid rimu mill houses back in sections towards Takaka for relocation.

After two years of doing an endless succession of jobs like this, I got 'promoted' onto the sowing truck, spreading superphosphate and lime on paddocks around the district. It was specialist four-wheel driving and I rose to the challenge, finding it highly addictive. I drove all over virtually every farmer's paddock, going places few people would ever see. Formed roads have always been boring for me since that job.

About this time I also began noticing that things were not quite right about the drive for increased agricultural production. Like the way that certain Rockville cockies put too much superphosphate on their paddocks, sometimes more than three hundredweight per acre (330 kg/ha) twice a year. As a stock driver I noticed that it was always the animals produced in this sort of environment that caused the most problems. Cull dairy cows in particular, fed a life-long diet of heavily superphosphated grass, appeared to lack stamina and tended to want to sit down in the crate. Once that happened it was nearly impossible to get them up again, and as a result they would become bruised and their meat downgraded. Drivers often got the blame for bruised meat, but part of the problem obviously was that cockies reared animals with insufficient stamina. Sometimes the cull cows even collapsed and had to be shot in the crate and dragged out with a tractor.

Unbeknown to me at the time, my appointment to the sower truck was due in part to the government giving out Farm Development Suspensory Loans to encourage farmers to develop their marginal land, including many of the swamps I admired. It was a handout: they didn't have to pay back any of the money, provided they used it to create productive farm-land. It was a win-only situation for farmers, and they went for it with their ears back, clearing land for cash that went into their pockets.

The underlying truth was that they were all farming a dramatically depleted environment. The soil's natural fertility was used up as soon as the last of the potash from burnt trees of the ancient forests was con-sumed in the first bright green flush of grass. Even today the common sowing mixture of ryegrass and clover is still called 'bushburn'. The first three years or so of grass and clover growth was usually spectacular, spurring much hope for the future of agriculture in the new colony. But the land would become leached and sour within a couple more years. In many places an ironpan would form, the water table would rise, and what had once been virgin forest became pakihi. Such a dreadful equation, struck with a match: hundreds of years of fertility, locked up in trees and layer upon layer of forest-floor litter, reduced down just like that.

As a nation, there was nothing we could do about it – not by ourselves anyway. When you shat in your nest, you had to sit in it. You couldn't move on like a nomad to the next fertile patch of ground. The solution was to import phosphate from Pacific islands like Nauru, Christmas and Banaba (Ocean Island). It was dirt cheap and unsustainable, but it underwrote the phenomenal growth of agriculture in New Zealand and Australia. The British Phosphate Commission fostered many a rural dynasty.

The 1970s saw the last of the cheap phosphate, as several of our Pacific Island neighbours found their lands laid to waste. Ask any Banaban today where his home island is, and he will tell you, 'Scattered all over New Zealand and Australia.' By the 1980s Banaba was reduced to a mess of uninhabitable craggy coral.

But meanwhile, to keep up with the mad rash of land-development work, Merv Solly bought a new prototype truck/tractor spreader for me to drive, called a 'Tructor', manufactured in Warkworth. Our mechanic immediately dubbed it the 'Fucktor' because of its incessant teething problems. Although all of us workers at Solly's had a remarkable camaraderie, I got on particularly well with two others. Bob MacMahon was an ex-Western Australian stock agent who loved engaging farmers in lively discussion wherever he went. Then there was soft-spoken Geoff Benge, who'd been hired as the new dozer operator after Animal had to quit because of severe diesel poisoning, presumably caused by rubbing the stuff on himself for all those years. Oily food now made him sick: even the smell of a burger cooking was too much for him, and the merest whiff of diesel fuel caused him to retch.

Geoff and I often worked together in the farthest-flung areas of Golden Bay on farm-clearance jobs. On his big D-6 bulldozer with a root-rake attached instead of a blade he would literally uproot the trees, raking them into long piles for burning later. Then he would tow a big set of concrete-weighted discs to chop up the debris before I would sow the cleared land with lime, fertiliser and seed.

At Snake Creek, out on the coast just behind Mangarakau, we 'brought in' a few remaining acres of flat virgin bog forest, a part of the Mangarakau Swamp that was privately owned. The D-6 made short work of the trees, smashing them off in blade-wide swathes and raking out all their roots. But it was deadly ground to work on, and we spent much of the time winching each other out. Even after a week of work with two huge machines we only had two cleared acres to show for our efforts, but the farmer urged us to carry on. He certainly didn't care about the delays, because he was getting paid by the government regardless.

Slowly but surely my attitude towards this work changed, for I was knowingly participating in the destruction of so much 'marginal land' that was more often than not pristine native bush, along with some of the last remaining lowland swamps left in the Bay. But I have to admit it was only after a health scare that I finally quit. My Tructor rode so rough that soon I was bleeding from my bum, a condition the doctor diagnosed as proctitis, a weakening of the bowel often caused by too much bouncing and shaking. Reading up on the subject, I discovered that scraper (Euclid) drivers in England were common sufferers of proctitis. It did not surprise me, for they drove a similarly rigid suspension to that of my Tructor.

Once I found that out, I gave in my notice. I was a free man. No longer would I have to inhale fertiliser as part of my job; no more would I be washing lime out of my hair; there would be no more digging trucks out of 'useless' bogs. And never again would I take part in the draining of a swamp.

CHAPTER 5

SUBVERSION

My second child Catherine was born into more indulgent times. After leaving my full-time, all-consuming job at Solly's, suddenly I found myself with all the time in the world. It enabled me to finish our 80-square-metre house positioned on top of the knoll, just in front of our little hut, which henceforth became known simply as 'the bach'.

Thanks to all the money I had saved while working as a driver, things had certainly gone up for us in the world. We now had the power on, a new dial phone with a five-digit number, a 15,000-litre concrete water tank, a flush toilet and septic tank, a bath with all the wetback-heated water we could ever desire, and even a second-hand Hoovermatic washing machine capable of thrashing our score of cotton nappies cleaner than clean. No more dragging water up or washing in the stream for us! What a treat in winter it was. All in all, the cost of our new establishment was just under $9,600.

Best of all, with mains power we could use our turntable, amplifier and big stereo speakers now, which had previously remained packed since we'd moved down. From our little knoll, Tukurua got blasted with *Dark Side of the Moon*, by Pink Floyd; *Guess Who Live at the Paramount*, *Eric Burdon Declares War*, and *Wave*, by Patti Smith, plus a stack of others. They were our sounds liberated. When building, I used always to put on Al Stewart's *Year of the Cat* album, which set a good pace but not too hurried for the thinking process.

Because I was suddenly home all the time building, and the local ambulance service was desperately short-staffed, I volunteered to become a part-time driver. This involved doing a standard first-aid course and then sticking by the phone 24 hours a day for one week in every three or four, depending on how many other drivers the Nelson Hospital Board had on the roster. Some weeks nothing much seemed to happen and I never even got a call, while in other weeks there would be three or four, taking mainly rural-related accident victims to Nelson Hospital in the old Dodge ambulance which was kept in a purpose-built garage at the Joan Whiting Rest Home in Collingwood.

My initiation involved collecting a sheep musterer called 'Rooster', who had fallen down an abandoned mineshaft up in the Collingwood goldfields. I drove as far up as I could along the pot-holed track, then we carted him down by stretcher. Next it was an elderly woman farmer who had been run over by her own runaway beast of a tractor. But what soon began to disturb me was the number of car accidents involving young hoons, invariably on Friday or Saturday nights. In fact it got so bad that I would simply stay up on Saturday nights, waiting for the inevitable call.

My worst-ever callout was to an accident on Waitapu Road in Takaka, just before midnight one Saturday. A local man who had been drinking heavily left the Telegraph Hotel with the intention of drinking more at the Globe, which often used to flaunt the licensing laws and stay open late. But on the way, this drunk driver crashed into the rear of a late-model car backing out of a driveway, immolating the two elderly occupants in a fireball as their fuel tank exploded. The policeman had already dealt with the charred remains when I got there, so all I had to do was take the drunk driver, who had suspected head injuries, to the A&E department at Nelson Hospital.

Next day, while listening to National Radio, I heard a Belfast doctor describe his feelings after treating a man who'd had some of his stomach and both his hands blown off in an 'accident'. This doctor realised from the wounds that his patient must have been assembling a bomb at the time. Simple compassion becomes replaced with all sorts of emotions at times like that, including despair and revulsion for the person you are trying to save. It was just like what had happened to me the night before.

On most Friday nights we would head into Takaka for a quiche dinner or raw salad at a new alternative café called The Wholemeal Trading Company that had opened up in the old theatre building. Unlike today, when this café is patronised by all sections of the community, it started out fully segregated. No one who considered themselves in any way 'straight' would be seen dead in there, even if it did offer the only non-instant coffee in town. Besides, we ate so much meat as homesteaders that the funky vegetarian food they served up was a change and a treat. We used to look forward to our Friday night out.

After dining, we would always show our support for the new organic bakery by picking up a Rangihaeata Red loaf, made with dark konini flour, before heading down to the Golden Bay Film Society that held its screenings in the library at the high school. The first film I saw there was a saga about two men on an emotionally tumultuous Brazilian road trip. At one point in the film, the lead actor stops his battered Volkswagen to get out and have a graphic shit on the red dust highway, an event which was filmed in its entirety.

'He's expressing his relationship with his co-driver, he wants to be rid of him completely,' someone whispered in front of me.

'No, it means he just wants to get rid of all the shit in their relationship, so then they can finally relax together,' commented another.

Two weeks later we were treated to a moving if slow-paced film from Senegal. The first feature-length film ever to come out of that country, it was all about a day in the life of a poverty-stricken family. The first quarter of an hour depicted nothing more than their waking and getting up. Then getting their grumpy skeleton of a cow out of its enclosure of woven sticks took the next half-hour. Milking it for a cupful and grinding some stale millet for breakfast seemed to take the rest of the show. Being many of us homesteaders, we could relate to it completely. And besides, anything in those alternative days that wasn't Hollywood was welcome fare. During the screenings our kids generally played merry hell through the library before dropping off to sleep one by one among the mass of sleeping bags strewn around up the front.

But the reality of our new-found family freedom and togetherness was that soon we were totally broke again. We were jobless and had two small kids. I looked around for work, but there was nothing going. Clare managed to get some part-time work in the laboratory at the Golden Bay Dairy Company, but there was nothing for me. So I had little choice but to apply for the dole one Tuesday morning when the woman from Social Welfare set up shop in Takaka for the day. I got it automatically, just like half the other alternative lifestylers around the place by then.

The welfare system was in full swing in the late seventies and early eighties. It was also well past its use-by date. Generous benefits in the form of the dole, largely ineffectual PEP schemes, sickness benefit and domestic-purposes benefit were all being supplemented with add-ons for medical and dental needs, house extensions, even home appliances. A few people, mostly Treasury economists and National candidates, were arguing that our payout-based system was severely under strain, but every worker collective around the country was still screaming that it wasn't enough.

I have always naturally been inclined towards the left: like swamp water, it's in my blood. My journalist father was active in indoctrinating me with worker sentiment, and no wonder: his father was Alfred Humphrey Hindmarsh, MP for Wellington South, whose election in 1911 along with four other independent Labour men was a considerable advance for the labour movement in this country. In August 1915, the Reform and Liberal parties formed a coalition government with Massey as Prime Minister and Ward as Minister of Finance. Five of the six left-leaning MPs at that time decided to form a caucus under the chairmanship of my grandfather, and became the official Labour opposition.

His formative experience as a barrister had come from representing the Blackball miners in the Arbitration Court at Wellington during their momentous 1908 strike, an experience which polarised him to the worker's cause. During his time as an MP, my grandfather also curiously revealed a passion for classics, when he became well known for his stuttering impromptu recitations of Greek tragedies in public parks around Wellington. Although tipped to become the first Labour prime minister, he was one of thirteen MPs who succumbed to the influenza epidemic of 1918.

At the time, signing up for the dole felt right to me, and to many others as well. Why should we feel guilty about not joining the wage and salary earners who carried the country's tax burden almost entirely upon their shoulders, who could expect no tax breaks or handouts like the upper echelons who were milking the system? Politicians did it with their slush funds, free air travel and taxi chits. Business people got development grants and were into tax evasion. Even farmers were in on it, milking their give-away suspensory loans – I had seen that myself, co-operated in it, even. But no more!

A cynicism about our so-called 'freedom' had permeated the consciousness of my generation. All the time we were being told we could do anything we wanted to, have anything our hearts desired – good jobs, flash cars, designer clothes and other consumer goods – but the reality was different. Sure, you could have it all – as long as you were prepared to run like mad with the pack, and what sort of life was that? A very high pressure one. Like the world, it seemed that everything was about to explode. Nuclear arms were proliferating; the first oil shocks had revealed how crazy our dependence was on imported energy; even water was already being predicted to become a diminishing resource. With toxic waste everywhere, clearance of the world's rainforests and a population explosion, society looked dangerously close to collapse. We knew the country could still afford to support us, just a few dole bludgers. And besides, we reasoned, by resisting consumerism we were 'contributing' – by not consuming what resources remained. Our time was best put to use solidifying our 'revolutionary' position, setting up a wholesome life and raising loving families, ready for the time when others would surely look to us as the example of how it should be done. We would be the inspiration for the collapsing society. Then again, maybe we just wanted to do a Jim Morrison and 'get our kicks before the whole shithouse went up in flames'. Looking back, we were just like any other human beings, justifying anything we wanted.

So I joined a veritable army of system-savvy hippies on the dole, able to indulge in sheer creative talent at a relaxing pace and get paid for it, before the screws got applied. A wealth of furniture-makers, painters, basket-makers and potters all fired up around this time, bringing the Bay to national attention as a growing hotbed of alternativism and creative talent. All sorts of exciting and innovative ventures got going, including the Golden Bay Workcentre Trust, which charged itself with creating new employment. Creativity oozed out into the streets as play. Aunt Fanny's Sewing Circle was a kind of madcap cross-dressing club that became the great adversary of the Christchurch-based Alf's Imperial Army, and held huge mock battles at Takaka. The old locals didn't know what hit them: even custard pies flew through the air in impromptu theatre on Commercial Street.

A definite rebellious streak among the newcomers began to make itself apparent fairly early on. Every societal group has its share of ratbags, and hippies were no exception, in fact the phrase that comes to mind is 'pro-actively bent'. *The First Whole Earth Catalogue*, issued in large format on newsprint by 'alternative' publisher Alister Taylor, touted all sorts of survival skills, including a whole page devoted to – wait for it – shoplifting hints! Like Abbie Hoffman, leader of the Yippies, whose aptly titled work *Steal This Book* was a manual of subversion and theft, the *Catalogue* advocated shoplifting not only as a means of living cheaply, but also as a protest against the rat-race and the exploitative capitalist system. As far as we were concerned, it was another legitimate (albeit underhand) form of guerilla warfare. Even among thieves there was some kind of honour, though: it was considered wrong to steal from family-owned shops; only those perceived as being owned by big business and outsiders were fair game. It was one raised index finger presented blatantly to the 'Establishment': Up yours, it said.

Lots of old hippies' bookshelves have the second and third *Whole Earth Catalogue*, but few have the complete set. That's because within weeks of its release, *The First Whole Earth Catalogue* was taken off the shelves by members of the New Zealand Booksellers' Association. We dismissed this as another act of censorship and capitalist arrogance, saying that it was 'of course' due to pressure from the staunch big-business bully boys of the New Zealand Retailers' Federation.

The recall didn't make much difference in Golden Bay anyway: some hippies had already made shoplifting their sport of choice, routinely rolling into the big farm-supply shops along Commercial St in Takaka and helping themselves. If you had a farm plumbing job on, you just took in your shopping list, filled up your bag with every part you needed and then just walked out. Need a new Swanndri? No problem at all: just try them on until you find one that fits, then nonchalantly walk out.

Everyone seemed to have some kind of a scam. One man I knew used to routinely swap his muddy old gumboots for a new pair at Wrightson-NMA. Another told me how he paid for a box of spanners and arranged to pick them up later. Minutes later his girlfriend shoplifted the already-paid-for purchase, so when the guy came back they had to give him another set. Two for the price of one! Hippy shoplifters left the teenage variety for dead, and I don't believe the honest retailers of Takaka were ready for them.

Not everyone got away with it of course, often because they got too greedy. One man installed a special flat fuel tank under the tray of his truck, which was capable of holding over a hundred gallons of petrol. Once a week or so, late at night, he would park where the tanker used to stop to unload petrol by the Takaka gas station, and go to the pub. But not before he had inserted a hose down into the ground tank and activated a small electric pump in his truck. By the time he came back to the truck and drove away, his tank would be completely full. There was even an automatic cut-off switch in the system to prevent overfilling or spillage. It was a scam that had originally been espoused by Abbie Hoffman in *Steal This Book* ('This trick is especially rewarding when you have a bus'). It worked fine, providing the guy and several of his mates with free petrol for nearly a year until the night when Nola Drummond, publican at the Junction Hotel across the road, noticed a man acting suspiciously. She called the police, who came up to investigate, but the culprit was gone. Inquiries next morning revealed that Hodgkinson's garage had been involved in a long-running dispute with the fuel company over supposedly short deliveries. Of course, the fuel company was delivering and billing the right amount, but some of it was being drawn off before it could go through the pumps. Nola had taken the vehicle's number and told the policemen that the man had driven up the valley, so all they had to do was drive up every side-road until they found the truck, and one guilty fuel-stealer sound asleep in a nearby barn.

Another man called Marcus was proud of his purpose-designed woven hippy bag with a Velcro fastener along one side of the top edge. He pulled the fastener open in the supermarket and slid in the odd block of tasty cheese and perhaps even a smoked chicken or a handful of Peanut Slabs as well. This was a variation on Abbie Hoffman's 'booster box', an innocent-looking but fake parcel with a flap on the side through which shoplifted goods could be inserted. He nearly got caught in Nelson once after going through the checkout, when he was stopped on the footpath by a store detective with the manager close behind. 'I have good reason to believe you have a block of cheese in your bag,' said the security man gravely. Marcus protested his innocence, making a big scene, then threw open his bag to reveal … nothing at all! Luckily for him, in the heat of the argument no one noticed the big bulge out one side. The manager foul-looked his security guard for wasting everyone's time and stormed off, and so did Marcus, leaving the incredulous store detective standing there, looking silly.

Marcus was still sweating when he got home and unpacked his ill-gotten cheese, and vowed he would never shoplift again. He didn't have to, anyway. Before he had emigrated from England, he had bought several stolen credit cards and filled a 20-foot container entirely with the proceeds of a momentous week-long spending spree. You name it, he bought it: blenders, bedside lamps, toasters, clothes, figurines, cameras, light fittings, several TV sets and three Persian rugs. Towards the end he was even throwing in things he knew he'd never use, like bowling balls and golf clubs, just to fill the container up. As far as he was concerned, the filthy conniving capitalist banks he was ripping off deserved it completely.

The day he left England, Marcus cut up his stolen credit cards, deciding to leave his major criminal urges behind and start afresh in Golden Bay. Going around to his place was always such a treat, spotting hash and playing with his 'toys'. But Marcus got tired of the place and all of us after a while, and left for Australia to do another big rip-off.

Of course even if the scammers stuck out, not everyone had illicit urges. In fact most had sincere good intentions, like Humfrey Newton, who had a passion for trees which he set out to indulge on seven hectares of bare land at Onekaka. A professional career had been pretty much on the cards for the young Humfrey, his Christ's College education preparing him admirably for a law degree at Canterbury University. But it was not to be. The sudden loss of both his parents was too great a shock for the 17-year-old, and he dropped out of university to roam the world. 'It gave me a new perception on life,' Humfrey recalls. 'The question that came up for me was: do I want to work in an office or do I want to plant trees?'

He opted for the trees and returned to New Zealand, where he used what was left of his inheritance to buy his largely bare farmlet, and set about planting, in particular timber trees. 'I stopped counting when I'd planted 15,000 trees,' he says. Dreams and pragmatism mixed easily in the modest version of an English estate he created as surroundings for his hand-built home, complete with a rowing lake.

Then there was a former Wellington librarian, Dick Nicholls, who shifted to Golden Bay in 1974 with the intention of organic gardening. However, his sights soon shifted from the car case he was squatting in near Parapara Inlet, to an unoccupied block of burnt-off coastal Crown land at Milnthorpe that no one seemed to know what to do with. His detailed proposal, headed 'Milnthorpe Revegetation Project', advocated the wholesale planting of native trees among the scrub, and received the enthusiastic support of Larry Russell, then Commissioner of Crown Lands in Nelson. Within a year Dick had established a plant nursery on the land, while living in a caravan with his wife Jane. 'It was relatively easy getting natives established in the sand-dune country, but shocking fertility over the rest of the place meant I got pitiful results elsewhere. Even gorse wouldn't grow on most of it.'

The influence to radically change his ecological strategy came from people like Neil Barr, best known for his trees column in *New Zealand Farmer* magazine and a passionate advocate of eucalypts. To Dick, they sounded ideal: they thrived in poor soils, broke up the ironpan with their roots, and enhanced fertility. They also attracted native birds to feed on their nectar-laden flowers and disperse native seeds through their copious droppings.

So Dick planted more than 90 species of eucalypt, at least 50,000 trees in total, at Milnthorpe over the next two decades. He raised nearly all of them on the property, from seed. It was a monumental effort on his part, and could not fail to inspire others. Bob MacMahon, who I had worked with at Solly's, became his right-hand man, slashing long rows and tracks ready for planting. Dick was always giving people bundles of eucalypt seedlings, so before long my place was covered in gum trees of all types, except of course in the swamp. I now say that I spent my first 15 years in Golden Bay planting 'eucs', and the next 15 chainsaw-ing them down. I don't regret it for one minute: scores of truckloads of the best firewood ever, not to mention endless poles, beams and flitches from chainsaw-milling the best logs.

However much I enjoyed socialising, the concept of communal owner-ship and living did not appeal to me as it did to some. Rainbow Valley today is a cluster of dwellings with a comfortable hand-hewn look to them, clustered on about 100 hectares of river flats up the Anatoki River. A breakaway group from Waitati helped start this community around 1974. 'We were influenced by reading William Morris and ideas of going back to the land,' said Mike Scott, one of those founding members, some time after. 'There were a lot of strong moral feelings among us back then, about how we should live.'

The new wave of innovation did not please some of the more entrenched locals though, who saw some of the new ways as nothing more than smart-arsed, unproductive behaviour. 'Reckon someone should take a box of matches to that Crown land at Milnthorpe,' I heard one of my co-workers at Solly's say soon after Dick Nicholls' first eucalypts had begun poking their heads up through the gorse. 'Those gum trees coming up everywhere are a menace – a fire hazard, not to mention causing dangerous windfalls along the highway.' Any argument about birds perched in the new trees, shitting a rain of native tree seeds that would eventually restore the vegetation, didn't impress this guy one bit. Ironically to me, it seemed that the greatest fire threat was this latent pyromaniac himself.

The divides grew deep. Golden Bay can today be regarded as a for-tunate backwater boasting a happy mix of hard-core locals and artis-tic newcomers. But it wasn't always like that. For a while it became 'straights' versus the 'hippies', the latter finally rallying under the banner of the Rural Resettlement Association (RRA) in 1976 to oppose the local councillors, who they largely perceived as 'the enemy'.

Much as I appreciated the way the old boy network had let me build on my land, that same council did not last long in my good books either. The councillors cottoned on quickly to the anxieties of the local people who had voted them in: undeniably the influx of newcomers was going to destroy the social fabric of their tight-knit cow-cocky and cement-making community. Within months their attitudes hardened as their desks were flooded by a mini tidal wave of applications for rural subdivisions and permits for wacky buildings like geodesic domes, yurts, log cabins and residential 'studios'.

Suddenly we had a new rule, invoked under some obscure clause of the Town and Country Planning Act 1953. Under the guise of preventing the fragmentation of productive farmland, subdivision into anything less than 50 hectares in any rural zone was suddenly disallowed, and nor would a building permit be granted to anyone who already owned such a block. Shock waves rattled through the alternative community. At our regular RRA meetings, held at the Onekaka and Puramahoi community halls in central Golden Bay, I joined other men with bushy beards, and an equal number of women in colourful hippy skirts, whose strong rhetoric fell only slightly short of advocating armed revolution. Mind you, there were also other important matters to be debated, like whether we could afford to send out the RRA newsletter with postage at seven cents a copy.

Collectively, we were laying siege to the Establishment, insisting that the council should wake up to its hypocritical stance on such issues as wholesale coastal subdivision, like one at Parapara which was backed by TNL, a big Nelson-based transport company. Two large residential subdivision applications were put in by councillors themselves, and duly approved – many of us thought that was inappropriate. We even hit out at the Holy Grail of the region's concrete-headed culture – the Golden Bay Cement Company – accusing the council of not doing enough to stop the enormous smoke and dust emission from the aging cement works at Tarakohe. As RRA members, we formed active alliances with the Maruia Society and Mining Monitor, and similar groups campaigning on Waiheke Island and on the Coromandel Peninsula. Those links empowered us, because they reminded us that we were not alone in our struggle.

A group of 'troublesome newcomers' set up the *Golden Bay Community News*, a worthy A4 stapled newspaper with aggressive reporting of council meetings. Needless to say, the councillors were not impressed.

To them, the public gallery was a token empty chair, never used by anyone except an old lady called Mildred who had to catch her breath after walking up from Sunbelt Crescent with their scones for morning tea. Suddenly the council had some feisty individuals wanting to sit in on the proceedings. One man got the council's back up when he asked if there was any contingency in the district scheme for an alien encounter. But their biggest worry by far was Lynn, the *Golden Bay Community News* reporter, who never stopped taking notes and reported every twist and turn as though it was some great farce – which it was.

'Put down that pen, girlie,' said one councillor to her finally when a contentious issue got raised. Lynn refused, saying they were not in committee, it was a public meeting, and they had no right to stop her. But she still got kicked out and banned thereafter from attending any more of the council's so-called 'public' meetings.

The council retaliated in other ways too, collecting some compelling photographic evidence to show that there had recently been some serious breaches of the Building Act, especially in regard to a rash of 'residential sheds', artists' studios and sleepouts. Both sides became increasingly provocative and confrontational. One young man named Tony, who was staying up the Kaituna, took his own photos of the building inspector who had come to take photos of an illegal dwelling. Tony kept jumping up in different parts of his patch of bush, acting like a big monkey as the official walked up the drive, pointing his camera and snapping the shutter before disappearing, uttering monkey whoops of excitement. Tony then tabled his photos of the 'council incursion' as 'evidence' at one of our RRA meetings, just as the council produced their photos at their meeting. Looking back, it was all pretty childish!

Initially, Chip and Hess Williams had felt lucky. At the head of the Pupu Valley, five kilometres west of Takaka, they had 109 hectares of idyllic, bush-clad hillside, so their property was well above the 50-hectare minimum. Hess was a trained secondary-school teacher and Chip was set to make a mark with his precision building and joinery skills. But when they applied for a building permit, the councillors tried to change the rules.

The 'no-subdivision-under-50-hectare' rule still applied, but suddenly they added a clause prohibiting building on any parcel of land, whatever the size, if it was not an 'economic unit.' That was the final straw! In the minds of these meat-head councillors, only large-scale farming scenarios were ever going to be allowed. Never mind that many flourishing hives of industry were up and running, producing copious quantities of everything from art to vegetables, nuts to woodwork, pottery to willow baskets, dried flowers to herbs. Clearly these efforts did not count. During one meeting about the issue, the still-incumbent pointy-nosed councillor had the temerity to ask what decent-minded people would want to settle up the Pupu Valley anyway – it rained too much!

I guess that was just democracy in action, which worked well for 'them' while there were plenty of them. But what they hadn't betted on was an increasing number of 'us'. Towards the end of the 1970s, the Bay bulged with more and more hot-headed hippies, all dying to exercise their democratic rights as residents and ratepayers.

The local election of 26 October 1977 was the first time in Golden Bay history that any newcomers had stood for public office. Previously you had to have been born there to even get nominated. The book *Golden Bay – One Hundred Years of Local Government*, published in 1975, must rate as one of the most boring books of all time, and gives an insight into the minds of the councillors who commissioned it. It's all summed up in the caption to the frontispiece, showing obviously posing councillors 'discussing a weighty problem' and describing them as 'all members of well-known families of Golden Bay'.

So plenty of feathers were ruffled when a whole lot of relative new-comers stood for council, proclaiming the coming of a new social order for the Bay. RRA representative Philip Woollaston was by far the most articulate. He lived on a 10-acre block at Parapara , which had cost him $3,500, first in a railway carriage that he shifted on to the land, and then in an adobe block house that he and his wife Chan built. Philip had the gift of the sincere gab that would be the envy of any politician, as we and the rest of New Zealand would find out when he went on to become MP (and later mayor) for Nelson, the architect of the Resource Management Act, and eventually Minister of Conservation in a Labour government.

Rather than preach to the converted, this well-spoken, level-headed man used a reasoned appeal to the 'straight' community, pointing out the narrow-minded follies of the incumbent council. *The Nelson Evening Mail*, sensing regional social upheaval in the making, was quick to report every twist and turn. The 'Williams saga' alone made two whole feature pages, spread over two successive nights.

Voter turnout was over 93 per cent for those elections, the highest turnout ever in New Zealand history. When Phillip Woolaston got voted in, not only as councillor but as Chairman a week later, the *Evening Mail* ran headlines of a size usually reserved for announcing the end of a world war:

Huge Upset in Golden Bay
Riley deposed

Shock waves rattled the province. In Motueka, the county council convened a special meeting to discuss the local government 'disaster' in Golden Bay and to discuss what steps they could take to stop the same thing from happening over there. But the ball was already rolling. The same turnaround was mirrored to varying degrees in councils all around New Zealand. The new Golden Bay County Council sent a ripple through the country when it proudly declared its territory 'nuclear free'. People laughed, asking what chance did Golden Bay – or Waiheke Island, the next place to follow suit – ever have of a visit from a nuclear-capable warship, or becoming the proposed location for a nuclear power plant. But it's amazing how quickly attitudes like that can change. Within only a few years it would become the most widely popular policy of David Lange's Labour government.

There were other spinoffs too from the change in council, especially in regard to plainly uneconomic and marginal land. Suddenly it was more feasible for farmers to sell small blocks of wasteland like mine. It was a 'win/win situation': the farmers hated these 'useless' swamps and pakihi scrublands, but ecologically-aware smallholders were more than willing to buy and preserve them. Since the alternative in the long run would have been to convert these lands to pasture, this new attitude undoubtedly saved many swamps and patches of scrub. Today, every swamp on a lifestyle block or reserved land in Golden Bay is still completely intact. The shift to 'softer' social politics led to a new guardianship of the land. Together with the artistic efforts of the newcomers, this was the first real outcome of the new social order in Golden Bay, and there would be many more to follow.

CHAPTER 6

GOING TO POT

Of course, all those ousted rednecked councillors had been quite right: most of us were dope-smoking hippies. Who in New Zealand didn't have a few plants in their backyard then, anyway? The cops were even finding them out the back of rest homes.

Within a few years Golden Bay became the number-one growing district in the Nelson region, and possibly top in all New Zealand, as one senior policeman claimed at the time. Despite the denials, that man was almost certainly correct. A conservative street value of $7 million was given to plants pulled by police in Golden Bay during the 1983 growing season. What that implies about how much police *didn't* get is anyone's guess, although there have been some curious attempts to make estimates. Opposition spokesperson on 'misuse of drugs' at the time, Graeme Lee, told a select committee that several serious cultivators of marijuana had told him their estimates of what the police got ranged from 30 to 45 per cent of the total crop. Although the police tend to jack up street prices to make it look as if they got a good sting, even taking $2 million off the estimated value of seizures meant cannabis was probably contributing around $5 million a year to the Golden Bay economy by the early 1980s.

This was reflected in retail sales, which began escalating around 1979 for no identifiable reason. In the year ending March 1984, Golden Bay County shops made a record total of $10,207,000 in sales, even though not much was happening apart from a craze for putting in massive kiwifruit orchards. So where did all that extra money come from? Even the largest employer, the Golden Bay Cement Company, paid out only $2.75 million in wages that year. Unemployment, DPB and special benefits would have added up to no more than another $1.5 million. Add the cockies' income, most of which was spent over 'The Hill' on new cars and tractors, fertiliser and the like, plus all other small businesses, and you still have a big shortfall that could only have come from dope.

Paul Bensemann, a reporter for *The Dominion* newspaper in Wellington, was sent down to Golden Bay 'to follow the police on the trail of the growers, and meet the alternative lifestylers who are thought to be part of the problem'. The first of his four full-page features was, predictably, headed 'Golden Bay Goes to Pot'.

The star of the story was Constable Tony Cunningham, a solitary country cop whose main purpose in life seemed to be pulling out dope plants and arresting their growers. We called him Cunning Bacon, or Sneaky Pork, or just plain Crafty, because of his uncanny knack for ferreting out information. He loved his work, and the poor reporter had trouble keeping up as he jogged around all the patches of gorse on Rangihaeata Head, pulling out plants at every turn. Bensemann described the haul as a 'typical' day after a tip-off. Someone had seen a cannabis plot but didn't want to get involved. All intelligence was passed on to the Air Force, whose Iroquois helicopters conducted raids once or twice a year. Already they had aerial photographs showing some huge plantations, notably one of 200-plus plants up the Aorere Valley in a huge fenced-off compound, where the soil had been raked into rows, with a sophisticated irrigation system. Because tall kanuka had been left scattered across the plot, it had been almost invisible from the air. Another of similar size, but with huge flourishing two-metre plants, had also been found growing beneath limestone bluffs in an untracked part of the Northwest Nelson Forest Park.

When the big air raids came, you couldn't help but notice. It was like *Apocalypse Now* without the death toll and heavy music. The comparatively slow rotation of those rotor blades mimics the beating of a human heart, albeit much louder: 'Thud, thud, thud', 80 beats per minute, faintly at first, then louder and louder. The choppers used to fly so low that they could take the nappies clean off your line and reduce all your fresh frilly lettuces to tatters. All the dope plants they pulled up, often numbering in the hundreds, got loaded into a high-sided trailer, taken to Nelson and immolated in a big bonfire. Some people kept themselves well supplied simply by picking up what got dropped at the transfer sites.

Constable Cunningham claimed that he couldn't recruit local aircraft companies to help with the spotting because they had received a number of threats over the years: 'One of those choppers could go up in smoke any time.' Nor did he bother to ask what any pilot had seen: 'I don't want to put him on the spot – he's a real nice guy. But he must see planting going on at this time of the year.'

His comments were backed up by Sergeant Rex Morris in Motueka, who said that although growers were scattered throughout the Nelson region, the cannabis problem had definitely become a compounded problem in Golden Bay: 'We seem to have a number of people with alternative lifestyles. Dare I say ... hippies.'

Next day in *The Dominion*, another full-page feature presented the other side:

Communities fed up with raids
Helicopter scene 'like Vietnam'

The colourful characters who were mainly the subject of this investigation were residents of the Happy Sam community, who had groovy names like Mole, Grub, Ben and Bunny. This community, which shared the same river flat as the Rainbow Valley Community, got its name from a very likeable dog one of them had once owned.

From their impressive communal house, which featured an enormous rock fireplace they had all pitched in to build, the 'Happy Sammers' wanted to go on record complaining about being harassed after three big raids in the last summer alone. They alleged police intimidation with riot gear and handguns, heavy search tactics and even photographing a woman in the nude against her wishes. Nelson police district commander Norman Stanhope replied that he knew nothing about the nude photographs, but added, 'I am advised, however, that it is not unusual for females to present themselves topless while police are carrying out cannabis searches.' Dope and depravity went together, so we were told.

In Paul Bensemann's next exposé, Takaka librarian Berna Soper was quoted as saying that she continually had to deal with people who were high on cannabis. Occasionally they were so bad she could simply not understand them when they tried to take out books. Many of them had young children, and perhaps worst of all, books were sometimes returned with cannabis leaf bookmarks inadvertently left in them. She resorted to keeping a plastic marijuana plant on her withdrawals counter. The sign attached read: 'Have YOU seen this plant?' It seems quite a few of her borrowers had.

Some people even claimed cannabis users had shattered their peaceful lives, and took direct action. Justice of the Peace Fred Page and his wife Rita discovered twice they had unwittingly rented out the spare house on their Puramahoi farm to dope growers. They even claimed that their young son had been tricked into watering some trays of young dope plants while the tenants were away. Suddenly there was dope everywhere, even in the rhubarb patch.

The last straw for them was when an Iroquois helicopter and seven cars descended on their farm. They saw their tenant run from the house and disappear into the scrub – the last they ever saw of him. All his possessions were left behind, including, to Fred's horror, a novel about drug trafficking and a map showing where some jars were buried in the garden. 'There was a big hole in the ground, the jars had gone,' he was reported as saying.

After the raid, hearing the house was vacant, a number of people asked to rent the place, but the Pages felt they could never trust any tenant again, no matter how innocent they looked. So they got their son Leon to burn down the old family home. Rita Page couldn't watch as it went up in flames: 'We lived in that house for forty years,' she said sadly.

County Clerk Warwick Bennett, whose covert mission we all suspected was to rid the Bay of every last hippy, said council had for some time been lobbying for more police to stop the new plague. The national policing average was one policeman to every 880 people, but Golden Bay's sole-charge constable translated as one to 4430. 'We're so lucky to have Tony Cunningham,' said Bennett. 'But he seems to be spending the majority of his time just tracking this stuff.'

I had never smoked dope before I came to live in Golden Bay, and didn't even try it for a few years until after my fisherman mate Jeremy drowned. A few weeks later, his widow turned up with a paper bag: 'This was his stash, you may as well have it.' She thought I had always been a smoker, but it wasn't until she was halfway down the drive that I actually started.

When the bag was nearly empty, I found some seeds in the bottom and sprouted my own *Cannabis sativa*, carefully nurturing the seedlings in planter bags until they were ready to plant out. And what better place than along the margins of the swamp: not on my place, but just over the unmarked back boundary and inside the forest park, a half-million hectares of wilderness that stretched all the way to Murchison.

A lot of dope these days is grown indoors, hydroponically and under lights. I don't know anything about that, because I was always an outdoors sort of guy. And every outdoor grower will tell you the best dope always grows in chicken shit, the best of all the barnyard manures provided you let it rot down for a few months first. It makes plants grow healthy and tall, three metres no trouble at all, not to mention giving those tetrahydrocannabinols a subtle edge. Other factors do come into it too, of course: growing marketable heads follows much the same horticultural principles as turning out a good wine, with climate, nutrients, harvesting and processing techniques to consider.

Small-scale swamp horticulture had its moments for me, staggering between the flax bushes, trying to keep my balance with a hefty pack of manure on my back. Falling clean over in the flax was always so undignified, but luckily no one ever witnessed it. Every now and then I would be rewarded with the sight of a fernbird that would come out to dance for me across tufts of tanglefern, oblivious to my illegal antics.

Planting out the seedlings was always an exciting day, and it was a relief to finally get them off the property too. My little patch would be already cleared, I would whip off any new shoots of bracken with a machete and re-dig the six manure mounds. Next I carefully peeled the pint-sized planter bags off to expose the cylinders of whirling white roots, desperate for release from their polythene prisons. Finally I would dig a hole for each and press the soil around them. To any gardener there is nothing quite like the feel of damp soil on your hands, no matter what the plant. Finally, just to lend an initial hand, I would stick bracken stakes alongside each seedling and tie them up with flax strips.

Growing a patch presented no great moral dilemma for me: it was just another zing in the swamp cocktail. Until I got caught, that was. The big bust of my life. Twenty D's (detectives) roared up my drive in four unmarked Holden sedans. It took their black labrador bitch half an hour to find my half-kilo of pure manicured sinsemilla (unfertilised female buds, the best dope you can get), hidden in a Tupperware container under five cords of docked rimu tailings. All next year's firewood. All next year's smoke, not to mention a small wad of 'green dollars' to supplement the family income. Fuck 'em! The entire crop gone in the whiff of a dog's nose.

They took me to the Takaka police station, where they fingerprinted me, checked I didn't have a belt to hang myself, then left me in the slammer for a few hours while they could do a proper aerial search of my property. Next door, in the safe storage room, went my drugs. I laughed out loud, recalling the story of Ted who had climbed onto the station roof, undone the skylight and used his kid's fishing line with a big three-pronged hook to retrieve the plants they'd pulled from his garden earlier in the morning. 'They're bloody well mine, and I'm going to get them back,' he told his family defiantly before setting out. No wonder they'd installed a heavy-meshed grille over the skylight.

Although the marijuana seized from me was in one cake-sized Tupperware container, the police confiscated all the other Tupperware from our kitchen cupboards for forensic testing. Clare was annoyed about that, especially since much of it was brand new.

I was charged with possession of marijuana for supply, indicted to stand trial at the High Court, and ordered to surrender my passport and report daily to the police at 7 pm. On the first evening I turned up at three minutes to seven and was told to come back in three minutes. The next evening I was five minutes late and the constable threatened to arrest me. Never mind that I had to drive 18 kilometres to the cop-shop. It was all designed to belittle you: the punishment had already begun.

A High Court indictment is for offenders whose crimes render them liable to more than two years' prison, so getting 'done' in the High Court was a serious business. I pleaded guilty, but strongly contested the weight of the stash. I knew the drug squad had confiscated just under 16 ounces of marijuana, because my scales were dead accurate, but the charge against me stated one kilogram of marijuana, around 34 ounces, making it look as though they'd caught a big-time grower. The evidence had already been destroyed, along with all the Tupperware containers, said the smirking police prosecutor.

I recall so well the white wigs, the speeches, not being allowed to say a word, and the police officers beside me when I stood up for sentence, ready to escort me down to the cells. The previous day had been a harrowing one, thinking about this moment. I had mowed the lawns, re-stocked the firewood and spent the rest of the time playing with my children at the beach until late, before coming home to pack a small bag in case I got put away. But with great relief (and a smoke-up on the courthouse lawn) I just got fined $1,000 on the supply charge and $100 for cultivation. My good probation report and a fair judge saved me that day.

The cops had tried to exaggerate the size of my stash, but at least they hadn't actually planted false evidence, the way they had done to a couple of my mates. One particular Nelson detective was infamous for planting drug stashes. Sadly, anyone who has ever had any unpleasant dealings with the police will know that they really do sometimes plant evidence, use dubious paid informants and even perjure themselves in order to ensure a conviction. To them, the end justifies the means, and if they were convinced you were guilty, they would get you any way they could. Look at what happened to Arthur Allan Thomas and Rex Haig.

'Takaka Man Sentenced for Big Drug Bust' reported *The Nelson Evening Mail* the following day. Everyone can recall their most embarrassing moment, and this will always be mine, especially living in a small community. A few jokes went around about 'Mr Tukurua' at a time when Mr Asia was becoming a household name. So much for the quiet life!

The following season I had the good sense to downsize to a three-plant crop – just for personal use. I couldn't afford to face a second possession-for-supply charge. These three female beauties were doing quite nicely in the swamp, in big black planter bags for easy shifting during floods or when a chopper visit was expected. The growers' grapevine gave at least a couple of days' warning of a police aerial cleanup operation, but it would still be a time of general paranoia and panic. Dope and paranoia always go together.

One morning in late February, almost a year to the day after the last bust, I was relishing the sensation of the breeze on my goosebumped flesh as I enjoyed my usual routine of waking up, stretching, getting up and wandering out, naked as the day I was born, to piss on the garden. Squirt of extra nitrogen for that pumpkin plant, red-hot poker, aspidistra, whatever: anything that could do with a 'growth spurt' was a fair target. Why waste it down a septic tank? My first trip to Asia had given me revelations aplenty, but I was about to get another one.

The atmosphere was charged that morning. What they call today a 'weather event' was on its way. A huge dump of rain coming straight in over the western ranges, cumulus kneading itself angrily into a filthy black watery dough, desperate to drop a million tons of condensed water vapour. The first distant rumblings of thunder came. Never had I seen the daytime sky so dark. I hoped the rain would hold off long enough for me to get to the beach and score another boot-load of my favourite firewood, southern rata, *Metrosideros robusta*. It's the sixth densest wood in the world, and floats in seawater just below the surface, until the surf finally chucks it up on a beach. Burns hellish hot. Remnants of ancient forests, sculptured by waves and shined steely grey by the sun. At Solly's we used to use it for truck decks when we carted big rocks, because it was the only timber that could take the pace without splintering.

But the driftwood mission was not to be, because my reverie was interrupted by the sound of crunching gravel, and I turned around to see four late-model Holden sedans hurtling bumper-to-bumper up my winding driveway. It was the drug squad again, and they weren't there for a surprise champagne breakfast!

I had 15 seconds at most before they'd reach the house. It was a moment of painful indecision: choose which sharpened horn of the minotaur you want to be impaled on. What was it to be: pants or patch? Dart inside and slip on my trousers, or streak through the swamp and get rid of the plants? Pick one: you can't do both. Embarrassment I could laugh off, but getting busted for the second time wouldn't be so easy, so I took off full-bore into the scrub towards the swamp.

'He's running! He's fuckin' runnin' away!' screamed the driver in the rear. 'Hurry, hurry! Get the fuckin' bastard!'

Adrenaline was pumping so hard I never felt the scores of gorse prickles that jabbed and snapped off in my hide, although it took me two weeks afterwards to pick them all out. How the senses flush at times like this! My ears were filled with sounds: car doors slamming, voices over walkie-talkies and heavy footfalls upon the hard pakihi lawn. *Dog.* A dog! I could hear the handler hyping it on at tight heel. My God! How was all this suddenly happening? Every second now counted. I didn't stop for a moment as I pushed through the prickly brush, the last gauntlet of flax and swamp, lacerating my thighs and torso.

I ripped the first plant mercilessly from its planter bag, roots flailing as I shied it over a patch of gorse. 'Over here, he's over here, this way,' came a shout not 20 metres behind me. I said sorry under a shallow breath as I repeated murders on plants number two and three. I biffed the bags too: couldn't afford to leave any fingerprints. Just in time, too. Through the flax bushes, glimpses of the dog handler … short cropped black hair … moustache … camo jacket. They always looked such mean bastards at times like this. Hyperventilating. Heart the loudest thing in my head. Feeling so naked, so vulnerable. Only two weeks before there had been a headline: 'Police dog bites off man's penis in demonstration.' How could I forget that now? Getting your arse bitten couldn't be half as bad as losing your dick, so I threw myself face-down in the swamp sludge.

Sheer relief as I made out not an Alsatian dog, but a beagle, just like the ones that slobber over your luggage at the international airport. I managed to crawl a few additional metres from the crime scene before getting wrenched up by my hair. Without clothes, what else was there for a police officer to hold on to?

I will never forget the look on the policewoman's face when she saw me. Primeval swamp-man, naked and covered in mud, being dragged along by his hair back to the house for a two-hour interrogation, which luckily for me proved fruitless for the cops. Still, I had experienced my second-most embarrassing moment, getting caught 'with my pants down'; or rather, not on at all. 'You guys never give up. You just get better at hiding it,' said the head detective. Dead right he was, too.

My last attempt at growing dope was along the Tukurua Stream, three plants tucked into a small clearing in tall gorse. But the one weekend I was away, a big storm blew down the gorse, putting the plants in plain view of the highway. By the time I came home they were gone. A week later, Constable Tony Cunningham was in the newspaper saying that growers had become so blatant they were even growing their plants in full view of the highway! What had Golden Bay come to?

After that, I got my 'shit together' as they say. It wasn't worth all the hassle, especially after seeing what some of my mates had been through. Like Kev, whose super-serious plantation of 230 irrigated plants in a big possum-proof cage got staked out for 23 days by an over-zealous detective from Nelson. For more than three weeks this poor cop had hung out in the bush, mostly under a piece of plastic sheeting in pouring rain, each day waking up in a sodden sleeping bag and hoping this was the day he would catch the big bad grower.

It was incredibly bad timing, because Kev had just taken off with his latest hippy spunk on a 13-day honeymoon escape package to Fiji. In the end the poor cop used up nine days of his annual leave, just to hang in there after the operation had ended so he could still bust the smart bastard grower. When poor old Kev finally came back to check his plants he found himself looking down the barrel of a handgun held by one trembling, promotion-hungry cop, demanding to know his name. Kev got 18 months inside for that one.

Then things got heavy. Every country has its price for a life. In Cambodia, someone might kill you for a couple of bucks, but in New Zealand it's a good rule of thumb that if you have around $80,000 worth of something that someone else wants, they could well be tempted to kill you for it. Especially if it's an illegal commodity and easily transport-able, like a big stash of dope.

Dave was a big-time grower who got his door knocked down at three o'clock one Sunday morning by three Christchurch skinheads wielding weapons and pointing a shotgun at his head. The one with the big axe demanded seven pounds of Dave's stash or he'd start chopping off his sleeping kids' toes one by one. They tied his wife up while they gave him ten minutes to come up with the goods, which he did of course. The two of them were left gagged and bound across the table for the kids to find in the morning instead of the Weetbix.

That was a heavy scene for sure, but nothing for me beats the story about Robbie (not his real name, I hasten to add). It was a similar-starting scenario, with skinheads calling in the night, demanding dope. The difference here was that Robbie was a big man who'd never been known to lose a fight. He led the two skinheads down to his pond, where he said his stash was hidden under a log on the bank. They bent down with him, but as he was pretending to reach down and get it out from its hiding place, he grabbed them both in a headlock, one in each arm, and deliberately fell forward into the pool with the intention of holding them under and drowning them. For ten minutes they struggled, gulping and thrashing for their lives. Unfortunately for Robbie though, he hadn't counted on one thing: there was a third man waiting in the getaway car, and when he heard the commotion and came down with his sawn-off shotgun he blasted a couple of toes off Robbie's foot that was sticking out of the water.

Poor Robbie: they tied him up and tortured him for five hours, stubbing cigarettes all over him. They found a cordless drill in his workshop and began drilling into his bum cheeks with a quarter-inch bit. When they finally gave up and left, their parting words were, 'You're lucky! We might even call you an ambulance when we get back to Christchurch. Well, if we remember that is.' Robbie recalls their evil, riotous laughter outside as they got back into their car. They never did get his stash: Robbie would rather have died than hand it over.

It wasn't all serious like that, though. Marijuana is a social drug: most people don't take it on their own. You build up acquaintances who for a million practical reasons regularly visit you, and vice versa, and while you're all together, someone rolls up a big hooter and everyone gets wasted. Growers and dealers never roll up those mean little 'racehorse' joints that characterise their city-dwelling counterparts. Country folk do them like Cuban cigars. At some of the early Golden Bay harvest parties, it was common to see single joints rolled up with a dozen carefully-licked-together cigarette papers. Then someone would produce another bag of dope the size of a small shopping bag and roll up an even bigger one. The biggest I ever witnessed used 40 papers and about a whole ounce of pure 'sinse', and went all night.

A remarkable camaraderie existed amongst the growers, although they were also highly competitive. Westhaven growers reckoned they grew the best dope because of their heavy hill-clay soils. Aorere growers argued that you could never go past their deep gravel-studded alluvials. You should have heard them when they got together, even in the Collingwood Tavern.

'You should have seen this trunk, man. It was as thick as my arm.'

'Yeah, but how strong was it? I got totally off my face just *smelling* my buds.'

In certain circles, to be regarded as a good dope grower was as prestigious as winning any A & P Show ribbon. People loved showing off their plants to visitors. A party up at Happy Sams one year had the stage for the band decorated on both sides with two-metre-high marijuana plants in pots. Again, it was one finger up to the Establishment. And if 40 per cent of New Zealanders had admitted to smoking the stuff at one time or another, who really gave a shit?

No wonder they got busted, one by one, all those growers – most of them simply couldn't keep a secret. Unlike just plain smokers, who tended to be secretive about it, growers often stuck out by their boastfulness. The police knew that too, and advocated all sorts of stereotyped images to identify the guilty ones who lurked among us. One day when Joshua was just seven years old he came home from school saying how a policeman had given them all a talk at assembly about drugs. Something that stuck in his mind was that the cop had said if people had incense in their home, then that was a good indication that they were smoking drugs. Suddenly Josh was embarrassed about our burning of incense, so I hid it all for his sake until he had forgotten all about it.

In Golden Bay, we still have lots of good laughs about all those 'heady' times, like when the Governor-General came to open our new school hall. As a High Court judge in his previous job, Justice Hardie Boyes had tried and sentenced me, most fairly I had thought, many years before. 'Haven't I met you somewhere before?' he asked me. It was one of those questions that sounded like 'I remember you. Nelson Courthouse No. 2, Cultivation of Marijuana and Possession for Supply.' Of course I was probably just another face to him when I'd been standing in the dock, but never before had I been so lost for a response!

To another man who was well known as a grower, he casually inquired whether he was a farmer. His reply was quicker than mine: 'Nah, not really. More a "farma-cist".'

For sure, the scene produced some good laughs, but it wasn't worth all the ongoing hassle. I gave up growing completely, and never looked back. I felt freed from my annual growing servitude, a routine built around paranoia, suspicion and seriously sly behaviour. Somehow, for whatever reasons, a lot became clearer again: my family, farm, community and friends. What's more, I still had my land and my swamp, the latter best left quite alone anyway, enjoyed for what it was: a primeval wonderland.

CHAPTER 7

WHITE HERON PASSING

Any way I looked at it, getting convicted in the High Court followed by another visit from the drug squad bearing yet another search warrant under the Misuse of Drugs Act was like being dealt a series of big kicks up the arse. I laughed it off to my friends and acquaintances, but it nevertheless made me feel like lying low, like a cat does to lick its wounds after losing a fight. I became highly introverted for a while, in particular avoiding going to Takaka unless it was absolutely essential. There wasn't actually much need to. Even pay-later groceries could be sent out in the mail car, and if I ever needed something new to read, I'd just wander down to Liz and Di's cottage at 'Pooh Corner' and borrow a book from the ever-changing stash maintained by the Country Library Service. When small community libraries still mattered.

In comparison with the Solly's years, when my son rarely got to see me during the day, suddenly the children were by my side much of the time, naturally following me on various projects I always had on the go around our farmlet. While Josh would actively copy me by banging in nails and attempting to saw timber with his own little handsaw, Catherine's style was completely different. She would be foraging wherever she went, picking manuka nuts and other seeds, flower heads and colourful leaves, to use as the main ingredients in 'magic potions'. I could not help but notice how meticulous she was in her collecting, counting everything by grouping them in fives. Watching the infant mind invent strategies was fascinating for me.

Joshua and Catherine were only 18 months apart, but what a difference that made. Once I divided up an orange and gave them half each. Joshua immediately noticed his half was actually one segment smaller than Catherine's, so he broke his in two and offered to exchange his two pieces for her one. She smiled and took it, thinking she was making on the deal. Both felt they were the winner. It was the ultimate conflict resolution – as long as the loser stayed deceived, of course.

Catherine's collecting around the garden fascinated me. Carefully she would tuck her hand-picked harvest into a fold of her long hippy dress, and bring it all back to the house. There she would grind or stir it all up in a bucket, or just leave it to ferment in water. Her recipes varied from day to day, but she would always pour the resulting mixture into preserving jars and leave them in rows, often in relatively inaccessible places among the scrub.

Whenever I questioned her about the purpose of her potions, she told me that they were 'for any reason you could think of'. They could make you happy, bring back some long-lost friend, save someone from having to go to school, or just make you smell nice. But it was a while before I discovered that *she* did not actually impart the potency to any particular brew: she was only the gatherer and mixer. Rather, it was the fairies who lived among the manuka who did the real work. They would only come when they were sure it was safe, which was why sometimes the potions took a while to get made. Many of these, of course, she would forget about, and for years after I would come across jars in the bush, still sometimes propped up on a quartz rock, and inside them was a black sludge of composting flower petals added to by a layer of tiny windfall manuka leaves.

It was at this time that I read what must rate as one of the most inspirational articles of my whole life, which completely changed the way I thought about bringing up children. My *National Geographic* collection fills around half of my bookshelves. They go back to the 1920s, and include every issue my father subscribed to in his 40-year career, plus all the subsequent years since I carried on subscribing after he died. The article I came across on the Wyeth family of Pennsylvania, called 'American Visions', struck me initially as just another patriotic 'first-family' bleat. But the haunting paintings by Andrew Wyeth, in particular *Christina's World*, drew me in. And as I got absorbed by the words, I could not put it down; in fact I ended up re-reading it several times in a row.

Three generations of Wyeths grew into perhaps America's most remarkable family, or what the author of the article, Richard Meryman, described as 'a dynasty of applied fantasy'. Five siblings, Henriette, Carolyn, Nathaniel, Ann and Andrew Wyeth, all developed an international reputation for creativity, in portraiture, painting, inventing and composing.

Undoubtedly it was their father who fired them up. Newel Convers Wyeth (known as N.C.) was an artist and illustrator, described as 'two men fighting in a sack', torn apart all his life by the opposites of his nature. At once he was both a questing intellectual, open to new ideas, and an untrammeled romantic with a virtuoso imagination that imbued whatever he touched with meaning, personality and excitement.

He considered the 'spirit of family reverence' a lost art, and when he had his own family, he set out to be the ultimate father. Until his death in 1945, he managed a hothouse of creativity to develop each of his children's talents to the utmost. N.C. succeeded to an extraordinary degree, his legacy continuing into the third generation, with 13 grandchildren all making names for themselves in the world of art and technology.

So what did he do that was different as a parent? What were his techniques? Obviously for a start he had a supportive wife. Carol Wyeth is recorded as being an overwhelming resource of warmth and fierce protector of the entire family, who kept their house like a polished shoe but left the daily details of parenting to her husband. 'Our father,' recalled daughter Henriette, 'was like a big nanny.' Certainly a nanny with a difference. He had a bellow that his children sometimes mistook for the railroad whistle at their town's railway crossing. But it was his vitality and enthusiasm that set this father apart from any other I had ever heard about.

To ingrain into his children his own 'sense of identification and unity with nature' and to develop their powers of observation, he took them on walks and picnics in the woods. They searched for mushrooms and birds' nests and found in the wet leaves of melting winter the first, starry spring flowers. In the woods they performed long-running dramas based on *Robin Hood* and *The Three Musketeers*. Driving the family in a big Ford touring car along the narrow roads of Chadds Ford, Pennsylvania, under a full moon, N.C. would turn off the headlights and exclaim, 'Look at it, look at it!'

Systematically stoking their imaginations, N.C. joined his children at play, helping them build dams in the brook below the house, then breaking them open to watch the torrent. Other times he showed them how to construct paddle wheels of wood, using their jackknives. In the evenings, with the children clustered around him, he drew pictures of giants holding children. 'Even eating the head off one,' according to Andrew. He drew 'old Kriss' (N.C.'s version of the European Santa

Claus, Kriss Kringle) sitting in the bathtub, elves sliding down his back and diving into the toilet. As far as creativity went, it was a house of no rules and no limits. When the young Andrew showed his own pictures to his father, he would study them gravely before perhaps demonstrating a better artistic technique or dispensing advice like 'Andy, you have to free yourself.' Or: 'Keep alive to everything.'

I took all N.C.'s advice on for myself. He became exactly the father I wanted to be. Of course I could never be exactly like him, but I could try. That would be enough.

However much I could inspire my children and encourage them to develop their own fantasy worlds, the reality of my marital relationship had become quite different. It would be fair to say hippy society in Golden Bay went through a big transformation in the early 1980s, and many established relationships – about half of them in fact – simply did not survive. New ways of looking at relationships, and techniques to improve psychological awareness, translated to extremely questioning times for many couples who wanted to travel the rugged road to so-called 'self-awareness'.

Vipasshna meditation courses, encounter groups, co-counselling, domain shift, neuro-link, neuro-linguistic programming and a host of other 'therapies' became the new methodologies of the alternative lifestylers. A new mini-wave of overseas immigrants came to the Bay about this time, many of them German families supposedly escaping the fallout from Chernobyl. 'Burn-your-bra' style feminism was already accepted, but now along came a wave of lesbians doing their 'clustering' thing. Autumn Farm at Central Takaka had already established itself as a guesthouse and retreat for gay men, and was attracting more and more patronage, especially over summer. Golden Bay's alternative society had it all: from fanatical organic gardeners to intergalactic energy counsellors and La Leche Leaguers.

Best of all, we had new drugs. Hashish was passé, acid had been cool, but ecstasy was making its first appearance as an awareness-heightening drug. And this was the real stuff, not full of speed like the shit you get today. Bert Potter, leader of the Auckland community Centrepoint, controversially stated that ten E's taken in the right context could short-circuit as many years of psychotherapy.

Clare and I had largely enjoyed our pair-bonded relationship, but we agreed after intense discussions and experimentation that this should now end. Bravely – or so we thought, anyway – we should venture forth as free people to find out who we really were. It was like what we had accomplished when moving to Golden Bay seven years earlier, but just on another level.

They say the only real constant is change. In a few short years, I had seen my relationship with almost everything – the law, the community, and my wife – go through dramatic change. Despite the fact I had considered myself 'alternative' to all those societal concepts, I was deeply affected by the changes. An onlooker who knew me well might have said that my life was breaking down but my touchstones were still intact. My backyard mountain, Parapara Peak, was still putting on a red tussock glow every sunset. The little stream along my boundary never stopped flowing with pure water; and best of all, I still had my kids, property and swamp, thanks to a well-qualified ex-wife who went to pursue a career doing chemical analyses for the Taranaki gasfields.

Around March every year a solitary white heron would return from its stately kahikatea kingdom up the Waitangiroto, north of Okarito, to spend the winter months at Parapara Inlet, just over the ridge from my house. Kahikatea trees growing in a swamp do not spread their crowns to nearly touch their neighbours the way they do in a forest. They stand solitary, their limbs reduced in size so that they look like brooding sentinels. But owing to the wholesale clearance of forest, Parapara had nothing like the tall trees of the Waitangiroto for the heron to perch in. Here, the low-lying inlet was its domain, which it shared with royal spoonbills, black shags, white-faced herons, variable oystercatchers, pied stilts and the occasional influx of black swans.

The first sight of that white heron every season used to be a great excitement for my children and me, perhaps because it provided a reassurance that some things never changed. On our daily trips to the beach, we would always stop along the causeway to watch it. Even surrounded by other birds, this elegant bird always stood out like a bride at a wedding. With no distinguishing features to determine whether it was male and female, it was only possible to speculate as to its sex.

'I'm sure it's a mummy,' Catherine would often say under her breath.

'No, it's a dad one,' Josh would say.

I was never sure. This bird had the gift of combining the female quality of supreme patience with the directional focus of a male hunter. If men were from Mars and women from Venus, then the heron could well be from both, in my opinion. Deadly still, it would stare into the whirling estuarine translucence of the incoming tide, as if gazing vainly at its own beautiful reflection. No such luxury for this bird though, for the fleeting flash of its yellow bill followed by a silvery flicker and bulging long-necked gullet would reveal its true purpose: it was a finely tuned fish assassin.

Until early September the heron always stayed in that rush-rimmed estuarine wetland, finishing off its stay by gorging itself on the flush of whitebait that passed through the culvert. Then it would flap off in that peculiar manner of flight, at once both graceful and lurching, to begin its 350-kilometre trip south to mate and nest once again. The maternity laws governing this bird's life were set in stone, or should I say carved in kahikatea: it just had to go back there every year.

Back at Okarito, 'our' white heron would undergo striking changes to which we were not privy as it dollied itself up for breeding. Long loose white nuptial plumes would develop on its back and wings, its bill would change from yellow to black, and the skin between the eyes and bill would become bluish-green. The birds would conduct elaborate displays and mating rituals before settling down to incubate a clutch of three to five eggs for 25 days on their untidy platform nests. By late summer, six weeks after hatching, the young would finally have left the nest and the tired parents would heave themselves skyward once again in loping flight and head off to various estuaries and coastal lagoons all around the country. These birds are big yet lightly-framed, so they are strongly susceptible to being blown off course and could end up anywhere if there were strong winds at the time of dispersal. Some occasionally even turned up on the sub-Antarctic islands, where they were unlikely to survive. The opposite also applied, with the local population occasionally being boosted by wind-blown strays from Australia. The year 1957 was a case in point, with more than 40 new herons counted at Rangaunu Bay, in Northland.

Birdwatchers cannot usually get up close to the shy, easily-spooked herons unless they have some sort of a hide, but Parapara is different. Ever since 1952, when road-builders laid a kilometre-long ribbon of curving causeway across the inlet, it has been an ideal place to view the heron. The bird seems not to be bothered by people inside vehicles, so you can drive close by and even stop to watch, but if you get out of the car it is liable to take off at once.

The road builders connected the two sides of the inlet with a single two-metre-diameter culvert, which was a bit Humpty-Dumpty-ish in that it never was quite 'put all back together again' properly. A single culvert was simply inadequate to allow for the sheer volume of tidal flow, so as a result the tides of the inner estuary were forever destined to be two hours out of phase with the tide outside. Without the full flushing effect of the sea, nutrients washed off the land tended to linger in the inner estuary, stimulating the intertidal food supplies for birds and everything else up the food chain. It also meant that the inner estuary was less prone to drying out at low tide. Compared to the scoured outer estuary, the inner one was swathed in places with a rich green carpet of seaweed (*Enteromorpha* and *Ulva*), and was clearly the preferred habitat for some 17 species of wading birds, including our solitary white heron. One ecologist I spoke to speculated that the inner inlet would end up a green morass of slimey goo, like that tactile, fluorescent-coloured snot we used to buy from Toyworld. But another pointed out that if such a thing was ever going to happen, it would surely have been noticeable within a few years after the causeway was built, and not still be wait-ing to happen more than 30 years later. The inner inlet was certainly a modified environment, but this was one case where the overall effect did not seem to be deleterious.

My mate John Mitchell took it upon himself to plant a row of 48 pohutukawa trees alongside the causeway where it gashed through the heart of the inlet. The visual effect of that kilometre-long planting was more dramatic each year, especially around Christmas when the curv-ing streak of crimson flowers became a wondrous hedge. For the rest of the year I didn't think they looked quite so pretty, especially bent over in strong spring winds, their pale underleaves fluttering like millions of knickers on distant clotheslines. Tarty, almost.

Transit NZ soon declared them a traffic hazard and wanted them all cut down, but a few locals rallied when Transit staff turned up with their chainsaws. 'You may as well knock off before you start,' they declared. There wasn't much choice either, because they intended to press them-selves against the trunk of every tree. That sort of action takes guts.

Humfrey Newton, the great tree-planter referred to in Chapter 5, once did much the same thing on Waitapu Road in Takaka. He, together with a few others, kept a sofa-sitting vigil in front of an historic laurel hedge that the old rednecked council were keen to cut down to make way for extra parking space. For days the standoff continued, until finally Warwick Bennett, the County Clerk, in frustration at 'the sheer stupid-ity of the situation', took one of the council chainsaws to the hedge at six o'clock one morning. He sawed it all up and left it lying all around. 'That's done it!' he declared to a few bleary-eyed residents who ventured outside to see what the commotion was about. Humfrey made sure all seven councillors got a rude wake-up phone call and a blast in their ear even before Bennett had finished.

I admired anyone who could stand up and say 'enough'. Like Heather Wallace, who got the local power board boys to come back out and collect the old power poles they'd simply left dumped on the soft mud of Parapara Inlet after putting up a new line. It was just another 'power trip' laid on the poor inlet, she reckoned. 'This isn't the 1950s you know: you can't just do that sort of thing anymore, leave old power poles lying in an inlet!' she shouted down the phone to the hapless area manager. First thing the following day, three workers in blue and orange-fluorescent overalls drove out from town, no doubt telling 'silly bitch' jokes as they went. After a long smoko while they waited for the tide to go out, they retrieved the sodden poles which they had initially hoped would just disappear into the mud, and heaved them on to their truck before heading back to the depot in time for lunch.

Going back to the pohutukawa trees, I should add that Transit wasn't the only threat to them at Parapara Inlet. Botanical purists protested too, because the pohutukawa, *Metrosideros excelsa*, was not on the list of trees known to be naturally present in the region. To them, this meant that while the pohutukawa was a New Zealand native, it was not native to Golden Bay. But these dumb buggers didn't realise that the reason for the absence was simply that the ancient Maori had used them all for timber. According to local mythology, Maori warriors had once fashioned weapons from the last big pohutukawa growing in the area, to kill Te Kai-whakaruaki, the dreaded taniwha that lived at the bottom of the tannin-stained pool just inside the mouth of the Parapara Stream.

This monster was said to be the most ferocious of any taniwha that had ever lived. Exploding out of its lair, it would devour any traveller that dared to attempt the difficult crossing. It could easily eat 200 people at a time. Finally, all the five tribes from the top of the South Island decided to combine forces, sending their best warriors to slay the monster.

Ngai Tahu contributed their most feared warrior, a man famed for being able to kill a big seal with his bare hands. 'Show me the taniwha and I will kill it with one blow of my fist,' he boasted. But charging forward, the big-brave-bro seal-killer got gobbled up immediately. The others, realising that they would need formidable weapons to vanquish this foe, cut down the only big pohutukawa growing along the beach nearby and devoted their energies to shaping stout spears and clubs from its many trunks. Clutching their treasured new weapons, some of the warriors hid in ambush while others crept forward to lure the monster out of the water. A terrible fight ensued, but finally Te Kai-whakaruaki lay dead. In its death throes, the monster gouged out the inlet with its enormous tail. The bones of many victims, along with treasured objects of wood and greenstone, were recovered from its dismembered body. A dramatic painting of this story can be seen in the Telegraph Hotel at Takaka.

Notices warning travellers of the danger of crossing Parapara Inlet were first erected in 1891 after a young man named Thomas Petterfer drowned there. A good swimmer, he was driving through some cattle with the intention of catching hold of the last one's tail for a tow across (a common trick of the day), but somehow he lost his handhold and his big knee-boots dragged him down. It was a particularly sad incident as he was engaged to a local girl at the time. Soon after, the troublesome ford became known as Bishop's Washout, which was a low punch at the local roading contractor of the time. It wasn't until 1917 that the council finally provided the materials for a bridge and the employees of a local mining syndicate erected it.

The gravels of the Parapara Stream – it's more of a river, really – have been turned over many times in search of gold, including a dredging operation in 1902. The Parapara Hydraulic Sluicing Company's 25-year stint is a record for the Collingwood goldfield. Some 80 tons of bagged cement were drayed in to build a 20-metre-wide dam in the Parapara Gorge, five kilometres inland, near Richmond Flat, in 1895. They obliterated a whole substantial hill and irrevocably diverted Glengyle Creek into the Parapara Stream.

Another company was floated in England in 1886 to work a Parapara mine called Red Hill, and this became New Zealand's worst-ever example of a 'wildcat flotation', according to every newspaper of the day. It sucked £150,000 of shareholders' funds into the pockets of its offshore promoters, for no return. Least restrained in its views was that most prolific source of goldfields gossip, *The Golden Bay Argus*, which referred to 'The Red Hill Swindle'.

No such fiscal excitement exudes from Parapara today, and the stream crossing at the mouth is no longer any more than knee-deep at low tide.

It is surrounded by a vast expanse of shellfish-studded sands and fringed by glaring white pavements of pipi and cockle shells raked up by the waves like some elegant Plimsoll line upon the beach. There are a few deep pools where a rogue taniwha could possibly lurk, but mostly it feels safe these days for those who fossick with bare feet and bucket in search of a feed of pipi and tuatua. On a spring tide, the water can drag out a kilometre on the near-level mud and sandflats here. It's impressive enough, but still nothing like the six or seven kilometres it can withdraw on the inner side of Farewell Spit.

I always used to get a tingle down my spine walking past the end of the sandspit that valiantly stretches out to block Parapara Inlet, and I know that I was not alone in my feeling about that place: something very Maori went on here, like a burial place. More than a few locals have dug up bones on their properties not far from here, some preferring to quietly re-bury them rather than risk getting a 'stop order' put on their building or driveway project.

Today the community is more coast-caring as people pitch in to plant patches of pingao or golden sedge (*Desmoschoenus spiralis*), hoping to reclaim the driftwood-studded dunes where the encroaching sea has made massive inroads into the end of the Parapara sandspit. Some square outlines of carefully-placed boulders get periodically exposed out of the sand, showing the efforts of the Skilton brothers, John and James, who sluiced the black gold-bearing sand on the beach here back in the 1920s.

Golden Bay is a wide, shallow bay like a big flat frying pan, around 15 metres deep. For the last 10,000 years or so it has been gradually filling up with silt from all the rivers and streams that flow into it. Reaching across towards Separation Point, Farewell Spit makes sure all the sediment gets trapped, and this protruding 'kiwi beak' at the top of the South Island grows up to 100 metres longer every year thanks to the currents sweeping sand up from the west coast.

Golden Bay is continuing to aggrade: that is, the shoreline is mostly building up and spreading outwards, rather than being eaten away by the sea. But climate change has dealt a wild card in the form of increasing easterly weather, which causes waves to buffet unprotected sandspits like Parapara. The sorry state of the mouth there today is nothing like what the Maori would have experienced, when bush was probably overhanging a much deeper crossing: a perfect haunt for a taniwha.

Just as the tale of Kupe's chase of the wheke or octopus through the

Marlborough Sounds provided Maori navigators with a verbal chart of the inland waterways, so the taniwha story reveals something about Parapara's past. To establish viable futures, we must understand these pasts, and none are more interesting than those from your own backyard. There was nothing I loved doing more than exploring the backblocks around my property, rediscovering remnants of the past to put together a picture of what it must have been like.

Historically, the bony ridge separating the Tukurua catchment from Parapara Inlet had been all done over by graziers, miners and timber-millers, in places leaving nothing but powdered puddles of grey silica sand that would emerge from its battered pakihi crust after rain. When I arrived, low manuka scrub was striving to establish itself, along with the prickly hakea and Spanish heath introduced by the Washbourn family, pioneers who had lived nearby.

I loved walking up there, letting the wind blow the clutter from my mind and gazing down upon my snaking swamp, the sight of which never ceased to enchant me. A small mill up here had just finished working when I moved to Tukurua. A wild woman called Valessca, who dyed her hair the brightest red imaginable, lived alone in one of the mill houses for a short time. I found a page of man-hating poetry that looked as though it had been torn out of a book, when I was walking up the mill road one day. I assumed it was hers, and kept a suitable distance thereafter. Silly me: who knows what I might have learnt from her?

The Forest Service made owner Harry Gates pull down his mill and two associated houses after he finished logging the rimu on his 600-acre enclave high in the hills of the park. Later he sold it to a North American recluse, who still lives up there. Harry had fingers in all sorts of pies and lived at Ruby Bay, where his trotter's training track was plainly visible beside the highway. Entrepreneurs like him were still actively shaping the countryside well into the 1970s, all the way from the swamps up to the hilltops. It was a shame though, that his historic mill had to be pulled down. My kids loved sifting through the timber and steel, or 'driving' the two old Fordson truck cabs that lay wheel-less on the ground. Sometimes I would join in and drive them too, complete with bellowing or siren sound effects, N.C. Wyeth-style.

When the mill was operating, a dammed pond supplied a steady stream of water down a narrow concrete channel under the saw blade, to wash the sawdust away down into Squires Gully. Today this spot is resplendent with a luxuriant crop of fine *Baumea* rushes that glint and sparkle when covered in morning dew. The little lake is still there too, loved by at least one pair of mallard ducks, much of its surface area pierced with the hollow stems of the sedge *Eleocharis sphacelata*. This sedge has long, thick stalks that, if you had to hide from someone, you could use to breathe underwater. Handy stuff to have around, I thought, so I pulled some out and introduced it to my swamp. What a shame I didn't have any to breathe under the water with and evade the police that day when they chased me naked!

There would not have been a hilltop, knob or gully around Tukurua that I did not fully explore, its human history always a big thrill to chance upon. A couple of miles up the stream which runs along my boundary is a narrow gorge where an impressive 10-metre-high concrete dam had been built between two rock buttresses at the head of Tukurua Gorge. Before a water scheme to Tukurua got put in 20 years or so ago, and the old road was opened up again, up there it felt like it was all my very own wilderness backyard.

There used to be scores of goats living up there, and every month or so I'd shoot one for dog tucker. It only ever took me a few minutes to bag one once I got up there: they would all be literally standing there waiting for me. I swear a few would even call out if they thought I hadn't seen them. So I always had plenty of time to explore. A decaying wooden tramway led me to more industrial relics hidden in the thick regenerating forest – cast iron wheels and an assortment of machinery bits including solid rubber wheels. But nobody I asked knew much about the operation, only that it started around 1915 and finished in the early 1930s.

I surmised that no one who ever worked there would still be alive, but maybe one of their children would be. After much inquiry, I made contact with an 86-year-old man named Charlie Blance; but as I suspected, his memories of being up the Tukurua were all childhood ones. His father, Jim Blance, had worked at 'Skilton's Mill', as it was known. Charlie remembers every weekday trudging over the heavily-wooded ridge with his brother and sisters to attend Onekaka School. At that time the tiny schoolhouse was full to bursting, with 37 pupils, mostly children of families working at the Onekaka ironworks up the road. The schoolhouse had been shifted from Rockville in 1924 as the ironworks moved into full production. Along with the residence for the ironworks manager John Ambrose Heskett, just across the road, the schoolhouse is one of the only two surviving relics of a thriving industrial community that once included a post office, single men's accommodation and a cookhouse.

The Murchison Earthquake hit at 10.15 on the morning of 17 June 1929, causing considerable damage in Golden Bay. Among its many escape stories, *The Golden Bay Argus* reported that the Onekaka schoolmaster 'showed great presence of mind holding the children in during the big shake until the chimney adjacent the porch collapsed, so that none of them were hurt.'

It has been claimed that not one brick chimney in the Bay survived that 7.8 magnitude quake. No wonder: the epicentre was only about 50 kilometres away, at Kahurangi Point, where the lighthouse keeper Arthur Page and his son Alva were cutting scrub up the hill when the booming noise came and they were thrown to their knees. In horror they watched as 200 acres of hillside slid down into the sea, smashing their house and several other buildings to smithereens as it went. Rushing back down, they dared not expect to find Arthur's wife Nellie alive, but luckily she had been taking a box out to the shed when the quake hit. She was forced to run ahead of the slip as it tore across the hillside, and narrowly escaped being buried alive.

Little Charlie Blance's teacher at Onekaka was a Mrs McNabb, who lived in a tin shack situated right where the Mussel Inn now stands. In winter it would still be dark when Charlie and his siblings set off from home in the morning, and dark again when they arrived home. Pouring rain was no excuse not to go: they just sat in wet clothes all day at school, until it was time for another drenching on the way home where at last, Charlie remembered, he would dry out by the coal range while sipping soup prepared by his mother Lena. So cramped was their cabin that all the Blance children had no choice but to share one big bed. Charlie recalls his eldest brother sitting up in bed smoking a long pipe, perhaps some sort of privilege that came with seniority. It was impossible to keep the bush rats out: 'Once the candles or kerosene lamp went out, we'd wait for them to climb over our bed, then heave the blankets to keep them off.'

On weekends and holidays, the children would climb up to the ridge so they could watch the coal boats come and go from the 370-metre Onekaka Wharf, which at that time was the longest wharf in the country. There was always some loading action to be seen as the little steam locos transported the coal along the narrow-gauge railway to the ironworks. Periodically there would be a 17-hour shift of men loading the 56-kilogram iron ingots on to the ship, and from Tukurua Saddle the wharf looked as though it was swarming with worker ants.

If there was nothing to watch up there, they'd walk down and climb the big pear tree near Tukurua Beach and pick some of the oversized pears that were always too hard to eat. One day Charlie fell out of it, landing on his head. 'The lump on my head where I hit stayed the size of a goose egg for two years!'

The mill was nothing short of hard, draining work. Logs were hauled out of the bush by snig winches, then loaded any way they could on to horse-drawn carts for pulling along the tramway to the mill. Two steam boilers powered the big jigger saws and cross-cutters to turn out big-dimension rimu and beech timbers, mainly for bridge-beams and planks that were insatiably in demand. Back-breaking indeed, but at 10 shillings a day, the pay was very good for the time.

Charlie told me how one of his father's mill-worker mates scrimped and saved so he could buy a brand-new Model T Ford, which he proudly intended to drive to Takaka every week. But on his first trip he pulled out onto the main road (just opposite what is now the Upper Tukurua turnoff) without looking. He crashed straight into an oncoming lorry, writing his brand-new car off, an event that made headlines in *The Golden Bay Argus*. At the time, no one could believe it: there were only a couple of dozen vehicles in the whole Bay, as opposed to around 1,500 working horses.

Despite 'dark and miserable winters' up the Tukurua, Charlie recalled his crammed cabin life was filled with happiness. No doubt it helped that his parents stayed madly in love. 'They always told me it had been love at first sight.' She had been 21 and he was 19 when they first met in Takaka. When Jim left he promised to visit Lena in seven months, the soonest his work would allow. But he turned up again in three. Charlie describes his mother as having long blonde hair, staying that way to the day she died. 'My parents enjoyed their life together, and if there was one thing they did, they passed that good feeling on to us kids.' N.C. Wyeth again.

They were a typical working-class family of the day. Charlie's father Jim had come out from Lancashire and his mother Lena was from an early Greymouth mining family. After Tukurua, they moved up to Bainham to work in another timber mill, and ended up rearing nine children altogether. Charlie left school at 14 to take up the life of an underground coalminer at Wallsend Coal Mine near Greymouth. He later switched to timber milling and farming at Maruia, another unsung hero of this country's great middle-development phase.

Hearing these sorts of social anecdotes filled the gaps in the story which the bare bones of industrial relics couldn't. Only together could the historical picture come alive. Slowly the interweave of local history started to become apparent. The Skilton brothers' name came up often as I delved into local history: they had done all sorts of cartage and contracting work at this end of the Bay, including the building of Washbourn Road for the county council. This once-busy road that gently weaves its way from the now-derelict ironworks, down and around the inlet to the wharf, was named after the pioneering Washbourn brothers, William and Harry, who ran the New Zealand Haematite Paint Company up the Parapara Valley.

Signs of iron deposits are widespread in the 'Washbourn Block'. The earliest geological map of the area shows my swamp marked out exactly as it appears today, with numerous small crosses indicating 'Chelybeate Springs'. These oily and rusty-looking patches would have particularly interested the geologist in Harry Washbourn, because they indicated the underground presence of iron oxide rock. In fact the name limonite comes from the Greek word for a meadow, and another name for limonite is bog ore.

Concentrated ochre pigments, literally rusting out of an exposed section of ore at Parapara, first attracted commercial interest in the 1890s. Later it would be discovered that there was a nine-million-tonne lode of highest-grade limonite ore behind Onekaka, Tukurua and Parapara. In the meantime the colony needed paint, in particular heavy iron oxide paint which would preserve any timber or iron it could be slapped on, and the Washbourns were determined to supply it.

They were not quite the first, though. The first owners had been ruined when BNZ Estates Ltd foreclosed on a development loan. A bullock track to the rich lode of oxide got dubbed the 'road into debt' by locals after it was gazetted with the bank's name, in the early 1880s. 'How dare they!' protested *The Golden Bay Argus* when the bank pulled the plug. Further south, *The Okarito Times* accused the BNZ of being no more stable than the sandbar at the harbour entrance.

The Washbourn brothers used a legacy to buy the business and property from the bank in June 1885. Under their auspices, the re-vamped New Zealand Haematite Paint Company made a name for itself by producing high-quality paint at a quarter the cost of the imported product. It was hot and dusty work that left them covered in the deep, rich red pigment at the end of the day. After digging the ore out of the hillside, the manufacturing process first involved calcining (heat drying) the ore, then crushing it to fine powder in a six-stamper battery. Each stamper weighed 340 kilograms and they were run by a giant waterwheel fed by water from a ditch which was 1.2 metres deep and dug by hand several miles up to the Glengyle Stream. After the pounding, impurities were removed by gravity-separation in water. The raw material for the paint was then kiln-dried and further pulverised through rollers before being bagged up. It was mixed with linseed oil to make the final product.

In the unpublished reminiscences of one A.T. Johnson, who went to work at age 16 at Franzens, freight forwarders, of Port Nelson, he describes how they used to store the 'hematite' from Parapara before it was shipped out. Although it was always in sacks, the finely ground powder permeated the place, and made everyone who worked there spit red. 'It worked through all our clothes to the skin, and I had to handle boatloads of the stuff, and cart it to the wharf for shipping – 10 tons in a day sometimes – and do all my other chores after it was finished.'

Without doubt it was a sought-after product. Its 80 per cent iron oxide content gave it good fire-resistant properties, and brought it to the attention of the government. New Zealand Railways became their best customer, and virtually every railway wagon and goods shed in the country was painted with their reddish-brown line, which to every older New Zealander is the signature colour of NZR. A brighter colour ended up on hundreds of woolsheds around the country, but the company's attempt to make a bright red roof paint for the domestic market proved unsuccessful.

The Onekaka Iron and Steel Company came later. They extracted some 40,000 tons of pig iron from 80,000 tons of limonite between 1922 and 1935, in the country's first successful attempt at iron production.

The paint factory closed around 1920, and the last pigment was extracted from Parapara in 1930 by the Nelson Paint Company, thus ending an era. There is one remarkable 'natural' feature left though, referred to on old maps as the Washbourn Dam. There is no water in this huge circular hillside basin today: it's just all choked with fine *Baumea* rushes laced with tanglefern, a most pleasing palette to chance upon when walking over the ridge, especially as it is inhabited by several pairs of fernbirds. In their own perfect kingdom.

CHAPTER 8

UNSETTLED TIMES

The description of N.C. Wyeth as 'two men fighting in a sack' could probably be said of any reasonable man. Sometimes I was happy to be at home looking after my kids, being with friends, wandering around some local history, checking out some slow process in the swamp. Other times I became desperate for change from my surroundings, feeling the need for some time to reassess things. I watched housetruckers come and go from the Bay, including many who parked up for long periods on my property, and became envious of their mobility. The atmosphere inside their trucks was subtly seductive. I had secured myself a property while they were like the proverbial snails getting around, albeit diesel- and petrol-powered. But at the same time, I could never imagine selling up. Tukurua was where I wanted to die; I had known that for certain since age 19.

I wanted a have-your-cake-and-eat-it solution, so I approached a couple at Collingwood, Geoff and Jenine, who I knew were sick of the prospect of another winter in their beloved house bus, but could not visualise selling it either. Together we came up with what we thought was the perfect solution: I would swap my house for their bus for nine months and go travelling in it, while they spent a comfortable winter at Tukurua. It seemed like the perfect solution.

The plan involved taking my two children away with me, as I couldn't imagine being without them. But Catherine had just joined Josh as a new entrant at Collingwood School, and her teacher was horrified when I told her. 'You'll ruin her education forever,' she said fervently. 'The kids that have the hardest times learning at this school are the ones who live with a solo parent. And you want to take yours away from their home as well.' Little did either of us suspect that dreamy Catherine would become a Cambridge scholar in due course.

The teacher could see my mind was made up, so she made the best of a bad job and implored me to take heaps of children's books, which I did – along with toys, clothes, fishing gear, tools, a small stash of firewood for the wood range, and even a few of my house plants to make the new home feel familiar.

Leaving Golden Bay on the first day out was hugely exciting. Almost immediately Joshua and Catherine discovered that the handrails running out along the ceiling, designed for standing passengers to hold onto, made the perfect jungle-gym bars from which to swing or hang like bats and monkeys as we trundled along. If they wanted to get my attention, all they had to do was pull the cord that ran above the window on each side of the bus, which rang the bell next to the driver's seat. The bus was perfect for them – so I thought – as we drove along they could lie in bed, make snacks or even stoke up the little wood range to keep warm on cold days.

We had a few mechanical mishaps along the way. Even on the first day while we were going over the Takaka Hill, flames and smoke starting coming up through the floorboards. Using some heavy electrical wire, I managed to bypass the battery lead that had chafed through its insulation and short-circuited on the greasy chassis, and soon we were on the road again. It reminded me of my old number-eight-wire fix-it days at Solly's, when everything that could go wrong often did. Then a week later we blew a head gasket at Ngaruawahia. I found a local diesel mechanic and helped him take the head off and replace it. Another time, a flying stone flew up and smashed the little glass fuel-filter bowl. Luckily I carried a box of spares and we could usually get on our way again in no time at all. One slightly annoying problem I put up with for the whole time was that any time the engine had been turned off for longer than two hours, the injectors needing re-bleeding to get it started again. This was not so hard really, with a spanner over the engine cowling that could be opened next to the driver's seat.

During eight months away we did thousands of miles in that bus, much of it travelling back and forth around our favourite communities in Coromandel and Northland. When we arrived at these places in our gypsy bus we were invariably welcomed, the residents often making us feel like long-lost members of their extended family, even if they hadn't met us before. Josh and Catherine would take on a wild gypsy air as we explored places and met residents one by one.

At Wilderland Community near Whitianga, everyone seemed to have something to enthusiastically show us, some symbolic gesture of effort pertaining to their 'dropping out'. Outside the community house, where we went to eat every night, I inspected a soybean grinding stone nearly a metre in diameter that had been painstakingly carved out of sandstone by one of the residents. It even had a small channel under the lower corner to direct the soy milk into a glass jug. An hour later I was talking to a woman who was milking a cow, and sampling her delicious cheeses. Next a long-standing resident was explaining to me the low-voltage solar power system that supplied his house and another just across the gully. Later in the evening we got invited to a jam session with about 20 local musicians. Not being too musical, I played the spoons. Joshua got right into it, banging a xylophone with ease. This was the first indication I had that he was musically inclined.

Like many alternative communities in New Zealand, Wilderland was superbly situated. In this case they had a 250-acre peninsula of scrub, mostly waist-high hakea and manuka regrowth, that stuck out into Whitianga Harbour. Dan and Edith Hansen had bought the hideaway in 1965, using Edith's inheritance as the deposit. When they cleared patches of scrub for gardens, they did something considered novel for the day and let it slowly decompose rather than heap it up and burn it.

From the beginning they opened up their place to virtually anyone that walked in. They were pioneers of a new type, because they believed in disturbing the ecology of the land as little as possible and were not limited by the idea of family 'territory'. Literally thousands of people came and stayed during the community's first 10 years, the number at any one time miraculously remaining somehow constant. Edith told me that she would wave goodbye to someone and then within a few minutes always seemed to be hugging the next arrival.

Everyone was expected to help out with producing food from the gardens, orchards and apiary. They had a stall from which they sold all their surplus vegetables, fruit and honey to the public, and at times this provided something like 90 per cent of the community's cash income. This money was used to buy groceries, petrol for community vehicles, seeds and anything else needed to keep the community going. If there was a surplus, the money went into a kitty on which people could draw for their own needs. I found out that some gave money to the community when they arrived, while others kept their savings intact and drew on the kitty. There was very little pressure to conform to any set pattern: Dan and Edith purposely did not have a 'policy' in regard to their property, because that would imply a set of conclusions, which to them was synonymous with mental stagnation. Dan in particular had been heavily influenced by the philosophies of Krishnamurti.

It sounds idyllic. In many ways I had a glimpse into a golden era of communities, a time when many were in full momentum, and when people and love were still all that mattered. But it did not take long for me to realise that many residents of communities had just as many vices and secrets hidden away as the rest of society. On the second morning I was at Wilderland, the district nurse from Whitianga marched up to my bus and asked to inspect my children, lining them up outside so she could check their general condition, fingernails included. 'Disease starts in communal places like this,' she said, definitely making us feel like 'dirty hippies'.

On our way up to the Hokianga, we ran out of daylight so we parked on the side of the road for the night. As the school bus drove past the next morning, a whole row of children leaned out the window and yelled out in unison, 'Fuck off, you filthy hippies,' as though they had practised it many times.

But most people we met along the way were welcoming, often letting us park on their properties in exchange for helping them complete some job around the place. At Kohukohu I stayed in the school domain and helped some locals renovate the community hall. At Ahipara I took the bus up the winding track to the gumfields and stayed up on those windswept moors for nearly a week, the highlight being a conversation with an old-timer who still hung around up there in hope of finding some more gum.

The Coromandel Peninsula drew me back several times, as its climate and alternative culture were to me more like Golden Bay than Northland ever was. Maybe it was also because I had spent much of my time as a mapmaker drawing a detailed 1:63,360 geological map of the northern Coromandel Peninsula. It was so complicated that it consumed virtually my entire three-year apprenticeship. My boss didn't care how long I took, saying, 'Geological time took hundreds of millions of years to form the place, so what's your three years going to matter?'

Every diatype name I waxed to that map made me feel like I knew each locality intimately whenever we came across it on the road. Despite memorising contour patterns over many parts of the map, some places still surprised me with the intensity of their geography, like at the Karuna Falls community near Colville, where we parked up for nearly two weeks.

At Tapu, on the road from Thames to Coromandel, we parked near the site of a huge Maori battle where hundreds of warriors had been killed – hence the name of the locality, which essentially means 'sacred place'. It was a spooky place, that Tapu. At night, huddled in the bus reading the books we had brought along, my children were sure they could hear people wailing in the distance, and I didn't even prime them for it! Though unrelated, I later found out that more than a few people in the area believed a spirit called Guinevere spoke to them eloquently through a local woman, and a whole cult developed around the interpretation of her words.

A few hours before we left Tapu I suggested to my children that we go for short walk up the Tapu-Coroglen Road, to find a pool in the river and have a bath. It was completely fine when we set out, but suddenly, about a kilometre up the road, thick black clouds rolled over the mountains and unleashed their watery fury upon us. It was simply the heaviest rain I have ever experienced in my life. None of us had raincoats and we got soaked to the skin as we ran back, screaming, screeching and singing in the rain. We got well and truly washed without having to go near the river. Back in the bus, we stoked up the wood range to warm up, then headed off to arrive several hours later at Hot Water Beach, which as the name suggests has thermal springs in the sand. I dug a huge spa-pool-sized crater in the sand at about mid-tide level, and we spent the rest of the day relaxing in the hot water before feasting on a stir-fry cooked up on the range in our bus.

I always picked up hitchhikers wherever we went, the most at any one time in my bus being thirteen. Invited to make themselves at home, they would make cups of tea on the wood range as I drove, read books to the kids, or just sit back and enjoy the ride. Whenever one of them wanted to get off, all they had to do was pull the cord.

For eight months we lived like this, going from one place to the next whenever the whim took us. Then it was time to come home. As we came back along the Desert Road for the last time, the falling snow got heavier and heavier until at last we had to stop. I had three hitchhikers on board that day, and we stoked up the fire until we were as warm as toast. Every so often we would dash outside to throw snowballs and build snowmen to run over later. Later, much to our relief, a snowplough came by and we followed it through; but I will never forget that day, the third to last in that bus.

Good to go, great to return. I was pleased to finally arrive back at

Tukurua and reclaim my house. It had been a wonderful adventure – or so I thought. In later years Joshua told me that going away was one of the most traumatic events of his childhood. His parents had broken up and then suddenly his dad had wrenched him and his sister away from the family home as well, and taken them off in some crappy bus: 'I just wanted to stay at home, Dad – didn't you realise?'

It isn't easy being a dad sometimes, even a hippy one.

CHAPTER 9

BABY DAYS

If you needed a new partner, then you couldn't go past the hippy scene. It was introductions unlimited, and there were plenty of good-looking men and women who were unconstrained by monogamy and repression of their inner feelings. It had been a liberating time travelling around in that bus, as all concepts of exclusive pair-bonding I had previously practised went out those sliding side-windows. Suddenly I was free to get close to as many women as I liked. Men too. And I'm not talking just sex here, although there was plenty of that. It was more about openness of feelings. Everywhere I went, people were receptive. The sharing of thoughts, experiences and emotions helped liberate me from old constraining notions of sexism and ageism.

But it was a fascination with a part-Maori woman from Auckland, named Rozena, that I have to say dominated my interest during that time away in the bus during 1983. I was simply besotted with her – which was strange, because we spent more time during those months breaking up than we did together. Still, I managed to get her pregnant – in the bus, as I recall, parked on top of Mount Eden one Friday night, our combined bevy of four children all asleep down the back.

It was not a happy pregnancy for me, and we didn't see each other at all during the last few months of it. I came back to Golden Bay with a heavy heart and got back into my old life thinking that maybe I would not have much to do with raising this new child of mine. How wrong I was! A week before the birth she rang me, asking did I want to meet up at Te Wairua Festival and be at the birth? I said yes without hesitation, and headed off the next day to have another baby.

Meeting together at Te Wairua put me on a roller-coaster ride of emotions. The festival, held on Ralph and Judy Brock's farm on the banks of the Owhango River, near Taumarunui, was one of the first big New Age celebrations held in New Zealand. The three hundred or so people who took part were not necessarily hippies, although many were, but what connected them all was a quest for a more wholesome and spiritual life. Rather than the rock concert and 'let's-get-out-of-it' mentality of the hippy music festivals, those who came to Te Wairua got off on holistic workshops and endless discussion and exchange of ideas. Before every meal, cooked for everyone in the camp kitchen, we all held hands in a huge circle and said an 'Ommmm…' for as long as we could manage on one breath.

I got into it too, all that peace, love and beansprouts, but occasionally the pragmatist in me couldn't take it any longer and I would head out for a bush walk in the Owhango Reserve, which was actually an ancient swamp forest full of huge kahikatea trees protruding sentinel-like from the water. When the wisps of mist rose in the morning from the forest lake, they wrapped around the trees to make it a magic place. It occurred to me that I had always managed to find a swamp – and solitude within it – wherever I went.

During the festival the time came for the birth. It was a hot day, 4 January 1984. We delivered our son with the help of a wonderful midwife from Thames and a funky doctor from America who happened to be attending the festival, so we totally bypassed the conventional health and medical system. We didn't even weigh him – he looked healthy enough. I buried the placenta among the roots of a huge matai tree. Predictably, Rozena and I could not agree on a name for him, a situation that we could not resolve for several months.

After the festival, it seemed quite natural to load up Rozena's Volkswagen Combi van, which was painted with a big rainbow on both sides, and head back south to my place. We were not 'together' as such, but an affinity with my new boy meant I wanted to be around for him. Along with our baby and Rozena's two daughters, Allannah and Bethany, we had somehow managed to pick up a cat which had just had kittens. Every time we stopped along the way, to everyone's alarm one of the tiny unweaned kittens would jump out and disappear, necessitating long but usually fruitless searches in toilet-stop towns like Te Awamutu, Feilding, Bulls and Palmerston North. By the time we got to Golden Bay we had lost every one of those poor little kittens. Looking back, it was totally irresponsible cat ownership, but I had more important things on my mind at the time.

Rozena and I did get back together for a while, and we had some good times, including a brilliant road trip around Queensland, where we joined a protest group called the Daintree Action Centre who were camped up trying to stop a new coastal road from being carved through the Daintree Forest, a pristine coastal rainforest in tropical North Queensland. Taking off by myself, I walked the full length of its gorgeously deserted tropical beaches. After a chest-deep crossing of Emmugen Creek, I spied a nice sandy spot under some palm trees where I decided to camp – until I saw some slithery marks in the sand. An old bearded tin-miner came out of the scrub and told me they were 'saltie' marks – made by a saltwater crocodile. You could tell from the marks that this particular croc was about five metres long: in other words, a big one.

'If ya do wanna sleep here,' the man advised me, 'just tie yer leg to a tree before you go to bed. The croc can only kill ya by drowning ya. He might hold onto ya for quarter of an hour, but in the end he'll let ya go if he can't drag ya into the water!' Needless to say, I didn't hang around. When I had to cross that murky Emmugen Creek again, holding my pack and clothes up high, my heart was thumping wildly as I thought of that croc returning for a feed.

But the real scare came when a small commando craft came zooming in to the shore as I emerged safely on the other side of the creek. It was the Queensland drug squad doing coastal surveillance, and so once again I found myself being caught naked by the cops. They had been watching me with powerful binoculars from a Coastguard boat way out to sea, and thought my behaviour suspicious when they saw me nervously pacing back and forth before I crossed. After emptying out my pack on the beach and searching it, they left, ordering me to put on some clothes. This was redneck Queensland after all, so it was no surprise that the road got pushed through later anyway. All our protests had been in vain.

Back in New Zealand, Allannah and Bethany became part of my family at Tukurua too. Clare had taken Joshua and Catherine down to live in her house truck in Christchurch so they could attend the Steiner school there, just as they had done in Auckland for a short time with Allannah and Bethany when we had house-trucked around.

But overall, my relationship with Rozena felt like a losing battle. In many ways, having got married so young, I had had little experience with relationships. Luckily all the practice we'd already had at breaking up came in useful for the final big bust-up, when we agreed to burn everything we had ever exchanged, like letters and cards, in one big purging bonfire. Big relief all around.

One thing we had finally managed to agree upon before we broke up was a name for our boy: Anesh, a Sanskrit name meaning 'bringer of light', which Rozena suggested. It immediately became shortened to Nesh. Some of my more conservative friends raised their eyebrows at the name, but somehow it suited my groovy third child quite well. His first words were not 'Mum' or 'Dad', but 'far out', largely thanks to the encouragement of numerous half-sisters. They loved dressing him up, right from when he was a baby. One moment he would be Rambo, touting a plastic tommy-gun; the next he would be a ballerina in a tutu. He loved it all.

I recall taking Nesh to the doctor when he was about one and a half, for some minor ailment. Trying to establish my child's medical history, the receptionist began by asking me who the baby's doctor had been.

'Didn't have one,' I replied. 'Delivered him ourselves.'

'What about the pregnancy test and scan: who did those on the mother?'

I racked my brains trying to recall something, but finally had to admit, 'Er … Rozena never had any tests or scans. She could tell she was pregnant without having to ask anyone – her stomach just got fat!'

'What about the baby's inoculations, then?'

I had to admit that my kid had missed out on these too, though he was perfectly healthy. And no, I couldn't produce a birth certificate either, because it had quite slipped our minds to register his birth.

The incredulous receptionist called the duty nurse for help. Here was a new patient who to all intents and purposes did not exist! No file, no card, no hospital number. This really threw them out, and made me realise with a certain sense of satisfaction that we had 'accidentally' managed to evade the system completely.

One outcome of the New Age philosophy that permeated Golden Bay in the early 1980s was the formation of Tui Community. Unlike the existing communities, Rainbow Valley and Happy Sam, this one was going to be different – or so they said. For a start, it was going to be drug-free, and espouse all the 'higher' callings: everything from permaculture to aromatherapy; from reiki to invoking tree spirits. Whatever holistic hit you were into, this would be the place for you, and the group certainly had a good combination of skills to implement its ideas successfully – it included chartered accountants, architects, beekeepers and marketers.

The group of around two dozen people that came together to form this community held several long meetings to hammer out their ideology and intentions. The talk went on and on without any resolution. Finally one of them, sick of the endless talking, just got up and said, 'Let's forget all these bullshit excuses: if we really want to do it, let's just start living together on Monday.' Half of them agreed and did exactly that, and as a result became known as 'the Monday group'.

Already they had sussed out a likely farmlet with a huge barn-like house at Tui, a locality near Tadmor from which the community took its name. But the big house wouldn't be vacant for another two months, and they needed somewhere fast – by Monday, in fact. So I invited them to move in with me at Tukurua for the meantime.

It seemed the natural thing to do. The Tui-ites were all good people who just needed somewhere to hang out until they could get on to their land. I'd already met them through Rozena, and Colin Iles, a successful beekeeper who was keen on joining Tui, was already living at my place in a double-decker bus with a wind-up pop-top. One of his specialities was making Bee Balm ointment, a business which the Tui community would later take over. The deal was that they would support me while they were there and pay for electricity, food and a share of the rates, and with that understanding they all moved onto my land. One couple slept in the bach, but mostly the eleven others – four couples and three singles – had their own house trucks and tents. It was quite a camp. I did my own thing and they helped out with various projects as required. It seemed at the start to work well.

But the sudden appearance of so many house trucks and tents on one property raised some serious concerns with the local council. I should have guessed this might lead to trouble. However, since the Tui people had a no-drug policy it hadn't occurred to me to warn them that in the past I had been the subject of several search warrants under the Misuse of Drugs Act. I should have done though, because on week seven of their stay, the drug squad turned up in force. It was the same scenario as previously, with four cars roaring up the drive, except that this time I had my pants on, although several of the Tui women were sunbathing topless on the deck of my house. The words of Nelson police district commander Norman Stanhope came back to me: 'It is not unusual for females to present themselves topless while police are carrying out cannabis searches.' It was hilarious watching some of the police officers making a poor job of pretending not to stare, more than one of them breaking into an excited sweat at the sight of a few bare-breasted women.

They went around all the Tui people, asking if they had any drugs in their possession. I had nothing to hide, so I took the visit in my stride, but not so the others. It turned out that every one of them had a small stash of marijuana, although they all denied it of course – except one particularly upstanding individual called Gordon, who believed in living his life by always telling the truth. He even told them where to find it in his tent. The result: he got busted and fined $600 in the Nelson District Court.

For me, the moral of the story was tell the cops nothing, deny everything and lie. But I still felt bad about it because Gordon had got busted on my land, and I should have warned them about my past. A few days before, the building inspector had visited us, with a policeman accompanying him for protection, causing us to wonder exactly what they had expected to find – some mad raving bare-breasted hippies perhaps? Whatever they had reported back had obviously triggered the raid.

The Tui-ites left after two months at my place, taking all their house trucks, tents and caravans, and shifted to their land at Tui. Later they moved, lock, stock and barrel, out to a permanent home, the old Crockford farm at Wainui Bay. Rozena left with them, became a full member of the community, and built a house for herself up on the hill. We shared our boy between us. It worked well.

Perhaps it was partly over marital problems again, but I found myself gradually becoming disillusioned with New Age communities. It was nothing personal against anyone, just that it seemed to me that many of them were kidding themselves about changing the world. What Jos Kingston wrote about environmental activists seemed also to apply to New Agers: 'The middle class eco-freak who refuses to recognise the extent to which he or she has been determined by class, by the privileges, the sense of superior self-confidence which being middle class bestows, can never do more than scratch the surface of the problems which face us.'

After the Tui people left, it was back to just me and the two kids again. Every morning Joshua and Catherine would head down to the gate to catch the school bus – or so I thought. One afternoon around home time I looked out my window and spotted them in the distance coming down through the neighbour's paddock. Obviously they'd wagged school. Questioning them, I found it had been nine-year-old Joshua's idea that day to take his younger sister and hide in the culvert as the bus pulled up. Amazingly, no one had spotted them – or rather, no one had reported their escape. Once the bus was gone, they had headed several kilometres up the stream through the thick bush to the old dam, which they scaled to spend the day throwing stones off it. When the sun looked about right in the sky, they headed back, hoping to arrive about the same time as the school bus, climb back up the culvert and casually walk up the drive.

I had sprung them, but my real concern was not about their missing school – far from it, I was almost proud that they had exhibited some real initiative of their own. I was just worried that they had gone into the hills without telling anyone. But if I was their role model, then they had mimicked me exactly. Whenever possible I took off to head into the hills around my house, often when the kids were at school. No one would ever know where I was, and that was all part of the thrill. One of my favourite pastimes was looking for pieces of ochre, the same stuff that was the base for the Washbourns' paint. Early morning and late afternoon were the best times to look for it, as the low angle of the light accentuated the rich red and umber colour of the loose chunks that had been eroded out of the ore body and washed down the river. Raw ochre has the consistency and density of an oil crayon, and can be daubed directly on to the skin.

According to anthropologists, for more than one and a half million years humans have been hankering for the blemish-free look that only make-up can give. When our earliest ancestors began plastering themselves with red and yellow ochre, brown limonite and black manganese oxide, at first they were probably seeking protection from the harsh elements and biting insects, but it soon evolved into primal fashion.

By all accounts, Maori used a lot of red ochre, or kokowai. At the Waihou River mouth, near where the town of Thames stands today, a surprised *Endeavour* crew came across locals painted from head to toe. Commented the botanist Joseph Banks, 'The reddish ochre which generally was fresh and wet upon their cheeks and foreheads was easily transferable to the noses of anyone who should attempt to kiss them … as the noses of some of our people showed.'

Wandering the Waikato in 1873, naturalist John Bidwell discovered a people 'who looked like they had fallen into a paint pot. I understand it is going out of fashion … but still so common that it is impossible to be carried by a native without getting your clothes daubed all over with the red dirt with which they had saturated their mats.'

A thick kokowai coating was mandatory on chiefs and elderly

matrons. But experimenting with multi-coloured facial designs became the prerogative of the young, especially females, although it seems males were actually allowed wider variation of design.

The best ochre came from deposits which had a rich colour and were free of grit. In places where there was no solid deposit, fern fronds were used to collect the red ochre scum which accumulated on the surface of swamps and slow-moving streams. But it was the solid ochre lumps rather than the scrapings that were most sought after. These could be roasted to make them more friable and bring out the colour, before crushing them to a fine powder with a kuru (stone pounder) on a large rock. The details of preparing kokowai were often a tribal secret, and often it became the work of one family who were traditionally assigned the task.

It is sadly no longer known exactly how the original Ngati Tama-takokiri people of Mohua (Golden Bay) utilised their renowned ochre, since successive raids by northern tribes finally wiped them out around 1827. But up Maori Gully, off the Parapara Valley, you can still see a big flat granite conglomerate grinding stone bearing the marks left by some ancient kuru.

Shark liver oil was used as the base into which the ochre was blended. The way they extracted the oil was ingenious. First they would weave a rough flax kete all around the liver, then tie it above a fire on an angle between two sticks. As the liver heated it was squeezed by twisting the top and bottom strings which had been roughly plaited from the two unwoven 'tails' of flax sticking out of each side, and the oil would dribble down the lower string into a gourd strategically placed to catch it.

The only problem with shark oil was the smell, as it quickly turned rancid. This was fine if you only needed it to repel sandflies, in fact it was the best repellent ever devised, or so some old Maori told the early ethnologist Elsdon Best. It also had the advantage of keeping away the dreaded patupairehe, or fairy folk, just as the vampires of eastern Europe were repelled by garlic. But in situations requiring a little more finesse, like clandestine meetings in the bush well clear of the family whare, the early kokowai cosmetics were made with pleasant-smelling vegetable oils pressed from the seeds of titoki, kohia or miro.

By the early 1900s, as European fashion held sway, traditional Maori make-up became a thing of the past. But it should never be forgotten that no other kokowai deposit in the country compared in size or quality with that which came from the 'rusting' hills around Parapara.

CHAPTER 10

GOLD FEVER

Without a doubt, life has a terrific see-sawing capacity. Now that my kids were away with Clare in Christchurch, I took up building, constructing in a span of several years some 24 haybarns, three houses and numerous sheds around the Aorere Valley, before trying my hand at forestry. The Forest Service had the job of planting out Pakawau Bush with pine trees after a disastrous fire had swept right through the hills and over to Westhaven Inlet. Much of it was planted by the time I got a job on the project, and I joined a gang doing 'blanking', which is planting out the missed spots, including all the steepest country, which had been left.

Each morning we would travel to the job in a van and spend at least an hour sharpening up our slashers with files. This usually took us until smoko. We did plant some steep country in *Pinus radiata*, including around rocky bluffs, but it was slow and arduous work just to get a clear line through the re-growth. We also planted a few hundred kauri trees in the thick gorse of the exposed Pakawau Saddle but I don't think a single one survived the incessant wind.

Then suddenly I contracted gold fever and immediately quit the forestry game. If you have not experienced the feeling of pursuing the precious metal, then you have probably not suffered the full gamut of high emotion. At its most intense, it is capable of causing a level of euphoria that exceeds all that gained from sex, drugs, rock-and-roll and chocolate put together.

Many of my friends felt the urge too. Growing dope for a living was going out of fashion as it was just too much hassle and risk. Suddenly it was cool to be a goldminer, albeit an 'alternative' one. The scene had been set by a surge in world metal prices that focused many big commercial interests on the Kahurangi region. The big oil shocks of the late 1970s had driven the price of gold up to a record high of US$870, and other metal prices skyrocketed too. By the early 1980s, the highly mineralised parts of northwest Nelson were a patchwork of prospecting, mining and exploration sites.

No single issue unified conservationists more than the Australian mining giant CRA's 1981 application to bulldoze a road up to the Mount Arthur Tablelands, an expanse of tussocky downs which had always been the main route into the park. Despite being ranked a state forest park since 1970, in recognition of its ecological values, it didn't have sufficient protection to keep out would-be miners, hydro-electricity developers, and even the Forest Service with plans for huge exotic plantings.

As a first step, the Native Forest Action Council proposed a series of ecological sanctuaries in the area. It wasn't until 1988, after further lobbying to the newly-formed Department of Conservation, that the 83,000-hectare Tasman Wilderness Area was finally gazetted. Now it could only be a matter of time before the adjoining pieces would be brought in to form a new Kahurangi National Park.

Outrage against the big boys mining in our patch had been fairly unanimous through the alternative Golden Bay community, and with many of the so-called 'straights' too. It felt like a serious invasion of our regional privacy, with little benefit to anyone in the area except a couple of Nelson-based helicopter operators, local cartage companies and the occasional unemployed geologist who managed to score a bit of work assisting the big-gun company boys who had been brought in to oversee the job.

If anyone should be digging for minerals it should be us locals, or so we all thought, but it took the gold price to hit the NZ$1000 mark before many of us finally became galvanised into action. Any river flowing through your backyard that historically had given up gold was fair game. A handful of residents of the Happy Sam and Rainbow Valley communities began sluicing in the Anatoki River, which has always rewarded hard work with good gold. In the old Aorere goldfields behind Rockville, about a dozen small operations started up in the early 1980s, working both riverbed and old tailings up the Slate, Rocky and Boulder Rivers, and also on Druggans Flat.

Danny Walker was one of the keenest of them all. Your might have thought he was born with gold fever, but in fact it wasn't until the age of seven that he got introduced to it by going out with an old-time goldminer, Arthur Richardson, who showed him all the likely spots you could expect to find the precious metal. It took him till the age of 10 to get his first half-ounce, which his mentor then sold for him, getting

$50, which was a fortune for a boy back then. Danny's next ounce took him two years, but he stashed it in a Coke bottle and then forgot where he had hidden it. He still hasn't found it after all these years, but that didn't put him off looking for more. In fact he's still gold mining, but he's across in Mongolia these days. His eight-year stint on the Aorere goldfield from 1980 established him as the archetypal digger, full of the optimism that has always typified workers on goldfields.

Gold is extremely heavy: a 35-centimetre cube of it would weigh a tonne (though of course you never find it in bits anywhere near that size). So alluvial gold – the kind that is found in nuggets, flakes and dust, all mixed up with gravel and loose rock – tends to work itself down through the gravel until it hits bedrock or the bottom of deep pools in the river and can't go any further. Some nineteenth-century miners on the Slate River used diving equipment with bell helmets and air pumped by hand while they extracted gravel from the river bottom and the crevices of deep pools. They put the gravel into buckets that were then winched to the surface for sluicing by hand, and got good gold this way.

The new generation of riverbed miners took this a step or two further. They used a suction dredge driven by a water pump, usually powered by a four-stroke petrol engine. It was like a big underwater vacuum cleaner that sucked everything up and passed it over a sluice box. When they worked deep, the sluice box could be suspended under the water to reduce the suction head required to lift the gravel. The sluice box had baffles in it to create an eddy zone where the gold would sink to the bottom of the box. At the end of each day the miners would empty the contents of the sluice box into a pan and have a 'wash up' to get the 'colours': one teaspoon of fine alluvial gold weighed around one Troy ounce. This was always the most exciting part of a day's work, because you never knew what you might find. I recall a hard afternoon spent up the Parapara with little Nesh in tow, shovelling vast amounts of gravel through my riffle box. For hours I hyped him up about all the gold we were going to get, but when we panned the fine gravel remaining in the riffle box we had only a few specks of colour to show for all our efforts, and on closer inspection they turned out to be fool's gold. So disappointing! And yet, a week later, just 50 metres upstream and by myself this time, I picked up a half-ounce nugget, the sight of which filled me with absolute euphoria and unlimited energy, spurring me on in a frenzy of further digging until it became too dark to continue.

They also used underwater breathing apparatus known as a 'hookah'.

111

This consisted of a compressor, usually powered by the same engine that drove the water pump, sending breathable air down a hose to a mouthpiece. Of course, a rubber suit was essential to keep an underwater miner from getting cold too quickly. A conventional wetsuit was best, because you could attach a big truck-tyre valve to the back, connect a hose that ran to a heat-exchanger on the engine, and have hot water circulating through the wetsuit. With this set-up a keen goldminer could work for hours on end in cold water, although there were some nasty accidents when temporary blockages followed by boiling surges in the hose line caused severe scalding. The diver also had to wear a weight belt with about 10 kilograms of lead to counteract the natural buoyancy of the wetsuit.

My friends Graham and John were masters at the art of gold mining, and managed six years of hard yakka up the Slate River, although I can't think of anything more exhausting. Just four-wheel-driving in with all their gear, then carrying and lowering it down into the gorge, was a marathon mission. Down among the deep crevices in the pools of the steep-sided river they directed their suction-dredge nozzle, using a crowbar to move the goolies out of the way. They even shifted the biggest boulders in relatively swift rapids, using triple-purchase winches. They took it in turns to supervise the compressor and suction dredge, and to dive.

It was not only physically draining work, but dangerous as well. Rocks could fall in any direction, pinning a leg or an arm. One man who worked alone got his arm stuck under a large rock, but luckily could just reach his crowbar with his free arm. For fifteen minutes he worked the rock, all the time knowing that if his compressor cut out or ran out of fuel he would be a dead man. Luckily he got himself free in time. Often your hands would be so numb with cold that you could do them quite a nasty injury without even feeling it until you got out of the water and warmed up. Then as the circulation returned you would find yourself bleeding profusely, or some enormous bruise swelling up. Quite a few new chums would get all keen and enthusiastic, imagining they were going to make a fortune easily, but would soon give up, disillusioned, as they discovered how arduous and dangerous it really was.

I loved the stories of the old goldfields. Golden Bay was the scene of the first of a number of gold rushes in early New Zealand, and thousands descended on the Collingwood field when it was discovered in 1857. Harry Washbourn described it like this: 'Imagine a large picnic with everyone in the highest spirits as if they had just come into a fortune or were just about to, that will give you some idea.'

Diggers were known by variations on their first names or nicknames, like French Charley, Scotch Charley or German Charley, or 'Ginger' No. 1, 2 or 3 as the case may have been. Pickles, Charcoal Bob and Jackie are a few other names recorded on shopkeepers' chits. These men would just record their addresses with *ad hoc* names that described their location or circumstances, like 'Dirty Mary's Gully' or 'Last Ditch.'

In the Golden Gully tragedy of 1861, a drunken miner was immolated with his dog in his hut after a quarrel with a woman. In the investigation that followed, the coroner asked if it was true that the deceased had only the day before brought a large quantity of gold. This was confirmed. So where was it? Surely he had been carrying it on his person? An old digger stood up, claiming to have panned the ashes of the man as soon as they had cooled down. 'And not a bloody colour either,' he offered as evidence. The subject of that missing gold was hot gossip for years.

Despite all the hard-luck stories, handsome rewards awaited those prepared to work hard on the goldfields in those early days. One man got seven ounces of gold in a day just by turning over rocks up in the Quartz Ranges. Another got a spectacular 135 ounces in one day, working a cradle in a section of the Slate River known as McKenzie's Bar. Miners joked that it was the men who rocked the cradle and not the women back then.

In search of gold-mining relics and new swamps, I had walked all through this country and knew it well. I formed a partnership with Dick Lamb, with whom I had done some building and logging work in the past, to mine over 23 hectares of river flat along Appos Creek, near the Devil's Boots. In our mining license application, registered number MLA 32 2047, we outlined our plan to dig house-sized holes using Dick's hydraulic backhoe, the bucket of which had a capacity of 0.4 cubic metres per scoop. Then we would put the gravel subsoil through a trommel, riffle boxes and jigs at a rate of around 30 cubic metres an hour. It was an ambitious plan, but not beyond the scale of what other gold diggers were doing at that time with powerful suction dredges and floating riffle boxes working directly over the river bed.

We weren't bashing around in the dark, either. We knew there was gold in that ground because a very experienced old miner had previously worked a hectare of our claim by hand. From his results we knew that on average we could expect a yield of 0.284 grams of gold per cubic metre. At that rate we could expect to win at least 500 grams of the precious metal out of every 2000 cubic metres we processed. That's 16 Troy ounces (a Troy ounce is 31.1 grams, slightly heavier than an ordinary ounce which is only 28), worth close to $20,000 in local currency at the time. We had it all worked out, optimistic theory fuelling more and more gold fever as we went along.

I went around driving in our boundary pegs and put up a sign describing the boundaries of the licence area, proudly staking the claim in the name of the Aorere Mining Company. But disappointingly for me, that was about as far as we got with it. The farmer who owned the land initially gave us his approval, on the understanding that we would re-plant his gorse-covered land in grass, but when he realised the scale of operation we were proposing he changed his mind. We were sunk before we even started.

I used to laugh about the fly-by-night goldmining companies, whose shareholders, often based overseas, would bankroll the initial operation for a year or so until it petered out and the company would be wound up, just like what happened with the Red Hill Swindle. But my goldmining venture was even more risible, because we didn't actually shift a single shovelful of gravel. Still, I had experienced a bad dose of gold fever, and how could I not catch another dose if I didn't know what to avoid?

Two guys called Henry and Dave were mining up the Rocky River until gold prices plummeted to a low of US$280 in the late 1980s and they abandoned their riverside camp. They still had a 44-gallon drum of petrol which had been airlifted in by helicopter but was not worth flying out again. So on the eve of their departure they took their vengeance on the thick black clouds of sandflies that had tormented them for so long. They poured the contents of the drum into the swiftly-flowing river and put a match to it. Henry recalls, 'Kapow! It was just like Vietnam, spreading down the river in sheets of ascending flame.'

One of the most colourful characters to emerge out of that 1980s mini-goldrush was a man who, like his earlier counterparts, was known only by his nickname, 'Boomer', a reference to an occasion when he'd accidentally blown the chimney off a timber kiln where he worked. His father was a hot-blooded Mexican who had served in the US Army and his mother was a one-legged publican from Westport. There was a story about how she had been out whitebaiting and filled her bucket to the brim, so she pulled off her tubular metal artificial leg and filled that up too. Then, apparently, she hopped back home holding her net plus the full bucket and leg.

Boomer liked the top shelf and could drink anyone under the table. Like many hard-core miners he always carried around in his pocket a 'skite tin' full of his best nuggets, which in his case were around $5,000 worth. Everyone seemed to have a story about Boomer, or a wife who had been screwed by him. He ended up going to prison for pulling a gun at a party in his little cabin. The revelry had gotten out of hand and his stereo had got smashed, so he'd pulled out a pistol and waved it around to calm things down a bit. When he left the Bay no one heard much of him again.

After the gold rush I took some time out to visit friends in Wellington, particularly a couple called Rex and Lorraine who lived in a big old two-storey house on The Terrace. Everyone just knew it by its street number, which was 242. This house was always full of interesting people, one of whom was a woman named Melanie, who was a year or two younger than me. When I first visited the house she was out, but the open door of her room revealed the new paint job she had done. The walls and ceiling were painted blue and red except for a big circular shape in one top corner, which upon closer inspection I discovered was occupied by a huge spider web.

Although I had not yet met her I was immediately fascinated by this mysterious woman who would paint around a long-established spider web because she obviously considered that the animal had as much right to be there as she did. I made excuses to come back and meet her, and before long we were an item. The first time she visited me at Tukurua was after she had walked the Abel Tasman National Park coastal track, painting as she went. When she turned up at the 'manuka nest', as she immediately dubbed my house, I wasn't home, so she just pinned all her pictures upon the walls as if the place was her own.

She shifted from Wellington to Nelson, where she got a job doing hospice work for Cancer Support, but it was pretty much a foregone conclusion that we would get together over in the Bay. Better still, Josh and Catherine took an instant shine to her, so it was not long before she moved in and came to feel just as much at home at Tukurua as I did. One modification she made, though, was to bring in some chairs. Previously there were just a few cushions thrown around because I seemed to be always busy 'doing things', and had no need for lounge furniture.

Melanie taught me how to relax properly, something I had not been able to do for a long time, and I in turn showed her around my swamp. At first she thought it odd but quaint that I should be so enthusiastic about a water-sodden part of my property. 'This is virgin ground, a hidden, untouched place,' I told her. 'Swamps change with time. They silt up and fill in. But chances are this swamp has looked much the same for hundreds of years. What other parts of New Zealand could you say that of?' Years later she said I had been 'so cute going on about my swamp like that'.

CHAPTER 11

SWAMP DWELLERS

Although Maori made some major modifications to the ecology of New Zealand, they did virtually no draining of the swamps that once covered more than ten percent of the country. To them, swamps were reliable sources of food such as waterfowl and eels, in any weather and at any season. They were valuable real estate just as they were, and the various iwi and hapu vigorously defended their rights to these mahinga kai. Surveyors and settlers from the 1800s have left us all sorts of descriptions in the form of survey maps, soil maps, paintings and written accounts that provide us with a fairly accurate snapshot of how much virgin swampland once existed, and how nine-tenths of it got reclaimed, or at least logged of its towering kahikatea.

Lorna Langford at the old Bainham Store always told me stories from the early days when I popped into her shop. How her grandfather Ned drained their hunk of the Bainham swampland with nothing but a shovel, and turned it into lush, productive dairying land. Or how one of their neighbours would drill a hole in the shell opening of a carnivorous native land snail (*Powelliphanta*) and tether it with a short piece of twine to a stick in his garden so that it would devour all the slugs overnight. He used to diligently re-tether it in a new spot every morning, so the garden stayed pest-free – well, free of ones that crawled slower than a snail, anyway. And how her parents, when driving in their motor vehicle from Bainham to Takaka, would always stop halfway for a picnic lunch and a check of the radiator by the ford through the Tukurua Stream.

One meaning of Tukurua is 'two outlets'. But according to another version it is 'hole made by two trees', and I think this sounds more likely, because early accounts describe a pair of massive rata that once formed an archway over the mouth of the stream. Sometimes after big easterly storms, remnants of the huge stump on the south bank can still be seen protruding through the sand at mid-tide level. Only once, after a particularly big storm, have I ever seen the second great stump exposed. In the past, thirsty Maori paddling across Golden Bay used to pull their canoes up into the big dark hole between those two great rata trees, because it was the only place where fresh running water could always be found close to the sea. All the other creeks coming out along this coast were liable to be brackish.

Abel Tasman's disastrous encounter with Maori off Wainui Bay in 1642, the first confirmed contact between Maori and European, was marked by mutual xenophobia and misunderstanding, and resulted in four of his crew being killed. By the time the first white settlers came on the scene, the Maori of Mohua (Golden Bay) were of different groups. Raiders from the North Island had wrought havoc among the Ngati Tumatakokiri people around 1827, killing many and driving the survivors away down the West Coast. Thus, by right of conquest Mohua became the preserve of Ngati Tama and Ngati Toa with their Ngati Atiawa allies, and chiefs such as Te Puoho at Parapara and Eneho (Niho) of Whanganui Inlet firmly exercised their jurisdiction. The big pa at Taupo Point, which had been occupied by the people who attacked Tasman, was by now long deserted, and had become supplanted by several smaller settlements around the Golden Bay coastline. Most notable of these was the Puramahoi pa, overlooking the mouth of the Pariwhakaoho River near what is today Patons Rock.

Up to 150 Maori used to live on the flat at Tukurua Point, where the New Zealand Haematite Paint Company later ran its little railway out to a short wharf they built here in 1907. That got washed away after only six months, much as the land around the point has ever since.

If you duck under the barbed-wire fence which is now suspended over the beach not far from a huge sprawling fig tree, after a short scramble through the scrub you will find a small lichen-covered sign inscribed 'Pirika Cemetery Reserve'. This one-acre square of consecrated ground is the last resting place of about twenty local Maori who converted to Christianity, and is named after the wily local chief Pirika, who was buried here first.

Connections again: the first time I heard of Pirika was in a handwritten account by the first European woman settler at Tukurua, who along with her husband eventually became the first European owner of my swamp. So naturally I became keen to investigate their lives.

Elizabeth Pringle Caldwell and her husband Thomas spent ten years in Nelson before moving in 1865 on to a block near my place which they bought from an Englishman who apparently hadn't managed to make a proper go of it and was desperate to return home. But Elizabeth just loved it, and described the building site they chose, 'close to the beach, just at the head of the Bay, commanding a lovely view from Cape Farewell to Separation Point, with the far-distant snowy cone of Mount Egmont in very clear weather.'

The whole family looked forward to it with great delight. But just as Thomas set out for Nelson to buy building materials, equipment to start a dairy farm, and to finalise the title to their land, the Land Wars broke out in Taranaki. In a highly articulate diary, Elizabeth recorded her fears growing by the day: 'Our Maori friends began to look very sullen and silent – old Piraka [sic] was busy casting bullets "to shoot the white man", he said when the boys questioned him.'

Thomas was still in Nelson when the first boatload of materials and equipment arrived, including timber and a cheese press packed in a wooden crate, which got landed on the dunes, probably about a hundred metres south of where the motor camp is situated today. But when Elizabeth and her older children went to fetch the timber, 'a band of Maori came along making hostile demonstrations – old Catherine with her hair cut short and standing upright a foot above her head, and whenever my people touched a plank, up she bounced, her tongue very far out, war fashion and relieved them of it at once. The women always headed the charge, and we could not proceed with any work. They claim to have never ceded title to the land – nor had they ever received any payment for it.'

Day by day the news from Taranaki got worse, and 'smouldering fires seemed gathering, even in our Bay, ready to burst into flame.' Still more boxes turned up by sea freight, and these too were stacked on the dunes, although the Caldwells were unable to be take possession of them. This was a story that might well have inspired the movie *The Piano*, I thought. The Tukurua version was not as elaborate and pretentious as the film, but being a true tale from my neighbourhood made it far more powerful, especially as further details unfolded.

Elizabeth wrote to Sir Edward Stafford, first Superintendent of Nelson Province, describing her plight and asking him to intervene. Stafford sent Reverend T.L. Tudor, of Nelson, to defuse the situation. Tudor had great influence amongst the 'natives', and implored them to not join the Taranaki insurgents. His visit also helped to reassure other anxious settlers in the district.

The sudden discovery of gold in a stream nearby made everything more complicated, because 'it had to be kept a dead secret in the present state of native affairs.' For months the impasse on Tukurua Beach continued, 'the timber lying useless and worst of all we could get no milk or butter, a most serious loss to a young family'. Thomas went back to Nelson to see if anything could be done to settle the dispute, but was told it would have to wait until Donald McLean, known as 'Makarine' to the Maori, came over, he being the unquestioned arbitrator in all native affairs:

> So we had no choice but to wait as patiently as the Maoris, for time is nothing to them – they hold the most wearisome endless koreros, "conversaziones" in more polite parlance, squatting comfortably on the ground, in either Town or Country, wherever they happen to be, puffing away at the inevitable pipe, men and women alike – thus they are in no hurry, and the longer they can spin out the conference the better they like it.

Obviously the waiting and the standoff did not bode well for Elizabeth. While Thomas was still away in Nelson, she finally in frustration grabbed some boards from the pile on the beach and laid them as a floor in her big tent 'which seemed very heavenly comfort indeed'. Next day some Maori turned up at her tent, demanding that she hand the boards back, but she refused and finally they left.

Her children whiled away the time gathering shellfish on the beach, or picking oysters and splendid large mussels among the rocks at low tide. But for Elizabeth, what was a rare delicacy like an oyster when the want of milk for her children was a far more serious deprivation? A large box of arrowroot served as a substitute, which when mixed with water made a nourishing drink for the baby. Fortunately they always had the lovely little Tukurua Stream, clear as crystal, so they were never short of fresh water.

Every night the family would huddle in their tent, listening to the far echoes of the Maori songs and chants rising and falling on the breeze, knowing full well that large war canoes were being sent away to Taranaki, laden with bullets and other materials of war.

One evening Elizabeth's eldest son Tom, who was the most trusted by the local Maori, accompanied them 'down the coast six miles to Puruahoia [sic], a well known Pah where "Edwin Stanton" and his father the old Duke of York were chiefs.' Her brave boy counted 200 Maori at the 'parliament', both male and female, and noted that the women were as forthright as the men. He listened to long speeches for and against joining the rebellion, but the group made no decision:

> This did not add to our peace of mind, for we had been told that the Maoris always as a preliminary massacred their best friends, so there was considerable reason for anxiety. Being at this time inevitably alone with my children, I never failed to call them around me at night to read prayers, and commit ourselves to the Almighty protecting care of the God of all Comfort and Consolation, so that should we never see the dawn of another morning we should assuredly enter the dawn of Eternal Day.

Days were a little more cheerful for the children. When they had finished their chores, they would engage in some sport, snare some of the plentiful kaka, or go fishing. On the warm summer nights they would wade out and spear flounders by the basketful, using torches of splintered wood tied into tight bundles with flax. The light attracted the fish, a trick they learned from the Maori.

Then disaster struck. One cold May night after the children were all asleep, her husband still in Nelson, Elizabeth was dozing off with her baby beside her in the still moonlight when she felt a violent shock as if hit on the head with an axe, and suddenly found she was paralysed all down her left side. The symptoms wore off for a time, but recurred another dozen times over the following day. She dared not get up, but managed to sew for brief periods:

> There was no pain but the horrible thing came on always when I began to feel drowsy, and I dared not sleep. I directed my eldest girl who was six years old to get out from my trunks some black things, as I had been mourning for a sister, put away.
>
> 'What for Mama? Oh you are so white Mama, do you think you will die?'
>
> 'I am afraid of it my pet,' I said. 'So you would want a black frock for Papa to take you back to Scotland, so get me out the stuff.' So as I felt able to sit up I made the frocks to be ready.'

Little by little, as she felt able to sit up, she made all the little frocks and outfits for her children to attend her own funeral. After a few days, the boys managed to track down a doctor, a young man from America who had recently settled at Takaka, 20 miles away. He examined Elizabeth and diagnosed her case as 'partial paralysis', saying, 'If your speech leaves you, don't be alarmed – that might come back, but I don't think you can last many days. I hope your husband can come back at once.'

By the time Thomas did return, a week later, Elizabeth was able to get around their tent a bit, but the 'awful, mysterious affliction' continued and it became imperative that she should be taken to Nelson for further treatment.

A small ferry, the *Lady Barkly*, regularly plied between Collingwood and Nelson, stopping at Waitapu and Riwaka along the way. Sitting on the beach, waiting for that boat, Elizabeth gave one last drink to her baby boy: 'such a lovely darling fourteen months old, who could run about quite nicely. I had made a calico hat for him with a wide brim, inserting around the edge a fine supplejack to keep off the broiling sun, my stock of straw hats being out.' She recalled this weaning of her last child with great fondness, describing:

> his little blue serge coat and big hat which I had put on, feeling his wee white bare feet before handing him over to his eldest brother. I then took a fond farewell of them all with many tears and much anguish of soul. An old Maori woman, Maria, who always said she was 110, and certainly looked it but was a kind old creature, promised me to 'look out' for them, as long as they did not get drowned or burnt!

Elizabeth's baby never forgot that parting scene on the beach all his life, and proved it too. When a tall fine young man, he startled a gay party at an evening assemblage who were discussing the power and memory and the length back to which it could go. 'I distinctly remember,' said this bold gentleman, 'the day I was weaned.' The ladies all blushed and the gentlemen shouted with laughter. No one believed him, but it was quite true as he found out comparing notes some time afterwards.

In fact Elizabeth did not, as she feared, die without seeing her children again, but returned two months later, well rested and nourished on the orders of two skilful doctors in Nelson. By this time her family had moved to a comfortable cottage at Motupipi, at the far corner of the Bay. There they remained until Donald McLean turned up in Nelson to settle the dispute, which he did in their favour.

It had taken two years of weary waiting, but at last it was safe to take possession of their Tukurua property. As compensation for their ordeal, the government awarded the Caldwells an additional 300 acres of adjoining land. This included what is now my swamp, and the surrounding slopes which had recently been all burnt off. They suspected that this land would be utterly infertile, but it didn't matter, as they were all overjoyed to be settled at last.

When they finally received word that the Maori in the district had taken allegiance to the Queen, they waited for the first fine day and set sail in a huge canoe packed to the gunwales with their belongings. Landing at the head of Tukurua Beach, they gathered their sun-bleached boxes, which were still stacked on the dunes, salvaged their warped timber, and immediately started building. 'There was a cottage erected near to the beach – a large kitchen with a spacious chimney, a famous dresser and I had the pleasure of arranging my long shut up dinner set on it, hanging up the teacups on little hooks with great pride and thinking how lovely to be home at last, and so near the sea too, an unspeakable delight to me.'

Coincidentally, I came across the remarkable story of Elizabeth Caldwell at the same time when Melanie came into my life, another woman who fell in love with Tukurua as much as her pioneering counterpart. The abundant birdlife was one of the things that made it special for Melanie, but this was just a recent development. When I first came, the denuded slopes of the surrounding land had been remarkably devoid of birdsong, except from blackbirds and thrushes that had taken over the nearby farmland. If it hadn't been for the weka and fernbirds, and the seasonal flowering of the flax which brought droves of tui to feast upon the nectar, it would have been very dull indeed in the bird department. Since then, natural re-growth and my planting of eucalypts, kowhai and tree lucerne had been a magnet for birds that fed on nectar, berries and fruit, including tui, bellbirds, wood pigeons, grey warblers and waxeyes. Fantails too seemed to suddenly flit about everywhere, performing their perky acrobatics in search of insects.

But I was sorry that a sudden decline of weka just before Melanie arrived meant she would not be able to get to know these cheeky birds and enjoy their company. It has been suggested that the decline of weka in districts where they were once so plentiful is probably due to a disease. The population in Canterbury took a tumble around 1917; in Taranaki they disappeared in 1918. In parts of Northland weka were plentiful in

1936, yet hard to find by 1940. They remained plentiful in northwest Nelson until the mid-1980s, and on Stewart Island until just a few years ago, while in Westland they are still common.

Perhaps they did succumb to a disease, but another theory is that introduced predators played the biggest part. Polynesian rats can break into a 60-millimetre-long egg, larger than that of most native birds, weka included, although these animals had disappeared in the late 1800s when the ship rat arrived and out-competed them. Anyway, weka can easily kill a rat, so it seems unlikely that introduced rodents were their nemesis. Dogs, cats and habitat destruction have all probably played a part, but it is most likely the mustelid family – weasels, ferrets and stoats – that have been the worst culprits. One theory is that ferrets escaped from a fitch farm in the Bay during the 1980s, and since the area has no wild rabbits (their usual prey) they gave the wekas a hammering instead. Other factors may be competition with possums and rodents for food, such as fruit and small forest-floor animals.

In the mid-1980s I began setting Fenn traps in long boxes on my property after Nesh made several sightings of what was quite likely a ferret running across the paddock near our chookhouse. But even back then I suspected we were too late to stop the tide, and I lamented that Melanie and the children would probably never get to surprise the stealthy weka at its mischievous antics, entering the house uninvited, intent on relieving us of some shiny, useless possession. They always went for the type of shiny stuff we did not really ever need but just coveted. Buddhists believe that all non-essential possessions only serve to make you unhappy. I could not help but muse that perhaps the weka's real purpose was to relieve us of such superficial cravings: Buddhist birds they could well all be.

CHAPTER 12

ISLAND SWAMP

The only thing Melanie missed about the city was not being able to stroll down to the corner dairy, and the fact that the nearest movie theatre was 120 kilometres away in Nelson. I had been active in the Golden Bay Film Society, as both a projectionist and committee member, and for a year was even an executive member of the New Zealand Federation of Film Societies. But even involving Melanie in all that could hardly be expected to satisfy her desire to keep up with the movies.

So with some enthusiasm we bought a big 16 mm projector from John Law, who had run the Greenlane Theatre in Dunedin before shifting to the Bay, and took over his business of screening popular movies every fortnight in the Golden Bay High School hall. It was an exciting if small-scale venture, renting 16 mm movies from Auckland-based film distributors, then on the night setting up, selling sweets, showing the film and then tidying up before we packed our gear and left.

But there was something we didn't count on, and that was the pent-up energy of the Takaka teenagers. Apart from sporting activities, a couple of church youth groups and the occasional school disco run with military discipline, there were no organised social activities for the youth of Golden Bay. So when something did come up like popular movies at the school hall, the atmosphere was often hyped.

Our first screening was the movie, *2010*, which was a sequel to *2001: A Space Odyssey*. The place was packed with over 200 people, mostly teenagers in a state of extreme excitement. Because they intimately knew every square centimetre of their school, many tried to sneak in without paying, via emergency exits, windows deliberately left open earlier in the day, passages through broom cupboards, and even basement crawl spaces under the stage. Anything to avoid going past Melanie, who was sitting at the main door selling tickets for $3. Great minds think alike, and I am pretty sure I caught all of them, because I had always tried exactly the same thing at the Ascot Cinema in Wellington when I was a lad.

The noise level was high enough when the movie started, but it got progressively more deafening. I felt for the handful of adults who had come to watch the sequel to their cult movie, so I stopped the movie more than once in an attempt to settle things down, but this had little effect. In hindsight, what could we really expect from these pent-up teenagers? There was nowhere else for them to socialise in Takaka unless you count loitering on one of the town's two street corners. And of course, we had hyped them up by selling sugary confectionery as well!

The next movie two Friday nights later, *Karate Kid 2*, was more suitable in that it attracted an audience made up entirely of young people. There was a storyline, but it didn't matter, and at times it was hard to tell where there was the most action happening: on the screen or in front of it. I quickly hit upon a formula: for every movie we screened aimed at adults we would show two for what we called 'the teenagers', although their age range was really more like 5 to 25. One Friday we'd show *Room with a View*, two weeks later *The Goonies*, followed by *The Three Amigos* a fortnight later. Neither audience demographic group need cross paths ever again – although my kids always came along, because we couldn't get a babysitter. Besides, I think the celluloid over-exposure did them good: it broadened their minds.

What I definitely couldn't factor in was the behaviour of some of the teenagers after their screenings. Let loose like a torrent, spreading over the little town of Takaka like a mini tsunami. Some just went home, but a few, maybe a dozen 15–17-year-olds at most, loitered around the school afterwards and did things like light the contents of rubbish bins so they had somewhere warm to stand around and get drunk. Young pissheads and small towns go together like pigs and a sty.

Just three months into our venture, the school's board of trustees held an emergency meeting, issuing a statement saying they wanted nothing more to do with these high-jinks, and abruptly terminated our agreement to hire the hall. I could see their point: they had property to protect, but I felt sorry for the majority of well-behaved young people who had just lost out on what was for many their only social night out. I approached the local Anglican church to use their hall, but predictably the ageing committee members turned me down flat.

Melanie and I did not like the way that the youth of Golden Bay were being lumped together as too irresponsible and immature to have their own night out, and decided not to give up without a fight. Like many small-town and rural teenagers, the youth of Golden Bay were already socially disadvantaged. Many lived long distances apart and their opportunities for learning to relate to one another in social contexts that were not heavily chaperoned by parents and teachers were pitifully few. Naturally there would always be a small minority who went berserk when let loose. But in time those teenagers would become adults, and mature and responsible adults need to have spent some part of their teen years learning to be mature and responsible. In short, the teenagers needed more opportunities, not fewer.

My anarchistic nature made me want to spew over the collective decisions of mainstream society. Being forever inspired by the magic and fantasy of films, I had long promoted the idea of putting a cinema back in Takaka, and the debacle with the high school was just the encouragement I needed. The Dalgety's farm store right in the middle of town had recently closed, and the building was up for sale. Its sturdy concrete construction, snazzy shop frontage, and cavernous interior made it a perfect building to convert into a movie theatre. So I bought it.

It was sheer lunacy to embark on this property and business path while I was still basically content homesteading, and I still don't know quite how I got myself into it. I am single-minded about all my projects, and nothing else mattered at that time except getting a cinema up and running, never mind that I had no money whatsoever. The price of the building and yard was $115,000. I claimed the GST back on the delayed settlement and used it for the deposit, then borrowed the rest at the extreme interest rate of 24 per cent. Some friends generously lent their time and money to help us convert the building into a cinema in what seemed like a record 12 weeks, including tiering the floor and building an elevated projection room. A group of us worked seven days a week, with 16-hour days not uncommon as we converted the huge warehouse into a cinema. I also converted the former Dalgety's shopfront into a retail shop which opened as 'Artisans' and was the first co-operative craft shop in Takaka's main street.

It was a big job, with fire regulations, plumbing and heavy cable wiring, paraplegic ramps and toilets, approved emergency exits and good security features. Even just studying the regulations was a big job.

Getting the furnishings and projection equipment was relatively easy. I was madly setting up a cinema at a time when many larger ones were closing down all over the country. The new trend was towards smaller, more intimate theatres, from small Rialto-type cinemas showing arthouse movies, right up to what the chains were doing, dividing their big theatres into multiplexes with a warren of mini-theatres. Technological advances in cinema projection technology meant that one projectionist could now show several movies at once. This also meant that old equipment and furnishings were going for fire-sale prices everywhere around the country.

For $1,000 cash I bought the entire contents of the Central Theatre at Papatoetoe, in Auckland, from a property developer just before the place was to be demolished. The power had been disconnected so Melanie and I had a rather eerie experience working by torchlight for three days in that huge building, rats scuttling everywhere as we unscrewed a hundred of the best seats and unbolted all the projection gear we could shift, including the two huge 1938-vintage German Walterdaw 5 projectors, which weighed about a tonne each. We also got electric motors, transformers, ventilation cowling, speakers and sound screen, which is a special kind of screen with countless tiny holes that let the sound through from big loudspeakers behind. Whenever I needed a lift I went out on to busy George Street and grabbed the first street kids I could find. Some told me to get fucked, but others were only too happy to help out. What we couldn't get on to our trailer, we trucked down.

Back in Takaka, the business community smiled politely while we toiled away, doubting of course behind their facades that we could ever make it work. They were nearly right. Putting all the Central Cinema stuff back together again was one mission, but learning from scratch to drive it all was another. I went all around the country, talking to projectionists and cinema managers and getting little crash-courses in the trade. A trip to Sydney took me into what was regarded as one of the world's most modern cinemas, Hoyt's Multiplex, where the projectionist I met was required to be no more than a computer keyboard nerd. It was all part of the picture I needed to be able to assemble a business back in New Zealand.

Cinemas in this country were still highly unionised, and usually the union made sure only licensed projectionists ever got to screen movies. This had its roots as a safety issue, because the celluloid film of old was highly inflammable and easily set off by the very hot projector lamps. But the union gave me a dispensation because our operation was so small. After that there was nothing that could stop us except the local fire brigade. Fire regulations meant that Melanie, as front-of-house manager had to train as a fire safety officer, but at that time it was not possible because she was a woman. We bickered and bartered until finally they deputised me so that Melanie could operate 'under' me. It was so stupid, and Melanie fumed about sexist regulations, but I told her not to worry: we were there.

The Village Theatre opened on Saturday 28 November 1987, with a weekend of solid screenings of *Footrot Flats – The Dog's Tail*. The laughter soon turned to cheers for the 'brave little cinema' as it was described in the newspaper, and Takaka become officially New Zealand's smallest town with a cinema. Karamea used to have that honour, thanks to Mark Christensen, but its theatre burned down not long before we opened.

By showing a rash of other blockbuster movies like *Crocodile Dundee* and *Good Morning Vietnam*, we immediately got a good cash flow to pay many of the debts I had run up. Virtually every screening was booked out in those early months, and we appealed to all the niche groups in diverse Golden Bay. We got sell-out audiences to music films people could get up and dance to, like the Talking Heads film *Stop Making Sense* and U2's *Rattle and Hum*, and arthouse movies like *The Milagro Beanfield War* and *Withnail and I*. Even late-night horror movies like *Texas Chainsaw Massacre 2* – we screened them all, appealing to a town that had been without a theatre for a quarter of a century.

I did most of the film bookings and all the projection work, while Melanie looked after front of house, where she painted two huge murals in the lobby: Humphrey Bogart from *Casablanca* for the older customers and Madonna for the younger ones. Melanie and I got married on our lawn one Friday afternoon before rushing off to show four movies in a row. Our first baby together (but my fourth), Nina, was born into the world of that cinema, and Melanie became known among cinemagoers as 'the breastfeeding ticket seller'. To our amusement, it was even mentioned in the New Zealand Motion Picture Exhibitors' Association Newsletter. As far as Melanie was concerned, if our baby needed a feed, selling tickets was no reason to wait.

We lived, worked and breathed that theatre for nearly four years, becoming good friends with many teenagers who came nearly every day. After the last screening on Friday night, many would wait outside like abandoned waifs, waiting for us to take them home. Melanie's orange Mini-Minor was perfect for commuting the 18 kilometres back home on screening nights, which were Thursday to Monday, but more often than not we packed in a few extra passengers along the way.

One Friday night we came out to find 12 young teenagers waiting for a lift home! But we had a policy of never leaving anyone young out alone after we locked up, so we somehow squeezed in the lot and took off. Before we were even halfway down Commercial Street, the new policeman stopped us for a routine check. Melanie was driving and I was in the passenger seat, counting a wad of takings scattered across my lap. That must have looked weird enough, but then he shone his torch in the back and started counting … one, two, three, four … twelve children! The smallest was squeezed across the parcel shelf at the back. I explained our predicament, suggesting that in the interests of safety he might like to take some of the children home himself, but he just let us go with a suggestion to drive slow. That was community policing before it became just a buzzword.

I think we managed the cinema and handled the social issues well, but we were under-capitalised, and interest on the enormous debt meant we were slowly but surely sliding under. In the first year of operation we paid the bank $28,000 in interest alone.

Ruth, my long-time mate from early days in the Bay, had come back to visit with her kids Frith and Sam. Her son had brought up his electric guitar and Josh had been fascinated with making it twang. Now aged 12, he really wanted an electric guitar, so the next week I just went out and blew the next month's mortgage payment on a second-hand Hondo guitar, a cheap Stratocaster copy made in Japan (a 'knock-off' in the trade) that came with a big Jensen Bass amp towering almost as high as Josh himself. He was so stoked, and looking back it was worth every cent, because it kept up his enthusiasm for the musical career that he would eventually pursue.

For a thousand little reasons like that, my bank balance only got lower and lower. Even selling the building and carrying on with a lease could not hold off the inevitable for long. Melanie managed to hold it together psychologically better, but I became more and more run down by the whole process.

We had to get out. I threw a big party for all our supporters and laid it on the line: the brave little cinema was not going to survive. There was an amazing response from the community, who rallied together and took it over as a trust, which still runs it successfully to this day.

It was a long process, extracting ourselves, and every so often during it Melanie and I would escape with our children for a well-earned break. Once we even went to Stephens Island, where we visited our mate John Mitchell who had just taken up the first DOC sole-charge caretaker position on the island since the lighthouse had become automated in 1980. He'd become incredibly lonely, so DOC had allowed the odd friend to visit him. Humanitarian good sense prevailed before the country went overboard on rule-bending.

For an hour we battled a stiffening northwesterly in a chartered launch to reach Queens Beach, the best landing spot on Stephens. I jumped waist-deep into the surf from the tender and walked ashore, two-year-old Nina firmly in my arms. A DOC man who was about to leave on the boat I came in on handed me a message: 'Your solicitor rang this morning. He wants you to ring him urgently.' My heart sank: I knew it was about a property law notice that was going to be served against me if I didn't sell the building by Friday. If anything brought home the craziness of my life at that time, it was that: landing on a near-deserted island covered in tuatara, dragging yourself up the beach and then getting a message to ring your lawyer. It felt like 'move over, Wacko Jacko' to me.

Other times we would take off to D'Urville Island, where my mother had been raised at Waitai, up the northern part of the island. Her stories about her parents, Angelina and Vincenzo Moleta, who had immigrated from the island of Stromboli, near Sicily, had always fascinated me as a child. So it was hardly surprising that I had the urge to explore that area, the idea for a book growing in my mind as I went. Messing about in boats was all part of the fun. I still remember young Nesh's horror when a gigantic seal popped its head over the gunwale of our dinghy as we were rowing along – a right smart-arsed fish inspector.

D'Urville made me see my own place in a new light. After several years of thoroughly neglecting it for the cinema, I found it necessary to re-establish my connection with my swamp, and others that I discovered during this time.

Much as I would like to be able to wave a wand and stop any swamp from being reclaimed, I also enjoyed finding out about what some land-owners had gone through in order to drain their swamps in the first place. Perhaps no other swamp story quite matches the saga of Len and Ruth Leov, who in 1949 began draining the enormous swamp running inland from the big sand-dune lake on their farm at Greville Harbour, on D'Urville Island. For a start, I could certainly see why: it would add 300 acres of flat and fertile pasture to their otherwise hilly farm.

This was never going to be a job for the faint-hearted. Late in the 19th century, an early farm worker there had been using a pair of horses to drag some gear on a sledge around the edge of this swamp. Suddenly to his horror, the horses and sledge collapsed through the soft surface, sinking completely out of sight under the thick ooze. At first the owner, who was hurriedly summoned to the site, refused to believe what his young worker was telling him, laughing it off as a joke. Surely he had the horses and gear hidden somewhere nearby. But then he saw the bubbles rising, and next day one of the drowned horses floated to the surface. This revealed the exact position of their gear, which they managed to salvage with grappling hooks and with the help of some horses, which this time were kept well away on solid ground.

Everyone else said the Greville Swamp could never be reclaimed. But the Leovs were not put off by the stories, and hopes were high as Bill Turner punted a ditch-digger onto the beach and their energetic farm worker Jack Kemp started it up to begin digging the first-ever ditch to drain the great Greville Swamp. The problems started on day one though. Progress in the sand country was painfully slow owing to continual subsidence, and more contractors had to be called in. Len Leov was soon keeping a diary of the project, such an impact it had on his family:

> When the Bryant Brothers came, Peter Bryant spent seven days pushing sand from a trench about 10 ft wide and 12 ft deep. He could not go too close to the swamp so Jack and I were forced to dig a trench about a chain long that let a lot of water go. Then we had to carry on ditching with shovels. Two miles of it. We made best progress when Jack used a hayknife to cut 2 ft square blocks of the peat surface. I had to lift them out. Bill Partridge was up to his waist in the ditch at all times – shovelling what he could.

When the swamp got a bit drier they burnt it all off, then went forth with their handy hydraulic Hopto Digger, attaching it to the back of a D-2 crawler tractor. But the surface was so soft they had to keep their rig from sinking by rafting it on a corduroy of manuka trunks, which had to be continually cut and laid ahead. If the tractor slipped off the saplings, it was a terribly tiresome two-day job, sometimes even longer, to jack it back up again; the worst incident took six men three days. At the end of each day every part of their clothes and bodies was filthy with sweat and mud. 'If we hadn't been brought up in the bush,' wrote Len, 'we would have been there still yet.'

As they progressed further into the swamp, where it was even softer, they were forced to carry two manuka saplings about 15 centimetres through and five metres long, which would be laid beside the tractor when it got stuck, and threaded to holes in the tracks with about 20 pieces of No. 8 wire. Then came the tricky part, jacking up the four ends of the saplings with Trewella jacks. To stop these sinking, trailerloads of smaller saplings were laid down under the jacks until they would not sink any more. Then slowly, using big wooden chocks, they would jack up the crawler enough to push the rails under, which were long and strong enough to finally carry the machine as it worked. Progress was measured in a few metres every day. They got bogged down so much that Len had to buy and punt in another crawler tractor just to be on hand to pull the first one out.

Frequently they had to go back to where they started, clearing the slipping that had occurred in the ditching through the sand country. With explosives they blew the original hand-dug ditches to 10 metres wide, scooping the debris out with their machines, which they frequently had to dig out from the slipping sand with shovels.

By 1954 they had reached the centre of the swamp. And as Len put it, 'That's when the real headache began.'

The big problem was pulling the rafted digger through the inner swamp, where conditions were almost impossible. The solution they came up with was nothing short of ingenious. First they got 32 chains (640 metres) of No. 8 fencing wire and ran it across the narrowest place, then attached it to another 32 chains of three-quarter-inch (18 millimetre) wire rope and proceeded to pull it through with the tractor. When the weight got too great the No. 8 broke so they had to double it, but after two days they got the big wire rope through. Then they tied it to the biggest tree, and attached the other end to the D-2 crawler, which remained on solid ground. In between it they attached the ditch-digger which, to stop it sinking, was rafted on two seven-metre-long logs bolted together into a rudimentary sledge two metres wide. For power to drive the ditcher they stripped down an old Fordson tractor until only the engine and gearbox were left, bolted it onto the sledge in front of the ditcher, and then connected up a power take-off. With this Heath Robinson contraption they were able to gradually pull the rafted digger across the swamp as the ditch-digging progressed.

Every time they needed to change direction they had to shift the D-2 and reattach the wire rope to a different tree. Taking up the slack just after shifting the 640-metre wire rope was a particularly tricky moment:

Len recalled the curve slowly tightening up as the D-2 took the strain, until the raft he was riding upon would suddenly lurch forward several metres. Timing was crucial, so they developed a signalling system using flags and yells. In places the scrub and flax were so high that a man had to climb the nearby hill to see Len's signal. When Len waved his jacket, the man up the hill would relay the signal to the D-2 operator to begin the pull. A second wave, combined with an extra-loud yell, was necessary to stop the tractor being pulled too far, because there was no way of backing up. Later Len attached a trailer winch to the tractor and this made the ditching easier.

Everywhere they dug, 'oodles of eels' would slither out and gather in the pools. In one tight area they found masses of a clear jelly-like substance which, when dried, turned into solid white matter. The whole area had obviously once been a forest: they found huge stumps growing on a mat of manuka logs and sticks, looking as though it had all been flattened by some cataclysmic event like a tsunami. When they burned off the manuka an overwhelming tarry smell filled the area for months.

Interestingly, Maori oral histories of this wonderfully warm and sheltered area they called Mo Awhitu tell of a disastrous tsunami called 'Taniwha tapu-arero-utu-utu' that swept through here and claimed many lives, possibly sometime around the 15th century. Generations later, an invading war party from northern tribes wiped out most of the remaining people. According to one version, the invaders chased the last of them across a natural rock bridge to what is now known as Bottle Point. Rather than surrender, they all committed suicide by jumping off the cliff onto the jagged rocks below. The rock bridge collapsed during a big storm in about 1916.

By the time the swamp-draining operation was completed about eight kilometres of ditches had been dug. Discing the drained area provided Len with enough firewood to keep them going for a decade. The lake level was lowered by nearly five metres as a result of draining the swamp.

Triumphantly they planted out the former swamp with their first crops of turnips and chou moellier. Wild pigs came out of the bush to feed on the flat, the largest mob counted early one morning being about sixty. Gradually they got their pasture established and it was a great source of pride to Len and his family, feeling they had finally won their nearly continuous two-decade struggle with the swamp.

Len and Ruth Leov retired in 1969, moving to manage a small farmlet at Spring Creek, near Blenheim. Their son Fred cut his first crop of hay at Greville, about six hundred bales, in the early 1970s. Within the next ten years he had so improved the land that he was cutting more than two thousand bales per season. In 1992 he sold the property, and it had two more owners before the government bought it in 2005, adding it to the conservation estate and securing its ecological and historical heritage for all New Zealanders. Not only is the extensive sand-dune system a rare feature within the Sounds, but it was once inhabited by a thriving Maori community who relied on the vast lagoon and wonderful dune-dammed lakes to provide them with all the eels, kokopu and waterfowl they could ever want.

So was all that energy directed at the great Greville Swamp worth it? Certainly it was well-intended – any endeavours to increase farm productivity and agricultural exports were regarded as heroic back then. But times have certainly changed: DOC's 2006 Draft Operation Plan for the farm recommends 'That ecological restoration of the lake and associated former swamps is carried out in expectation of restoring the eel population.'

Perhaps that too is a sad thing. Despite my feelings about swamps, there is also a part of me that rages against bureaucratic policies that mirror the see-saw attitudes of society. Some would argue that perhaps our new ecological bent is just as destructive of our proud and well-meant agricultural heritage, as those early pioneers were on the land. Fickle, shallow creatures we sure are.

CHAPTER 13

THE BROS

After finishing with the theatre, I got two three-month contracts with
the Golden Bay Work Centre running training courses called Skills of
Enterprise, for people wanting start-up business skills. Business has as
much to do with attitude as it does with specific techniques. Then I got
a call from Vi at the local Onetahua Marae, asking if I could urgently
help out tutoring a building-skills course they were running. Why not,
I thought? I needed a job, so I said yes over the phone.

That simple decision led me into what must rate as possibly the most
challenging period of my life, even though it was just for a couple of
months. The practical outcome of the course was supposed to be building
a toilet and shower block at the marae. But the six 'at-risk' teenagers,
who came from all around New Zealand, daily ran me ragged with
their antics. One day I got so frustrated I actually challenged one of
them to a fist-fight! Luckily for me he backed out, because I was about
20 kilograms of muscle lighter than him. The attention span of these
guys was remarkably short: for a quarter of an hour we'd be building,
then we would have another quarter-hour playing touch rugby in the
mud, and after that we'd be having a boil-up of something like puha
and pork fat, or for a real treat, docked lambs' tails. We never had a
meal: it was always a 'feed'.

But just exactly how much we bonded, how much they were all 'bros',
and how much I earned their respect as their boss, was revealed dramatically one afternoon when a Talley's Fisheries truck appeared on Pohara
Gully Road, on which the marae was situated. Two men standing on
the tray of the truck were scanning people's yards as they slowly went
along, looking for any sign of the light-blue fish bins stamped 'Stolen
from Talley's'.

The Motueka-based fishing company was missing around 30,000 bins
at the time. At $30 each, it amounted to nearly a million dollars' worth.
The root of the problem was of course, that the bins were extremely

useful. I'd seen them used for every purpose to which a container can be put: from baby cribs to toolboxes; from clothes baskets to plant-pots and retaining walls. Unfortunately for the fishing industry, crews did not take particular care of the bins and used frequently to lose them overboard. When they washed up, beachcombers went for them with their ears back, applying the 'finders keepers, losers weepers' rule. In this situation, of course, 'stolen' wasn't quite true, although no doubt a lot of other bins were taken deliberately off boats and from around fish depots, or conveniently 'fell off the back of a truck'.

From time to time, fishing companies would have a crackdown. In both Motueka and Takaka, Talley's regularly sent some of their, shall we say, 'larger' employees around to systematically check private backyards. When they found any bins they'd swiftly tip out the contents and load the bins on to the truck.

As far as the police were concerned, the bins constituted 'found property' so they always belonged rightfully to the original owner, and the company was quite within its rights to ask anyone whether they had any. In so doing, there was nothing to stop them coming on to your land to ask you – that is, until they were asked to leave, at which point they became trespassers. A complaint to the police that you were harbouring 'stolen' property could result in a search, but I never heard of it happening. I think the last thing police wanted to get involved in was more fishy business.

We watched from the driveway of the marae as the truck came closer and closer. Every so often it would stop as the men dashed up someone's driveway and came out with another bin or two. As for us, we had a heap of bins: all our tools were in them for a start, but there was no way we were going to hand them over if we could avoid it.

'Just give us the word, bro,' said the biggest of my bros. The other five stepped forward to completely block the entrance. Several had brought out their taiaha practice sticks and began whirling them around. They were preparing for battle. The truck pulled up short when they saw us. The standoff lasted five seconds before the driver did a hurried U-turn and drove back down the road. We had won. One word from me and I could have unleashed them upon the hapless fisheries workers. For a moment there I had experienced the intoxicating power of having a gang at my disposal.

At night my bros slept down in the disused offices of the Golden Bay Cement Company, presided over by a Maori warden to keep them out of trouble. Which didn't work all that well, because the local policeman one day described them as a 'mini-crime wave' in the Bay.

A week before the course was due to finish, Vi rang me early one morning. 'The course is over,' she said. 'Last night they all got into a big fight and started bashing each other with iron bars. Three of them were taken to hospital, the others treated and discharged.' It must have been one hell of a fight. Thank goodness I never did unleash them that day!

Just a month later I crossed paths with one of them again. I was on the inter-island ferry just a few minutes out of Picton when the captain came on the intercom and advised that we were turning back to drop off a stowaway who had just been discovered hiding in a lifeboat. I sauntered up on deck to see who he was. Sure enough, there was one of my bros being led away.

One of the most wonderful things that happened for my family around this time was that a tame female bottlenose dolphin made its home along Onekaka Beach. Old Scarry (sometimes also called Doris) had been rescued after a stranding incident in Golden Bay, and for two years was regularly seen swimming around before she joined swimmers near the old Onekaka wharf. As word spread, more and more people came to see her: 50 at a time on weekends was not uncommon. The dolphin became more and more daring, jumping out of the water, towing people around, even throwing them a big fish on the odd occasion. At a public meeting convened by interested parties at the Onekaka Hall the creature's name was officially changed to Aihe, meaning 'dolphin' in Maori, but everyone just kept calling her Old Scarry.

It was like Opo all over again. Sometimes a first encounter with her could be pretty scary, this big black shape rushing directly towards you under the water at great rate of knots. At the last second, just centimetres away, she would suddenly stop, rest her beak in your hands and shake her head as if to say, 'Come and play with me.' Children adored her. For two and a half years my kids had her to play with any day they wanted. Then the dolphin got ...well, bored, we think. Tired of us all, bored by the crowds and the incessant attention, and just left. On her last day she even nipped a woman on the leg who she knew very well, who swam with her most days. Like some ageing rock star, Old Scarry had simply had enough of the limelight, perhaps even felt pissed off. She was seen briefly in Nelson, then along Paraparaumu Beach, but that was the last we heard of her. I do hope she hasn't forgotten us and comes back to retire in sunny Golden Bay one day.

CHAPTER 14

TWISTS AND TURNS

My new career as a journalist came right out of the blue. I started writing as another creative endeavour, and certainly didn't ever expect the roller-coaster ride that it turned out to be. Fate fetched me to Auckland's glitzy Sheraton Hotel to pick up the inaugural Cathay Pacific Travel Journalist of the Year Award for something I'd bashed out on an old typewriter nine months previously and got published in *New Zealand Geographic* magazine. Part of the prize was a trip to Hong Kong.

'Ring me when you arrive – I'll shout you a drink. And for Godsakes get yourself some bloody business cards!' Kevin Sinclair never wasted words. And who could blame him, having to croak through a hole in his throat - a tracheotomy. Smoked himself to near death, but did it set him back? No way. Arguably the most accomplished and prolific journalist ever to leave New Zealand's shores, Kevin had left in 1968 to cover an escalating conflict in Vietnam and never found a reason to come back home. Except to present me with my award, that is.

Of course, his vocal problem meant someone else had to read out his judge's speech at the award dinner in Auckland that night. I still couldn't quite believe it was me they were all talking about. Ten months before I'd been totally broke and burnt out after that business with the Village Theatre in Takaka. Although I had managed to sell it, it had been a close shave for me both financially and emotionally. Melanie had to go back to cooking at the Junction Hotel to pay our bills, while I earned a bit from my Access courses. We were just treading water to keep afloat at this time.

My successful story was about a five-day trip with three mates – John Mitchell, Andrew Dixon and Brian Cooper – along a particularly rugged and untracked northern section of the West Coast which is now part of Kahurangi National Park. My 'to hell and back' account followed the footsteps – and handholds – of Charles Heaphy and Thomas Brunner, the first European explorers to traverse in 1856 that 'frightfully rocky precipitous coast ... which none but those who have travelled over it can conceive the nature of.'

This particular stretch of coastline, from Kahurangi Point to the Heaphy River, was generally regarded as impassable. When we set off from the old Kahurangi lighthouse keeper's house, local farmer Brett Hart jokingly said, 'See you back this way Sunday. They all turn back.' One recent entry in the hut book simply said, 'Karamea or bust, and I bust!'

At Kahurangi Point, the geology changes from fossiliferous clay and limestone to hard pale orange granite with precipitous bluffs and offshore outcrops of rock. The most difficult section lies between Kahurangi River and Heaphy Bluff, one of the last unmodified primeval coastlines left in New Zealand. It had always attracted me: so harsh and inaccessible, so depriving of comfort, yet so replenishing of the soul. Sheer bluffs forced us on many occasions to climb up through the bush, but this was an even more unpleasant experience than getting around the cliffs. Most of the bush was kiekie (*Freycinetia banksii*), the same plant we met with in Chapter 4 where Animal introduced me to its fruit. But now it was not fruiting season, and the kiekie formed an almost impenetrable, interwoven barrier of half-scrambling, half-climbing stems and crowns. In some places it took 10 minutes to go just 10 metres. Swearing and cursing, we alternated between walking over it, crashing through it, and crawling under it. The only good thing that could be said about it was that at least you were never short of something to hang on to.

At the end of our first day we managed to reach Christabel Creek, near Otukoroiti Point, but couldn't find any shelter from the incessant wind, so we were forced to construct a driftwood barricade just to stop our tent blowing away in the night. We dined on paua (abalone), kina (sea urchins) and sea lettuce while watching the blood-red sun sink into the Tasman. Just as we were relaxing, a seal charged straight through the middle of our camp in a mad dash for the sea. It must have been hiding up in the flax ever since we had arrived. We hardly slept a wink that night, the tent flapping like crazy. John Mitchell made the best decision to sleep under the stars along the beach, a couple of seals not far away keeping him company.

In 1820 Otukoroiti Point was the scene of a great battle after the Ngati Toa chief Te Rauparaha had dispatched a crack raiding party from his Kapiti Island stronghold to corner the precious greenstone reserves of Tai Poutini, on the West Coast. Their intentions were genocidal: this was definitely a 'take-no-prisoners' mission.

Exhausted from a week-long journey across Raukawa (Cook Strait) and around Cape Farewell, they pulled up on the stony beach immediately north of Otukoroiti Point just as the sun set. Next morning they planned to wipe out the hapu who lived at the mouth of the Whakapoai (Heaphy River) before moving south to make their next surprise attack.

But the Ngai Tahu had been waiting for them for weeks. How astonished the half-awakened Ngati Toa party must have been on that beach next morning, looking out on half-a-dozen canoeloads of Ngai Tahu warriors bearing down on them. It's in the nature of surprise warfare that the advantage can suddenly change sides.

Unable to launch their canoes, and pinned down by perhaps a hundred warriors swarming the beach, the outnumbered but still redoubtable battle-hardened Ngati Toa could only hold a defensive position with their backs to the cliffs. By the end of the day, dozens of bodies from both sides lay around and the rocks ran red with blood. Only as the moon rose did the surviving Ngati Toa manage to fight their way down to a canoe and escape. Today, the recognised northern seaward rohe (tribal boundary) of Ngai Tahu is Kahurangi Point, which was basically as far north as they could defend.

As we progressed further south we found our way barred by steep headlands dividing the rocky bays. We had to scramble up and over through the bush, often belaying with a rope. Then we came to the cliff at Tauparikaka, the most daunting obstacle of all, and which the wily chief Eneho (pronounced Niho) of Whanganui Inlet had warned Heaphy and Brunner would be the absolute southern limit of their journeying. Climbing around it certainly scared the hell out of me. Heaphy's account says it all:

> Against this projection the waves broke on the perpendicular face
> of the rock, so as completely to prevent it being passed below, while
> inshore the mountain rose steeply and high, presenting in that direc-
> tion as impassable a barrier. About 80 feet above the sea, however,
> where the point jutted from the mountain, was a place where it seemed
> as if it might afford footing along the summit: to this we ascended by
> a difficult rocky way, through karaka bushes and large fragments of
> granite. On the other side, the appearance of the way was appalling,
> and we certainly for a time deemed the descent impractical without a

ladder. The sight of a rotten native-made rope ladder which dangled over the precipice made us perhaps imagine the descent to be more critical than it in reality was. At length, after looking down several times, we perceived a rock ledge and some holes in the face of the rock which might enable us to descend, and we summoned up the courage to make the attempt. The worst part of the way was around an overhanging rock, where it became necessary to lean backwards in order to get from one ledge to the other. Below this way was less dangerous but great care was yet necessary to avoid slipping from the slanted rock into the tide beneath.

I found the mention of the 'native rope' interesting. Not only was this one of the regular routes to the greenstone country, but it is known that Eneho regularly sent his slaves down this way in late summer to collect the karaka berries as they ripened.

But the West Coast had not quite finished with us yet. Beyond Seal Bay we came to a particularly obtuse bluff. The cliff rose vertically from the water so we could only strike upwards as best we could, and hope to cross over to the mouth of the Moutere River. At the very start we had to scramble up a few metres of loose, crumbly granite through the steep transition zone between bare rock and scrubline, where no foothold or handhold could be trusted.

It was here that I experienced the most terrifying moments of the whole journey, inching upwards in toeholds I had cut with my trusty bowie knife, unable to call out to Andrew nearby for help because the words wouldn't come out. To finally grab the lowest flax and pull myself up through the steep kiekie was sweet relief indeed.

A few kilometres south, at Toropuhi, I tried to imagine the hardship of the early European sealers on this coast: around 1830 a sealing boat was stove-in here and just two of the crew survived. Some of Eneho's people kept them as hapless prisoners for two days before smashing in their heads with boulders to avenge the loss of their chief's child, who had gone to sea in the vessel and never returned. Not to be put off, sealers established a small sealing station at Turopipi a few years later, but abandoned it some nine or ten years before Heaphy and Brunner came through because there were too few animals.

As we rounded Rocks Point, we had to grab onto the rock and pull ourselves into the wind, it was so strong. On the beaches the skin was sandblasted off our faces by the coarse wind-blown granite sand. Every time the burden of our packs seemed too much, I thought of Heaphy: 'Our loads consisted of 35 lbs of flour each, with tea, sugar, pearl barley, powder, shot, instruments, books, spare boots for when the first pair wore out, two blankets, amounting to 80 lbs each ... being exceedingly fatiguing.' In an earlier passage of this amazing journal, he also mentions the 12 pounds of tobacco that he took to bribe Maori for safe passage, much of it going to Eneho at Whanganui Inlet.

Early sealers had largely wiped out the fur seals by the time Heaphy and Brunner came through here in 1846, so they saw only half a dozen at most. But their numbers have greatly recovered, and this area is now home of New Zealand's largest northern breeding colonies. There are two sensations I particularly remember from along this coast: the incessant, salt-saturated winds, and the fetid smell of the seals that lived along here in their thousands.

Why hadn't anyone warned us that mid-November was smack in the middle of the mating season? During this annual flush of hormones the horny bull seals turn into fierce packs of wolf-like creatures. It was bad enough that as they fought among themselves they could easily tear out a whole kilogram of flesh with each bite, but as far as they were concerned it was open season on human intruders too. Keeping low, submissive postures as we had been advised to do made no difference: they lunged wickedly at us as we negotiated past their every haulout. What's more, they could charge along for short distances faster than we could run. No wonder the early sealers called them 'sea dogs'.

It was terrifying beyond belief, the first time I have ever been chased by a pack of wild animals. We had no choice but to engage them in battle, fending them off with sticks and rocks. In one place half a dozen of them bailed us up against a vertical cliff. Every time one of our stout sticks came near their heads they would rear up, open their mouth and snap off another quarter-metre with their huge fangs. When they had shortened our sticks enough they pressed home their advantage and we could smell their fetid breath, but each of us kept a rock ready in the other hand to bash the dreadful creature on the head and stun it just long enough make a run for it. Worse still for us, a seal's gestation is almost exactly one year. Birth and mating happen at much the same time, so newborn pups were everywhere, their mothers murderously postnatal as we progressed. What a lethal combination of sexes!

But those seals proved a lesser obstacle than the huge rollers which thundered in from the stormy Tasman Sea. Impenetrable coastal jungle and steep cliffs prevented any attempt to find even a slight inland diversion route along this part of the coast. There was nothing for it but to run between bluffs and sea. The technique was to read the wave patterns and watch for the occasional wave that would recede far enough to allow a headlong dash across a memorized series of boulders before the next wave surged in and covered the whole area up to four or five metres deep. This sounded great in theory, but if we got it wrong the consequences would be dire in the heavy surf. There would be no hope of rescue if any of us were struck and swept out to sea by a rogue wave.

Seaman are fond of saying every seventh wave is bigger, but you can also count on a rogue roller about once in every five hundred. It was just my luck to strike one of these, or should I say to be struck by it. This monster wall of water engulfed me completely as I was clambering around a near-perpendicular bluff. Waves surging below me had already confused my senses before it hit. I remember feeling as though I was hanging off a moving cliff with stationary sea below, then this big wave bashed my face against the rock before plucking me off and sucking me out to sea. I remember going round and round in the surf like in a washing machine, desperately trying to get the pack off my back, with just two thoughts in my head. The first was that the camera I was carrying was now wrecked and all the film was ruined. The second was that I was surely about to die!

Luckily only the former would prove correct, for another wave flung me up and dumped me like a big lump of driftwood on some loose boulders around 15 metres down from where I'd gone in. Badly bloodied and spluttering, I scrambled to safety. Alive, yes: but with my camera twisted around my neck and oozing seawater. The first roll of film was in it and obviously ruined. I called out to my companions, but they were already around the next point. The whole incident had happened without their even noticing.

I could celebrate being alive, but without pictures we couldn't publish. I rang *New Zealand Geographic* editor Kennedy Warne the moment I dragged myself through the door of my Tukurua home: 'Kennedy! We got a great story, just that I drowned the photos.' The benevolent, exacting tyrant barely paused: 'Go back and do it again, just this time wait for a cyclone. I want some *really* dramatic photos to go with this story.'

The next favourable combination of moon and low spring tides meant it would be another two months before we could tackle that coast again. And we got the cyclone that Kennedy ordered. It hit us with its full fury as we climbed up through thick coastal rainforest around the mouth of the Moutere River. The tremendous waves exploded against the cliffs and splashed high into the bush. A driving deluge of salt-saturated rain added to this assault, finally forcing us to weather out the tempest under a dense grove of karaka trees.

'Fantastic photos!' Kennedy rang me after seeing them 10 days later. 'The one of you holding onto the cliff for dear life, seals below and tempest all around – I just love it.' Andrew Dixon had been in charge of the cameras this time, with impressive results. That trip changed my life – and his too, for it was on it that he decided to build a small bush tavern on his property at Onekaka and call it the Mussel Inn. I can still recall the bay where we camped – 'Our Bay' we called it – where he announced his intentions.

By the time we forded the Heaphy River and got on to the Heaphy Track, we had run completely out of food and still had 55 kilometres of walking back to the Bainham end of the track. I have never known hunger like it. I recall bursting into Saxon Hut, unshaven and unkempt, and going straight to the rubbish bin where the first thing I found was an empty drink sachet whose sugary lining I proceeded to lick hungrily. Turning around, I realised there were four German backpackers at the table, horrified at the sight of such a wild man in their midst. But I had no shame that day, I was desperate as never before.

Setting out again early the next morning, we covered the rest of the track by the afternoon, nearly dragging ourselves into Browns Hut at Bainham with exaggerated handshakes, cheers and humour, before collapsing one by one in exhaustion. But we had succeeded. We had beaten the odds and experienced a level of adventure and comradeship that only a hostile environment can offer. We had all excelled in different skills, at times rescued and assisted each other, explored and pushed the limits, and witnessed first-hand a terrain few have traversed.

Whoever said, 'Travel writing is just turning your worst moments into money,' was dead right. One minute I'd been clinging to wave-battered cliffs by my fingernails, fighting off homicidal bull seals on heat and very nearly drowning. Next thing I was clutching my prize – two return air tickets to Hong Kong and Vietnam.

Ironic really: my writing about survival in a primeval wilderness had not only turned a profit, but propelled me smack-bang into the world's most densely populated region. My new path was revealed. Or to put it another way, I got a new job, which I badly needed.

I'm a great believer in destiny. Opportunity knocks every day, some say; it just depends whether you answer the door and let it in. Put another way, good luck is where opportunity meets preparedness. With the average human lifetime little more than 25,000 days, we can hardly afford not to seize the day or let wonderful opportunities go begging. I had used up around 13,000 of mine at that stage, and I didn't want to waste any more.

My journalist father may have inspired me in the twisted art of storytelling, but it was Kevin Sinclair at the awards dinner that night back in 1991 who gave me the game-plan. 'Number one,' he waved his hands around to include the entire hotel lobby. 'All this glitz is the bullshit part! But don't forget to send a thank-you card. Number two. Be prolific. I get up every morning at 4 am and write two stories before lunch. Then I drive into town and get two more. Number three. Order another bloody round, will you?' I liked this man! He became my mate and mentor.

The following weekend I would make a few lines in an item Sinclair wrote for the *South China Morning Post*. He described me as a 'virtual recluse who lived in a remote, self-built house on the South Island of New Zealand and took to writing at a mature age'. Melanie laughed at the 'virtual recluse' bit when she read it. The report went on to describe how my winning the prize had raised the ire of New Zealand's 'professional' travel writers, who took exception to an outsider winning the prize and gave the organisers a bit of stick about it. 'It's a damn sight harder to judge one of these things than to win one,' Sinclair was quoted as saying as he 'fled back to Hong Kong'.

My new-found ability to come up with marketable yarns meant travelling was made easy because the travel and hospitality trade were desperate for exposure in the media. I travelled relatively effortlessly around Asia in particular, cruising from country to country for stories. One month I was in Myanmar (Burma), the next I was in Hong Kong or Macau, or up in Nepal, China, even Tibet.

Despite this new existence of freelance comings-and-goings, my life continued to centre around my four hectares of paradise in Golden Bay, with Melanie well able to keep the home fires burning during my frequent absences. Along with Nina, we now had another daughter, Lucy, who was delivered at home, in our lounge, with the assistance of our midwife Celia. Seeing that the new girl was OK, she turned to me and asked, 'What gravel do you use in your driveway potholes? I always find oversize works best.' Like the dog jumping at the window at Joshua's birth, that tiny incident reassured me: she was so laid-back, matter-of-fact and obviously experienced. Life had to go on, and Melanie was extremely capable of making it work, especially in my overseas absences.

Last-minute jobs for me before each trip away became mowing grass and stacking a mountain of firewood beside the fireplace. I worked hard to combine normalcy into an exciting new phase that lasted nearly 10 years; a time during which I barely needed a car, just put my bum on a seat in a 747 every few weeks.

Although much of this work was business-related, covering the so-called 'unlimited opportunities' open to New Zealand entrepreneurs, it was the aesthetics of Asia and its natural world that truly inspired me.

In Japan, the zen gardens I visited in Tokyo, Osaka, Kobe and Otsu were breathtaking. The raked stones, the differing-sized bushes all trimmed to perfection with scissors, rocks so carefully placed amongst the moss: everything so simply perfect. In the most perfect postage-stamp-sized garden jammed between two buildings in Tokyo, an inscription chiselled into the rock commemorated the most celebrated haiku of the 17th century poet Basho:

An ancient pond;
A frog plunges,
Then sound of water.

I had heard this most famous of haiku many times before I saw it there, but to see it inscribed in the context of that perfect surrounding of zen beauty took my breath away. Basho, the pseudonym of Matsuo Munefusa, was born into a noble samurai family but early rejected his elegant life for the pursuit of poetry during the most formative years of the haiku genre. He quickly became famous in Japanese society for his ability to infuse a mystical quality into much of his verse and for attempting to express universal themes through simple images.

But it would be in Cambodia that I would find the greatest inspiration for practical application in my own patch. They say that to understand Cambodia, you must wade in the mud of the rice paddies and explore its rivers. Land mines provided me with roughly ten million reasons to opt for the boat ride. My destination was the great temples of Angkor Wat.

'It may take two days, maybe five. The river is very, very low,' I was told in Phnom Penh. The sturdy Khmer river boat, inscribed '1964', was divided into two decks, each barely big enough to crouch in. Down below, assorted freight, mostly motorbikes and sacks of salt, filled any space not taken up by the huge single-banger diesel engine. Those lucky enough to swing a hammock became unwitting first-class passengers as the rest of us filled the spaces among more cargo on the shaded upper deck. Later in the day, when it was slightly cooler, I clambered onto the 'sun-deck' roof with half a dozen other tourists and watched life on the Tonle Sap River go by.

Everywhere there were birds: huge cormorants and egrets roosting along the jungle-clad riverbank, thousands of them in almost continuous colonies. Perhaps the only positive thing about the Khmer Rouge occupation that had taken the country back to 'Year Zero' was that the birdlife had been allowed to live. I felt a natural sense of poverty, thinking of the solitary white heron which was probably gracing Parapara Inlet back at home.

The nutrient-laden waters, fed by the huge inland Tonle Sap ('Great Lake'), support vast numbers of fish. Several that jumped out beside the boat must have been over a metre long. This strategically located lake lies in the heart of Cambodia, its arterial rivers coming in from all directions, with many craft plying back and forth. It swells to four times its normal size during the rainy season, when the flood-swollen Mekong backs up, reversing the normal flow of the Bassac and Tonle Sap Rivers. Along a shifting shoreline, lake and river dwellers kept pace with water levels by moving their thatched huts up and down stilts. Whole villages appeared to float, and fish drying on the thatched roofs glistened like new corrugated iron.

Our first night on the water was spent tied to a sandbagged police station, complete with mounted machine guns. This gesture 'for our protection' made us feel like sitting ducks, even if the sporadic gun and mortar fire in the distance 'wasn't close enough to worry about,' as our nonchalant skipper advised.

We spent the next two days in various stages of alternately getting stuck and unstuck on the muddy bottom, with a horizon of shimmering water that turned gold at sunset. Though immense, the Tonle Sap is desperately shallow in parts, and our helmsman's two sons earned their keep wading ahead to finally find a passage.

And then the firing started. Our skipper had tried to run a government patrol-boat checkpoint, and while we westerners crouched behind sacks of salt to protect ourselves from the hail of machine gun fire, the Cambodian passengers all climbed atop the roof to get a better view! Evidently they do not share the Western penchant for ducking under fire. As the three dozen or so bullets whizzed over our boat, the locals on board became more and more agitated. When the patrol boat came alongside I could not resist poking my camera out through a rip in the canvas awning, intending to record the event, but was stopped by a French tourist who roughly pulled me back: 'Please monsieur, I beg you, do not aggravate them: it is all of our lives at stake here!' In the end it was just a low-speed chase, Cambodian style, and once they boarded and we paid the bribe, a mere $2 each, we were free to go.

But if I had to remember one thing from that trip, it would not be the threat of guns, or even the birds, but rather a brief stop-off at a little lakeside village on the fourth day. It was desperately dusty, every footfall raising a small cloud as I explored the open lane behind the long row of shacks teetering over the riverbank. At the end, an old man beckoned me, offering me some sticky rice he had just boiled up in a battered aluminium pot that looked suspiciously as though it had been beaten into shape from an old section of aeroplane fuselage. I indicated a small amount, which he scooped onto a banana leaf and handed to me with a big smile.

'How much do you pay for your rice?' I asked him in a mixture of English and an attempt at sign language, not really expecting a clear reply. But suddenly he became animated, grabbing me by the arm and leading me to his backyard at the end of the village. There he proudly pointed to his rice paddies, four ponds with water trickling from one into the next, no more than quarter of a hectare in total. The highest was the biggest, and it had a tiny island on which a small boy perched, presumably his grandson.

He waved and smiled at me: 'Hello Mister, where you from? America?'

'New Zealand,' I replied, 'where we do not grow rice.'

The boy looked at me quizzically. 'My family grows all rice we need in these just four ponds.'

In the parched landscape, the sight of those ponds was positively beautiful, like a little oasis. The two lower ponds were thick with green rice shoots and the upper two were partially drained, ready for planting the new season's crop. Once he had borrowed a water buffalo to plough up the bottom of the emptied pond, the old man needed only one piece of equipment, a combined planting tool and harvesting knife that looked as though it had been carved from a specially bent crook of a tree. Shaped like an 'S', it had a handle at one end and was pointed to make holes for the rice plants in the mud. In a middle pivoted a serrated knife that, when folded out, could be used to cut the mature crop. I noticed the blade was made from thick aluminium, probably from part of a downed US warplane. It was ingenious, that tool: so simple yet so effective.

Bamboo pipes brought water from a small ditch running alongside the town and featured rudimentary crossover taps from one pond to the next. Ponds could be diverted or filled in any combination before the water was allowed to drain out down into the river. The whole set up was ingenious, and aesthetically beautiful.

Even before the boat blew its whistle for us all to get back on board, I knew that I wanted to have ponds just like that at home. Even if I couldn't grow rice in them, at least my children would love playing in them, just like this old man's grandson obviously did.

Back on the riverboat, now suddenly sick from drinking contaminated water, I was reminded of the Central Asian proverb: 'Travel is a foretaste of hell.' Our river journey ended exactly four and half days after it started, with the boat stuck hard on the muddy bottom just off-shore from the tiny fishing village of Phum Kan Trap. The skipper just shrugged: 'We have to wait for rain,' he said. 'Maybe a small boat will come and get you.' The following morning saw 23 of us perched on a small teak dugout designed for three. The 300-metre paddle to shore cost us as much as the big boat ride, but they had us by the short and curlies: 'No pay, you walk; mud worse than quicksand,' the boatman just kept saying when we tried to argue.

My final ride to Siem Reap was as a pillion passenger on a motorbike taxi along a jungle road with potholes capable of swallowing a small truck. It took me a week to recover from my stomach pains, lying under a mosquito net in the tiny annex of the Aspara Guest House. Daily I listened to the manager recalling his 'happy months', 18 of them in a row, when UNTAC (United Nations Transitory Authority in Cambodia) had rented his 10 rooms for US$1,760 per month, paid in advance. It was a boom time for everyone. One memo that went out to UN staff advised that their conspicuous white 4WDs crowded around brothel entrances were becoming an embarrassment: 'Go around the corner to park if necessary.'

When I came alive again, I rented a bicycle and took off for a week, coming back each night to the guest house for a welcome cold shower and a simple feed at the little outside 'restaurant' – really just a wok, four tables and chairs – situated just along the road.

What an explorer I felt! One could spend months exploring the 72 major architectural wonders scattered over 200 square kilometres between the Kulen Hills and Tonle Sap. Although the 880-hectare complex of Angkor Thom is the largest, Angkor Wat is the most artistically accomplished and best preserved. As with Indian temples, the layout reflects elements of the cosmos. When the 12th-century subjects of King Suryavarnan II crossed the grand causeway over the crocodile-infested moat, they believed they left the earth and entered heaven. The king converted to Buddhism halfway through his reign, changing the architectural plan for his temple residence almost overnight. Cambodians still come here to pay homage to the Buddha today.

In the galleries, which can be measured by the kilometre, detailed sculptures in bas-relief unfold visions of heaven and hell. One prophetic frieze, kept lustrous by touching hands, depicts an entire people being starved, bludgeoned and led away in chains. More tempting for me were the 1700 asparas, or celestial maidens, carved into the stone tapestry, each with a different face, that danced their way around the outside walls.

In 1940 the German social critic Walter Benjamin postulated that the treasures of civilisation came from two opposing yet interlocking sources, humane creativity and dehumanising toil: 'There is no document of civilisation which is not at the same time a document of barbarism.' For every great artefact – the Pyramids, the Great Wall of China, a Fabergé egg – a price has to be paid, exacted from the less fortunate labourers, in blood, sweat or even lives. From Angkor Wat to Pol Pot, Cambodia for me had seen it all.

Of particular interest to me though, were the huge barays or reservoirs. It was Angkor's sophisticated waterworks that had enabled its rulers to hold sway: those who controlled the water supply for rice-growing also controlled the people. Cambodia has seen much oppression.

All the way home from Siem Reap in Cambodia to Tukurua in New Zealand I thought about the rice ponds and reservoirs I had seen over the previous week. I sketched several different site plans, putting orientations and elevations in my notebook: forever the cartographer. Even before I hit New Zealand soil I had in my head a feasible plan to dig a series of ponds to tap into the natural water flow running through my swamp.

Usually the transition back to Tukurua from some exotic place like Tokyo, Rangoon or Delhi would render me a little stunned. Seasoned travellers say you should be careful not to 'burn out on re-entry', and indeed I would often feel a little stunned and disorientated on arriving back to my family, community and work, however glad I was to see everyone again. But this time was different. Within hours of arriving home I got out my shovel and started digging along the side of the paddock. My children all came down to watch, slightly in disbelief.

First I dug the smallest, lowest pond, adjacent to a section of the swamp which had a natural fall. It took me four full days, because I had to cart all the soil away in a wheelbarrow and make a selection of mounds on which I would plant tussocks and alpine plants. The theme of the planting was going to be 'mountains to sea'.

Melanie's eyebrows raised slightly as my obsession drove me to start the second, more circular pond, next to and slightly higher than the first one. The first pond had already filled with water while I was digging it, because it was at the same level as the water table, but the second pond would have to wait for the third and fourth ponds before I would develop a scheme to fill them in a series.

I dug and dug almost without respite. By the time I got to Pond No. 4, which was by far the biggest one, my children and even some of their friends had come to help me. Catherine and one of her friends shaped the island in the middle, using the turfs that I supplied them. It must have looked like a scene from one of those big diamond pits in Brazil: human mules working flat out up to their knees in a mudhole.

After I had spent three months digging from dawn to dusk, Melanie thought I had gone completely bananas. I hadn't written a word on my computer. But I was now ready to tap the water from the swamp and fill the ponds. It only took a few hours to dig the little inlet trench along the side of the paddock to tap the swamp. It was a great moment when I took out the last spadeful of earth and a modest rush of tannin-stained water burst down the trench and into the waiting pit. It took four hours just to cover the bottom of the 12-metre-diameter hole, but slowly, millimetre by millimetre, the water level of the new pond crept up the sides and encircled the island. It was slow but at the same time so exciting to watch, just the same way that children on the beach so enjoy watching their hand-dug canals filling up as waves roll in with the rising tide.

Three days later we were all waiting and watching as the water level reached the outlet channel I had lined with stones, and started to dribble over the edge into Pond No. 2. It was just like the Mediterranean 'valley' filling in when sea levels in the mighty Atlantic rose quickly, but on a smaller scale, more like 1:1,000,000 – that's just the mapmaker in me again! We all cheered as it covered the bottom of the excavation. Three days later it dribbled over into Pond No. 3 which, being smaller, filled up quite quickly. Finally, after a week I had water flowing incessantly through all ponds, coming out of the swamp at the top end and going back into it again just 20 metres downstream. Taking out my little notebook, I compared the ponds with the sketch of the ones I'd seen in Cambodia that had inspired me. Proportionally they were exactly the same. They even flowed the same. But of course they would never grow rice: Golden Bay's climate was too temperate for the tropical, water-loving plant. Western Australia is the closest rice-growing area to New Zealand.

It was also my birthday the day we 'opened' the ponds. Lucy gave me one of her sweet homemade cards. Each letter of my name stood for something, the way kids like to do. Thus I was Gorgeous Exciting Rascal Adventurous, Rascal again, and Digger. And so I became known as 'Rascal Digger' to the family after that.

As a passionate gardener, I had achieved exactly what I wanted: to build on my most abundant natural asset, the moving water. I could now fill the new ponds with water lilies and all manner of aquatic plants.

My kids will never forget that summer. We spent so much time with nets and sieves, marauding the local ponds for frogs to populate our waterway. The swamp was soon reverberating to the high-pitched trill of tiny whistling tree frogs and the twang of southern bell frogs. We had been extremely resourceful, catching around two thousand of the critters: from big adult frogs down to tadpoles. It was a joy to see the new pond suddenly so alive.

Then the white heron came.

First it circled wide, keeping its distance as it sized up this new habitat. Then closer and closer it came, not believing its luck. Landing 50 metres away in the paddock, it sneaked up in purposeful slow-motion, head down, to position itself on the edge of the biggest pond. It stayed for nearly an hour in that one spot, completely motionless as it surveyed the smorgasbord before it. A pond packed full of thousands of freshly introduced tadpoles and frogs.

Suddenly it struck: not once but many times, with arrow-like precision. I could see the bulge sliding down its throat after each kill. It came four days in a row, gorging itself silly from early morning to evening. At the end of each day it could barely lift off, its belly was so full of frogs and tadpoles. After a week it came again, this time accompanied by another white heron. News travels fast, even amongst solitary white herons.

Two weeks later my children and I thought we had better do a frog inventory of our ponds. We searched under all the big rocks and combed the weed which was establishing itself all along the fringes. We couldn't find a single frog or tadpole. The herons had completely wiped them out, around two thousand of them, in a single concerted hit over a three-week period.

After that I decided never again to interfere in the processes of nature.

CHAPTER 15

MORE ON SWAMPS

Unlike Nina who came into this world to wake us all up (in the nicest possible way), Lucy followed in Catherine's footsteps as a dreamy youngster, she too becoming a great collector of ingredients for magic potions. One day when she was six years old, she said to me, 'I really wish the fairies would leave me notes to say "thank you" when I leave them magic potions down by the ponds.'

I could not resist. That night after she had gone to bed, I wrote a simple note, carefully disguising my handwriting: 'We know what you do. Thank you Lucy for all the magic potions.' I folded and placed it sticking out from under a rock by her potion jars.

Next day after school she came running up, yelling, 'Dad! Dad! The fairies wrote me a letter!' She immediately sat down and wrote a reply: 'I am your friend too. Please write back and tell me your names.' Suddenly I suspected I had made a terrible mistake, a bit like telling the kids about Santa but going one step further by faking some evidence.

The exchange of letters went on for some weeks as I responded underhandedly and the plot thickened at every turn. The fairies revealed themselves to be called Cynthia and Tabetha, and they were kept extremely busy going around all the potions Lucy was leaving out. I began hoping that she would tire of it all, but she only got more enthusiastic, asking increasingly complicated questions that required more devious answers.

Finally I knew I had to pull the plug. I composed the letter carefully: 'Dearest Lucy, it is with great sadness that I have to tell you about our sick fairy aunty, Tennyfrae, who lives a long way away, near Nelson. She sent a fernbird to tell us that she needs our help, so we have both left today in a hurry. Sorry we did not get a chance to meet. It may be many years before we can return. Please accept these four chocolate bars as our farewell gift. We will remember you forever. Love always, Cynthia and Tabetha.' There had to be a payoff, and Lucy loved chocolate.

When she come home from school I saw her from a distance reading the note for a full five minutes, trying to understand it. Then she bolted for the house, where I was waiting with feigned nonchalance. 'Dad, Dad!' she screamed excitedly, 'The fairies left me four chocolate bars!' She barely mentioned the fact they had left, but I promised myself I would never get into that situation again.

I watched the Bay change as the 1990s rolled along. The old hippies (some would hate me calling them by that dog-eared name) had slowly turned into respected members of society. Perhaps the 25-year residence rule did apply. Time took its course. On the way there had been plenty of marital settlements. I reckon just over half those original hippy couples got through, probably not much different from the average population. The 'hippies' changed along with the 'straights' at around the same rate, gradually seeming to merge together, co-operating and combining their talents.

The newcomers learnt lots of good skills from the cow-cockies, the Sollys, the RSA guys and the like who all made up the Bay. And the old-timers benefited from fresh, young creative talent, even when it was only spent as employees helping out in their cowsheds for some extra cash. Something artistically vibrant began to happen. All those experimenting, flourishing artists came of age, their creative talents helping to redefine the Bay's demeanour. Artists' studios began to flourish along the main streets, filling old farm supply stores and hand-built churches, and craft trails proliferated.

It would be too easy to say the acceptance of alternative lifestyles had to do with how much money all their combined talents were starting to bring in. Just as the redwoods of California were saved when their tourist dollar-value was finally realised. But I think more it was because Golden Bay finally matured as a society, a process that is still going on, and has only been made possible by mutual acceptance from both sides.

When the Golden Bay Cement Company finally closed in 1988, there were huge howls from the established community about how the Bay would die. For so long they had been hooked on the big wages from that smelly, polluting plant that they couldn't see the alternatives. For a while Golden Bay had more money on term deposit per head of population than anywhere else in the country, as former cement workers wondered what do with their big redundancy windfalls, in many cases over $100,000.

Some squandered theirs in the pub; others set up marginal businesses like bungy jumping and quickly went bust. Quite a few established themselves in more sustainable businesses and exist comfortably today. It wasn't only the hippies that changed: everyone was going through it on some level. Rogernomics too had its influences, sometimes painful but often better in the long term. All the doom-and-gloomers were proved wrong; Golden Bay successfully reinvented itself, the way it has time and time again since the first gold rush.

The same could not be said about the weather. Scientists have speculated ever since the 1950s about global climate change, but it wasn't until the early 1990s that ordinary people on the land, in New Zealand, started waking up to the fact that strange things were beginning to affect the growing of their crops and plants, and hence their livelihoods and lifestyles.

I recall an old-timer from up the Aorere Valley who told me how his father talked about the 'rata floods' that came down their mighty river most summers. When the rata flowered profusely at the start of summer, leaving the cliff-hanging rainforest of the Whakamarama Range looking as though it had been brush-stroked all over with daubs of red, that was when you knew the summers would be full of surprise floods. There haven't been the same rata flowers, nor the same summer floods, for years now.

For me a closer indicator of weather changes became the cabbage trees (ti kouka) which were scattered throughout my swamp. Normally their flowering started in November and went through to late summer. Suddenly they began flowering several months early, and more profusely than ever before. The density and size of the cabbage tree flower head is regarded by some as an indicator of how dry the summer will be. The bigger the flower head, the drier the summer you had to look forward to (or not look forward to, depending on your circumstances).

Those cabbage trees heralded the El Nino weather pattern of wickedly hot summers and tempestuous winters and shoulder seasons. In light of the repeated spring flooding, councillors in Takaka debated again whether to shift the town to Pohara. The huge flood of October 1983, which flooded through nearly half the town's houses, gave everyone a hell of a fright.

Vicious hailstorms suddenly seemed common as they cut their annual swathes through Tasman orchards. On 22 February 1994 hailstones the size of dollar coins fell in a storm just as orchardists were in the full swing of harvesting, and caused $3 million worth of damage in 10 minutes. Seven cows sheltering on a slight rise at Rockville were found dead the following morning, struck by lightning. These weather events were not confined to the Nelson region, either. Surging floodwaters tore away the nearly-completed, 'indestructible' Opuha Dam on 22 February 1997, causing 200 nearby residents to be evacuated. There seemed no rhyme or reason to the weird happenings. Most curious to me was the story about three scuba divers being hit by lightning while diving in the Bay of Islands. Five metres under the water they were, yet it jolted them just like a super-powerful electric fence.

Anything could happen, it seemed now. On 15 June 1991 Mt Pinatubo in the Philippines erupted, putting enormous amounts of fine particles into the upper atmosphere and affecting weather all over the world. Evidence could be seen all over New Zealand two months later in the form of brilliant sunrises and sunsets. We were always out on our deck to watch as many as we could. Better still was the occasional Aurora Australis or Southern Lights, that would fill our night skies uninterrupted by the light pollution that one gets near cities.

But it was always the smaller 'downward' perspectives that could be relied on to hold my enduring fascination. Like my ponds. They were so full of life, and so inexorably linked to the swamp. Each enhanced the other immeasurably, feeding life back and forth as fast as the cycles would allow.

The more I began appreciating the sodden part of my property for what it was, a wonderland of teeming life, the more all its commonplace inhabitants began to enthrall me. Like the extended family of 14 pukeko which would periodically move in from an adjoining farm to bring the swamp alive with their screeching, strutting antics. Over a period of several weeks during 1995, I watched a group of four males together and singly build a selection of nests on outcrops of flattened rushes. My five children and I could cover a lot of ground searching, so it did not take long to find them. All of the nests had been done 'on spec', because as it turned out only one would be chosen by the females, which then all shared and laid a huge clutch of 15 red-blotched eggs that both sexes incubated.

Early naturalists were completely unaware of the communal tendencies in pukeko and expressed nothing short of dismay at the huge clutch sizes. One 1890 report noted that 'a single' female pukeko had managed to lay 19 eggs in one single breeding attempt. We now know that these massive clutches are the result of communal breeding. This can be verified easily, even with the untrained eye because each female lays eggs with a distinct colour and spot pattern.

When roaming space is unlimited, female pukeko will nest individually and usually lay up to five eggs. But when they nest communally, the average clutch size jumps to seven eggs per female, so it is not unusual to see 25 eggs in one nest these days as competition for nesting space becomes intense. Some researchers believe joint nesting females are revealing a subtle form of competition here.

Many people see pukeko as brainless road fodder, and it is true that many get themselves knocked down by cars, but I would say their intelligence must be near the top end of the scale as birds go. I came to that conclusion when I first saw one using a stick as a tool, grasping it by the spindly toes of one foot and manipulating it through an old fishing net I had thrown over some ripe strawberries. The bird was definitely trying to extract them.

With movements akin to ballet, their blue- and scarlet-feathered bodies elegantly balance on long slender legs as they go about stripping seed heads. Once they went for my big crop of sweet corn, and reduced it to cobs on stalks, sheaves all peeled neatly down like multiple banana skins. Every kernel had been picked off every cob of the 350 plants.

When they spotted me that day, they scrammed, flicking their white tails and uttering their ear-piercing cries of alarm, *kwee-ow* like an old rusty hinge, as they took off flying, legs and feet dangling, into the thick of the swamp to perch gangly atop some spindly manuka barely big enough to take their weight. I'd swear they were all laughing at me too.

Let's face it, no one likes getting their crops ripped off. In the moments following my discovery of that pillaged corn, I felt no conflicting emotion, just an incredible deadly desire to wipe every pukeko off the face of the earth. Luckily I do not own a gun now, for I surely would have. It is an emotion that motivates many farmers, and hunters to shoot them in high numbers during the season running from May through to the end of July. It has been going on for years. Maori gardeners spent much time chasing pukeko from their kumara and taro plots, throwing the catchcry insult as they went: 'Hie, hie! Haere ki te huhi, haere ki te repo.' (Away, away! Go off to the swamp, go off to the bog.)

Luckily this feeling did not last long for me, and within days of being rendered cornless I was once again admiring the birds' antics. How could anyone decimate their numbers? Members of this wandering band of pukeko that visited my swamp were probably all related: two or three adult males, four adult females that bred promiscuously with each of the males, and seven non-breeding helpers who assisted with the raising of the chicks. Despite all their posturing and minor skirmishes, the pecking order was well established, their co-operative behaviour a challenge to the concept of the nuclear family.

New Zealand's biodiversity plummeted following the arrival of humans. But this does not quite begin with the arrival of the Maori in the 13th century AD: there must have been some earlier human visitors because carbon-dating has pushed back the arrival of the kiore to around 2000 years ago. These rats could only have arrived with humans, although those early people have left no other evidence of their coming. They may not have stayed, or died out for some unknown reason. Perhaps they were seafarers blown off course; perhaps there were no women among them although they had rats for food on their journey. But however the kiore got there, they must have swept like a tidal wave across the land, devouring anything they could tackle, from forest-litter animals to small birds, eggs and nestlings. Their depredations had been in progress for well over a thousand years by the time the Maori arrived. Many endemic birds were already extinct and once-huge colonies of ground-nesting seabirds on the mainland were in decline.

The Maori were just the second stage of this process. They burned off large areas of land, supplanting much of the bush with bracken, grass and tutu. They introduced another, larger predator in the form of the dog (kuri). Within a couple of hundred years they had driven all 11 species of moa to extinction. One of these, *Dinornis giganteus*, was the largest bird ever to walk the earth, eating as much vegetation each day as a large bullock.

European settlement and the drive to develop pasture saw another nine bird species vanish. Forest cover went down from 75 per cent to just 25 per cent. But despite the adversity faced by many birds today, the pukeko stands out as a true survivor. Before 1850, they were only patchily distributed, in small groups, but they increased rapidly in the late 19th century as more swamp forest was cleared, and are now common in all open wet or lush land up to 400 metres altitude. The pukeko is among the few animal species that have done well since the coming of Europeans to New Zealand.

After the birds I had all the fish to discover. So-called native trout, that began their lives as whitebait, found sanctuary in ankle-deep braided channels overhung with dank vegetation. They were elusive at first, leaving only ripples as they streaked for cover when I approached. That was until I discovered 'Fishville' some years ago, a knee-deep pool scoured out by periodic flooding, where fish would congregate. These I encouraged with daily feedings of crushed-up dog biscuit, until I could count on a swirling mass of some 50 fish to turn up. Then one day the white heron spotted them, and circled discreetly down to look. Within a week they were all gone. Once again, as with the frogs, I had tampered with nature, and the small guys had paid the price. I stopped feeding the fish after that.

What species they were I did not know until a regional freshwater survey of mudfish was carried out. Nelson-based ecologist Belinda Studholme set cage minnow traps throughout my swamp at the end of one long dry summer. 'Even if the swamp all dries up,' she said, 'these tough little fish go into a torpor-like state, and can survive for months in the mud.'

Next morning I helped her pull up the traps. We had no mudfish, but a gasping booty of banded kokopu, which we released after careful recording. This, I discovered, was one of five species of whitebait that live out their adult lives in swamps and secluded waterways like mine.

Occasionally in the season I still go out to the Parapara Stream with a scoop net and fish for whitebait, but not as often as my friend Chris, another draughting cadet who worked with me, along with his wife Rosie. I watched them fall in love just two desks in front. After I shifted to Golden Bay they came down to visit and ended up buying land and settling at Onekaka, just along the road. Chris started whitebaiting as a kid in the Hutt River and carried on his obsession when he came to live in Golden Bay. He still lives for the start of the season, which runs from mid-August to the end of November. His working wife gets a bit mad at all the time he takes out from his joinery workshop, but he doesn't care. His ploy is to get home before her so he can pour a bucket of sawdust over himself and make it look as though he's been hard at work all day.

More experts came and went, all keen to observe and to share their secrets about my swamp with me. I felt like such a late starter. Department of Conservation botanist Simon Walls came and did a flora survey and through new eyes I realised I had a veritable Garden of Eden! I had never even noticed some of the plants before, as if they didn't exist. Flourishing between the stout swamp flax I now knew I had fine baumea rushes (*Baumea tenax*) and large baumea rushes (*Baumea rubiginoas*) – these were my 'ball spikers' from Chapter 2 – and another called *B. terelifolia*.

In the fern department I now could formally celebrate knowing how well endowed my land was. Speared through by the elegant rushes, kiokio ferns (*Blechnum* sp.) and tanglefern (*Gleichenia dicarpa*) filled much of the available space between the towering flax bushes. Hard fern (*Paesia scaberula*) was predominant around the fringes, competing with the rather politically-incorrectly-named 'niggerheads' (*Carex virgata*) and introduced Spanish heather that gave the appearance of creeping in around the edges.

Swamp coprosma (*Coprosma tenuicaulis*) grew out at random inter-vals everywhere, its wiry, divaricating, almost impenetrable branches protecting it from grazing. The berries go through colour stages of white, orange, to red and finally black. Not quite black, because crushed through your fingers they stain your hands the richest purple.

Other plants took my fancy too. I celebrated the discovery of a swamp hebe (*Hebe gracillima*) and a thick grove of toetoe (*Cortadaria* sp.) at the very head of the swamp that I had somehow completely overlooked before. Others were not so exciting really, like when I spotted an *Astelia* masquerading as a flax, looking like some sulking crossdresser severely out of place. If I cared to look below, I knew now how to find the swamp herbs of *Dichondra* sp. and *Contella uniflora*, not to mention little darlings like *Schielema* and *Myosotis* cowering low, as though saying, 'Please, please, don't notice us.'

The greatest spectacle of course came every November with the flowering of the flax, when the five-metre-high stalks would erupt in masses of red flowers. Droves of tui would descend from the hills to slurp the delicious nectar, soaring off to perform fluttering acrobatics and plunging closed-wing dives as they got drunker and drunker. Their resonant and fluid song notes that interspersed these frenzied feedings were mixed with all their usual harsher sounds, variously described as croaks, coughs, clicks, grunts, rattles, wheezes and chuckles, which were most entertaining to hear while hanging out the washing.

In the old days, these birds had to compete with Maori children who roamed the swamps in summer, extracting the nectar by tapping it from the flowers into a gourd for use as a beverage and food sweetener. A big plant might produce up to 250 millilitres of liquid. Diluted with water, it was used as a soft drink or mixed with a meal made from the roots of cabbage tree and rhizomes of bracken fern. The phrase 'me he wai korari', literally 'like the nectar of the flax,' might in today's hip argot be translated 'Sweet as!' I tried extracting it myself once, but couldn't cope with the gritty aftertaste.

How could the swamp not be your friend when you knew its plants so intimately, could even taste them? They all belonged together, in a wondrous picture. Bush-bashing up the steep valley sides above the swamp, I could clearly see the association of darker, spindly manuka along the swamp fringe, giving way to the more robust kanuka trees on higher ground. It fascinated me how it all fitted together, harmoniously, complementary, in perfect balance. Inwardly, I thanked myself many times that no excavator had come to wreck it.

A thickly vegetated swamp is not an easy thing to get about in. Our horse Shorty ventured in and quickly came to grief, falling over in the soft mud where it was impossible for him to get up. As he struggled, the short but sturdy legs to which he owed his name just dug him in deeper. Despite our frantic efforts to help him on to hard ground only four metres away, he was going downwards with every new struggle. Finally, I had to put a slab of timber under his head to stop it too from going under, while we recruited the effort of 10 neighbours.

Two of them, Geoff Lamb and Harry Wilson, were old hands with horses. Harry, who had been a roadman for much of his long life, took one look and told me he'd buried 29 horses in his lifetime. I wondered whether that meant he expected he was about to bury his thirtieth. Finally we hooked a big strop around the animal as best we could, and hauled him out with a tractor. But the strain had taken its toll, and although we got him out and sitting up he was dead by next morning. An undignified end at age 38 to a noble if stunted horse. He had spent much of his life with his previous owner packing deerskins out of the forest park, only to end his days ignominiously in the Tukurua Swamp.

That swamp may have been soft, but the ground beside it was rock-hard and I spent the next three days digging a hole with shovel, pick and crowbar before I decided it was big enough to bury the horse. But when we rolled him into it and backfilled it, his legs stuck out above the ground, set by rigor mortis. I had no option but to get the chainsaw and saw each one off at ground level. Geoff and Harry said it didn't matter, because Shorty was already in horse heaven.

But when I had to rescue my eight-year-old son, the second time he'd been stuck in the swamp up to his thighs, I made a decision. My next construction priority became a wooden walkway that we could use as a safe swamp crossing. It took a year of weekends, labouring knee-deep in mud, driving posts deep and nailing boards on to rails. Because there was no solid bottom for the double row of two-metre foundation posts, I could often push them all the way in by hand, and I was forced to nail three more to each post, going off in different directions. The triangular structure that resulted gave as good holding as solid ground. It was laborious, but worth doing properly because at the end I had rock-solid foundations, and all in a jelly-like swamp.

When it was all finished, I gathered family, neighbours and friends and called on Nina to cut the ribbon. Melanie declared the structure open for anyone who wished to savour the delights of a swamp from a slightly elevated perspective.

That new platform gave us all a remarkable insight into the workings of the swamp. Spring would see channels flush with returning whitebait, and long-finned eels in slithering pursuit. Sunrise was the best time to view insects like the darting dragonfly, long-horn beetle and ghostly white widower moth. Often in gentle mist lifting off the flax, they would climb to the top of the undergrowth to catch the first rays of the sun and begin their daily rituals. You could see them drink dewdrops off their bodies before practising a few beats of their wings and then stuttering warm-up flights. Soon, with little percussive bursts, the insect orchestra would strike up to begin a new day.

Water levels rose as winter approached, flushing out the detritus of a previous growing season. Insect populations would decrease, then bounce back in greater numbers than before. An extended summer dry season in 1998 led to a bug 'baby boom'. Insects like the green-headed leafroller managed four generations over their breeding season instead of the usual three. Garden snails had proliferated to alarming numbers. Where were all the tethered carnivorous land snails (*Powelliphanta* sp.) when you needed them?

It was all like magic to me, but could I rely on the enthusiasm of others to protect it after I was gone? I decided that no one else should make the mistake I nearly did and destroy this fragile world. I applied to the Queen Elizabeth II National Trust to establish a covenant over the area, recognising its ecological value and binding successive owners to keep it intact.

CHAPTER 16

DISCOVERIES

It was one of those reported findings that made me drop everything and investigate: a huge, possibly ancient rock enclosure found amidst dense scrub in a remote reach of the Milnthorpe Revegetation Project, between Parapara and Collingwood, just a few kilometres from my home.

It all began in July 1998 when the Community Taskforce worker Matt Kausch literally bumped into it while cutting a new track through a particularly thick section of bracken and gorse on his way down to the coast. Clearing around the structure had revealed its full extent, and I could not believe what I saw. Accurately constructed out of large rounded rocks, the clay-filled wall was a square enclosure measuring 20 metres (one chain) along each side. I mapped it carefully, transcribing all the measurements on to a 1:100 scale map. It was about a metre thick through the base and came up to about a metre above the ground all around. Apart from a few boulders that had tumbled off, it seemed remarkably intact.

Although one news report labelled it an 'exciting discovery', the find was more of a rediscovery. Revegetation Project manager Dick Nicholls showed me an aerial photo of the property taken in 1950, which clearly showed a perfect square poking out of burnt scrub: 'I've been aware of its existence for some time,' he explained, 'but actually uncovering it made it both accessible and redefined.'

Plainly visible close by on the photo was an extensive network of strange trenching that turned occasional right angles with little regard for the lie of the land. Could this have been the Skilton Brothers collecting water to sluice the gold-bearing sands along the beach? Only one thing was certain: the poor fertility of this Crown leasehold was further diminished by the repeated burnoffs of manuka regrowth, intended to keep the land clear for grazing.

I began talking to all the old-timers I could think of who might know something about the stone structure. Retired Collingwood farmer Wattie Solly recalled mustering the area as a lad back in the 1930s: 'The stone enclosure used to be a kind of landmark. In those days it was surrounded by rough pasture. It looked ancient even back then. There was a neat pile of rocks nearby we used to think could have been a grave.'

Frank Soper, of Takaka, recalled seeing the 'stone square' on his way to work every day when helping to build the Ferntown bridge: 'Coming up off Bishop's Saddle towards Collingwood, you'd always glance down at it, an impressive square structure situated on a prominent and well-chosen ledge looking out to sea.' There was no bush to block the view back then.

Memories may abound of its existence, but historical details as to its origin were sadly lacking, taken by old-timers to their graves. Suddenly I had a mystery to solve, because confronting such a monumental effort can only make you ask: Who would have gone to such lengths? When was it built? What purpose did it serve?

Clues weren't far away. On the nearby property of Clem and Mona Randall there is a 20-metre-long clay-filled rock wall, 1.8 metres high in parts, that stretches between a gully and a bank, to divide off a part of their property. They have always just called the area 'the cow paddock' because there is a small dug-out section in the bank near one end that they speculate could have served as a rudimentary cow shed. This basic but effective attempt at confining livestock is thought to be the effort of the Scadden family, the first Europeans to settle the Milnthorpe area, around 1850.

'Back then,' says Clem Randall, 'all fencing, wire, waratahs, staples, anything metal, had to be imported from England. Timber or posts had to be pit-sawn or split. Rocks, if easily available, were a viable alternative for fencing.'

Milnthorpe's profusion of large round boulders, totally covering the ground in places, are what rock-hounds call a 'geological curiosity' because the odd mixture of quartz conglomerate, granitoids and sedimentary rock does not match the geological complex of the immediate area. Rather, they resemble rocks from the Aorere River, which we can speculate once flooded out to Milnthorpe before uplifting of the flattened, eroded land re-routed the river towards Collingwood. This would also explain the absence of the fine gravels among the Milnthorpe goolies, so abundant and river-worn. These rocks could be rolled around, even single-handedly, and a horse-drawn sled would make them easier to gather. Just roll them on the sled and let the horse do the shifting.

Clay was characteristically used to pack in the middle of the wall as rocks were stacked up on both sides. The result: an almost indestructible wall. Close inspection along the eastern side of the enclosure reveals a gate-sized gap, the only way in. Since it is in line with rectangular mounds outside, these are almost certainly the remains of the foundations of a small house, with fireplace and a garden plot.

It seemed unlikely to me that the square enclosure itself, being slightly south-facing, was any kind of garden. Probably it was just an elaborate pig-pen or a holding paddock for horses. Its slope certainly precludes its uses as any kind of reservoir. Metal items found on the site include an old teapot, a single ploughshare and a piece of drainpipe. A towering blue gum has avoided immolation over the years.

All in all, this site exudes masculine efforts. But a single red English rosebush and a small patch of thriving agapanthus indicate that a woman too may have lived there. My search of Land Information New Zealand Records in Nelson shed much light on the subject. The first surveyor's handbook, with field details recorded in 1881, records the existence of the house and a fence enclosing a 1.6 ha paddock.

How long this house had been there by then is anyone's guess now, but there is still no mention of any rock wall. It is worth noting that the surveyor (Mr Lewis) wrote 'poor land' across every block – it was obviously not desirable country. The earliest recorded leasehold on this crown land is in the name of Harold John Exton, later transferred to his brother Leopold. Their father, Timothy Edwin Exton, born in 1853, was an assisted immigrant from Bishopstrow in Warminster, England. He arrived on the ship *Chile* sometime in the 1870s and first bought land at Collingwood in 1876. He married Florence (Flo) Lucas, a daughter of a prominent Nelson family, in 1880, and made several more land purchases around Collingwood after that.

They settled on their farm at Swamp Road, just out of Collingwood. This entrepreneurial family also built a stately house along Beach Rd in 1907, still standing proudly as Mary and Dave Taylor's 'Chocolate House'. Timothy Exton died in 1925 and is buried in the Collingwood cemetery. Could it have been this original Exton family who built the stone enclosure at Milnthorpe? Harold John Exton was the earliest lessee I could find, but a look through the Registry of Births revealed he wasn't born until 1895. Brother Leopold, the next registered lessee, was actually 10 years older, but died young, in 1915.

So who built the stone structure? Surely anyone who put in so much labour would have registered a lease? Squatting was not tolerated back then. My mind began stretching the parameters, certainly more than any formally trained historian would have permitted himself to do. Maybe it wasn't Europeans at all who were responsible? Certainly these rock structures are uncommon in this part of the country.

I should confess that I had just come back from visiting French Polynesia, where I had visited several marae, a term which over there means the characteristic fence-high square or rectangular stone structures used for ceremony and sacred rites, including human sacrifice. Captain Cook witnessed such an event inside a low stone marae which looked remarkably like the structure I investigated at Milnthorpe.

It has been suggested that Golden Bay was originally colonised from islands around Tahiti, and if you look for circumstantial evidence to support this belief it certainly can be found. For example, there are localities with names that match – Ta'a'a and Motue'a (the consonant 'k' is absent from Tahitian) – just a few kilometres apart on the island of Ra'iatea. The original Ngati Tumatakokiri were wiped out by about 1827 by successive genocidal raids from northern tribes. Who knows what secrets went with them, or what stone walls they might have left behind? I could almost imagine some early European settler not believing his luck when he came across a ready-made pig-pen!

Or was I going too far? Not knowing definitely who built it does not of itself constitute evidence that the wall was built by Maori. If it was a Tahitian-style structure built by Maori, you might expect to find other archaeological evidence at the same site or in the region to corroborate it – especially during the two hundred years that Europeans have been tearing into the landscape. As I grow older my romantic side fights an increasingly uphill battle against the sceptic within me. Increasingly I am aware that there is sometimes a fine line between what fits the facts and what one would like to believe.

It still amazes me that I keep discovering things to enthrall me. I came late to one of my most exciting discoveries: the flax, or harakeke. Not a discovery in the sense of finding out that it existed of course – with its lofty flower stalks stabbing the sky and leaves as broad as waka paddles, flax crammed my swamp from top to bottom – but for too long familiarity had bred contempt. It was not until the late 1990s that I developed a growing awareness of its significance. A bit of book learning to begin with helped.

There are two distinct species of flax. The common flax found in lowlands and swamps like mine, *Phormium tenax*, was called harakeke. Its long blade-like leaves grow in upright clumps, with taller leafless flower-stalks growing up among them in spring. When they open, the waxy red flowers can be seen borne distinctly erect on branches of the flower-stalk or scape, and later the spindle-shaped seed-pods too stick up from the branches. The smaller mountain flax, *Phormium cookianum*, or wharariki, rarely exceeds two metres in height and the leaves tend to droop more. Its flowers are more greenish, yellow- or orange-toned, and distinctively hang down. The upright versus hanging-flowered habit is the most consistent point of difference between harakeke and wharariki. Otherwise they can be hard for the untrained eye to tell apart. Common on rocky outcrops in montane areas throughout the country, but also along the coast, wharariki often has a weatherbeaten, scruffy look that easily distinguishes it from the larger and more stately flax of swamp habitats.

But before I could think all harakeke was much the same, it was time to think again. I went to the flax plantation at Payne's Ford Scenic Reserve, beside the Takaka River, and was amazed by what I discovered. Rock climbers on the nearby limestone bluffs get the best view, but I had elected to wander among the bushes at ground level, to discover what I could about one of New Zealand's most important native flowering plants.

There are 60 varieties of harakeke in this planting. Some have drooping, floppy leaves; others grow as stiff and upright as spears. To the touch, they vary from a silky fineness to waxy and coarse. The tallest flower stalks reach to over four metres, although many are only half that size, and the leaves are correspondingly almost as tall.

At first glance, they seem to be mostly shades of green on green, but a closer inspection reveals subtle variations. Leaf margins range from orange to deep purple, even black, and the keel running up the centre of each leaf may be yellow, bronze or red. The basic colour of the blades can vary from a blue tinge of driftwood smoke through to the rich green of spring growth on a pohutukawa. A few plants are strongly variegated, erupting streaks of crimson and sulphur-yellow.

The tips of the leaves vary too. In some plants the leaves taper very gradually to the finest of dagger-points. In others they are blunt, like a trowel. I noticed that the leaves of most types are split back along the midrib for 20 or 30 centimetres, so there is a gap or open notch, but in a few varieties the two halves hold together, causing the tip to pucker into a shallow skiff.

The plants at Payne's Ford are all traditional Maori cultivars, selected on the basis of strength, softness, durability, colour and fibre content. Harakeke was the most widely used fibre before Europeans arrived with all their fancy textiles. When they did, traditional use of harakeke plummeted almost overnight. Flax couldn't compete with the warmth of wool, the versatility of cotton, and the durability of hide.

Maori recognised more than a hundred different varieties of harakeke. They had a flax for every purpose. Heavy duty, long fibred tihore, similar to what grew in my own swamp, was ideal for ropes and nets, and even salt-resistant. The short, finer takirikau flax, stripped easily even by a thumbnail, was ideal for making piupiu (a garment worn around the waist with a free-swinging fringe). Very long, bendy varieties such as atewhiki were used for making wharaki (mats) and kete (baskets). Black-edged, slightly droopy blue-green flaxes yielded the long ribbons of soft, silky muka, which might be further processed by an immensely laborious process of soaking, beating and rubbing. This dressing process, called haro, was the first stage in the manufacture of the warm, beautifully crafted garments that so impressed early Europeans.

Pakeha materials came as cloth or finished clothing. Making a garment from scratch out of flax could take months, even a year or two. As a result, the mass-produced woollen blanket supplanted the hand-made fibre cloak in the Maori wardrobe. Harakeke fell from everyday use, if not from grace, its special cultivars largely neglected; its importance became mainly ceremonial rather than practical.

These days, then, it is indeed a wonder that each of the clumps that you can see at Payne's Ford is labelled with a stout stick, inscribed with a traditional name: matawai, taniwha, takaiapu, makaweroa, pango, motu-o-nui, and all the rest. For someone like me it was a complete revelation. This particular plot, tended by local enthusiasts over the past 15 years or so, is one of half a dozen replications nationwide of what is known as the Orchiston collection – flax plants originally gathered from the East Coast, Waikato and Taranaki in the North Island and planted in a small paddock on a family farm at Hexton, near Gisborne.

As a young woman, Rene Orchiston became fascinated by the flax-working skills shown by local Maori weavers. 'It wasn't so much the process of weaving that used to excite me, rather all the different qualities of the flax fibres they produced. The more I delved into it, the more I realised that many fine craftswomen were using inferior materials because of the extreme shortage of specialised cultivars from which to extract good fibre.'

Orchiston was also concerned by the general loss of interest in flax-weaving, particularly among young and middle-aged Maori around that time. 'Special flax bushes had been totally neglected – just left to die out in many areas. I could see that in years to come there might be a revival of interest in traditional arts and crafts. Saving as many of those special flaxes as I could became my passion.'

Over the next 30 years, she crisscrossed the North Island, visiting old settlement sites and marae, gathering information from elderly weavers – especially the original Maori name and use of each flax variety. She describes how she willingly swapped plants from a selection which she carried in the boot of her car for the purpose:

> A typical marae had close access to only two or three different types. I'd trade them a flax variety that was, say, much more suited to fine kete-making than the material they were using, and they'd give me one of their local varieties which was ideal for cloak-making. In this way I built up my own collection, and then I in turn donated thousands of these plants to marae, schools and botanical gardens all around New Zealand.

Every one of Orchiston's flaxes has a personal story: where it grew, who donated it and its particular history. For example, while searching in the East Cape high country she came across an old Maori camp. Nearby in a swampy piece of ground were three battered clumps of harakeke, all different – a sure sign of a pa harakeke, or flax plantation. Pig-rooting had damaged the plants, so she carefully replanted them after taking a small fan from one, a cultivar she had never seen before. Its straight green blades were unevenly striped with white. The variety was later identified by a Whakatane woman as motu-o-nui, while Orchiston already knew the other two varieties: the short-leafed oue and the yellow-striped pare-koretawa. 'Harakeke was not indigenous to that particular locality, so I knew those flax bushes had to be of high quality, since they must have been carried there on the backs of travellers from swamps elsewhere.'

For many years, Orchiston's work was known only to a small circle of weaving enthusiasts. When the former Department of Scientific and Industrial Research (DSIR) started a small ethnobotany project in 1986, one of its first jobs was to send out the husband-and-wife team of botanists Geoff Walls and Sue Scheele to identify and rescue as many traditional Maori flaxes as they could. Imagine their delight when they first drove up the long, winding driveway of the Orchiston farm. There, laid out before their incredulous eyes, were over 50 distinct varieties of harakeke, all carefully catalogued. The job had already been largely done for them.

'It was a fantastic find,' says Scheele, 'but what gives this collection even greater significance is that it was made available to the public of New Zealand.' In 1987 Orchiston donated her entire collection to the DSIR to form the basis of a national collection. Landcare Research (Manaaki Whenua) took stewardship of the Orchiston collection in 1992, when the DSIR was disbanded. Ongoing research into taxonomy, fibre properties and management will ensure we will continue to become even more knowledgeable about flax.

The collection now has been replicated on sites at Havelock North, Rotorua, Taupo, Gisborne, Lincoln, and Paynes Ford in Golden Bay. Since flax varieties do not necessarily grow true from seed, the plants are best propagated vegetatively, from suckering fans. These are made freely available to weavers, and thousands of new plants have found their way into the gardens of marae, community groups and schools – a heritage saved. The importance of flax to early Maori is perhaps summed up by the story of the chief who, when informed that flax did not grow in England, asked, 'So how is it possible to live there?'

To the first settlers, the size, shape and strength of flax leaves would have immediately suggested a use for plaiting mats and baskets, skills well represented in all Polynesian culture, where hitherto they mainly used coconut and pandanus leaves. Harakeke would soon become transformed into platters to eat from, containers to carry soil and sand for gardens and fortifications, lines and nets for fishing, mats to sleep on and to cover floors, lashings for canoes and dwellings, snares to trap birds, sails for canoes. Babies were given rattles made from flax, and every boy knew how to flick a flax dart. (In recent years whole books have been published showing how to make traditional Maori flax toys.) Splints for broken bones were made from the leaf base, and flax fibres or strips used for sewing up a wound.

The first Europeans were quick to recognise the export potential of the fibre. The first major shipment to London of New Zealand swamp flax, a sizeable 60 tons valued at £2,600, left these shores in 1818. By 1830, a regular export trade was well established, with some £50,000-worth auctioned in Sydney alone in the four years up to 1832. Flax remained New Zealand's biggest export by far until wool and frozen mutton kicked in late in the 19th century. Entrepreneurial flax traders employed Maori workers to hand-strip the flax in exchange for blankets, trinkets and, most importantly, muskets. The price for one musket quickly became set at one ton of dressed flax, with still more required for powder and ammunition. Inland tribes, desperate for the muskets their coastal brethren and enemies possessed, exchanged three to five slaves for a single musket. Slaves were useful as flax-stripping machines.

Suddenly swamps became a commodity, a way to power. Maori even settled nearer to the swamps, often suffering poorer health as a consequence. Muskets and flax changed their whole way of living – and dying. And for what? In 1831, one ton of New Zealand flax fibre was fetching between £18 and £25 on the English market, mostly destined to end up as cheap rope. Today it is impossible to imagine how laborious the hand-dressing of swamp flax was. Colonel Theodore Haultrain, one of the flax commissioners appointed by the colonial government in 1870 to investigate the full potential of the industry, wrote:

> It is difficult to get any accurate estimate of what quantity a Native woman can prepare in a day, but it is not much. At a large meeting near Waikanae I asked that question ... some could do 1 lb, some 2 lb, and others as much as 4 lbs, according as they were fortunate or otherwise in quickly finding the proper leaves.

It was menial work for menial wages, and Maori knew it. Haultrain would soon be reporting back to his superiors, 'The Natives of Otaki are not preparing any of the fine flax, they think the price insufficient. I tried to induce Te Rauparaha to take it in hand ... but he seemed to think the attempt was useless.'

Haultrain travelled the country tirelessly, canvassing various tribes in his feasibility study. The answer seemed always the same: 'The Natives of Opunake, after some consideration, decline to prepare any fibre ... They said that the work was too much, and the price too little.' 'If Europeans won't do it for a pittance, why should we Maori?' went the cry. This not unreasonable position hardened during the Land Wars.

173

Between 1860 and 1866, the average annual value of flax fibre exported plummeted to a mere £150.

It took a conflict on the other side of the world to stimulate the flagging industry. The American Civil War created an unprecedented demand for manila rope, produced almost entirely by dirt-cheap manual labour in the Philippines. The price of the product skyrocketed from its customary £21 a ton to a peak of £76 during the height of the conflict. Such high prices stimulated attempts to introduce New Zealand swamp flax as a direct competitor to manila.

International conflict has always stimulated technology, even in New Zealand. By 1868, the problem of how to separate fibre from flax leaf was solved by the invention of the flax stripper, a machine which used a steadily rotating drum to scrape and beat the leaves into yielding up their fibres. Within just two years, export receipts for our flax had skyrocketed to £132,578 a year. By 1906, there were 240 flax mills dotted throughout the country, employing over 4,000 'flaxies,' who collectively produced export fibre that earned over half a million pounds a year. Most mills were sited near swamps and could be recognised from a distance by the high-pitched scream emitted by the strippers. Outside, vast quantities of drying fibre could be seen hanging on fences.

The country's largest flax mill by far was Miranui, built in 1907 in an area known as the Makerua Swamp, or simply the 'Great Swamp'. This area of 5,800 hectares stretched from three kilometres north of Shannon, along the Manawatu River up to Linton, and once supported a huge crop of flax. During the height of the swamp-flax industry in 1916-17 there were 19 mills in the swamp, operating 42 flax-stripping machines and employing over 700 workers. Many older people in the district still recall the multiple convoys of 50 or more 'flaxies' riding their bicycles every morning out from Shannon to work in the swamp.

But not all flax entrepreneurs saw their future in the seemingly endless swamps of the Horowhenua. The Prouse family of Levin were successful flaxmillers who early began casting around the country for new swamps to work, Percy Prouse making hot local gossip throughout Golden Bay in 1902 when he visited Westhaven Inlet to find a suitable location for a new flaxmill. He must have taken back favourable reports, because in October 1903 *The Golden Bay Argus* reported, 'Arrangements have been practically concluded with a North Island syndicate for the establishment at "Karaka" of a flaxmill.' This was big news for the remote area.

Karaka was the name given to the reserve at the mouth of the Paturau

River by N.L. Buchanan, attorney for the Taitapu Gold Estates. Paturau translates as 'many clubs' or 'many killed', a reference to the bodies lying in heaps there after the Ngati Tama chief Te Puoho, of Parapara, led a war party to kill the sizeable hapu who lived there.

It is no longer known what dispute had caused this, but Te Puoho had gone into a terrible rage when several of his tribal members described to him how they had paddled a waka around to the Paturau reef and got caught on the rocks. Instead of helping, the locals had just watched and laughed as the waka split into two, floating ashore that night with the survivors clinging to it. They made their way home via the 'Maori Trail' through Te Hapu, and thence to the south end of the Inlet and home. When Te Puoho heard their sorry tale, he issued his death warrant for everyone living at Paturau. The fierce warriors crept up on the locals, who were no match for them and were slaughtered in mere minutes.

Today the carpark at the mouth of the Paturau attracts a few camp-ervans and the odd druggie looking for the hallucinogenic mushrooms called 'gold-tops' that used to grow here in profusion at certain times of year. The Takaka policeman went around a few of the Paturau locals once, asking them to report any suspicious-looking individuals and their car registration numbers. Of particular interest were members of the black-jersey brigade who could often be seen on their hands and knees, combing the sand country covered in rank grass and marram for the little prized gold-tops. 'Boganville', we began calling the place, because of all the 'bogans' that came out here. Someone once counted 24 of them at once, all on their hands and knees. Now that sight is a thing of the past, and the psychedelic fungi are long gone.

The population along this wild stretch of coastline today swells to several hundred in summer. No matter where I went in the world, nothing would come close to the experience of family camping beneath the groves of nikau that can be found all the way down to Kahurangi Point. Paturau, Puna Paua, Sandhills Creek, Anatori, Anaweka, Ruakawa: all are top-class locations in their own right.

Immersing myself in the history makes it even more glorious whenever I stay down there. I have often tried to imagine the excitement at the Paturau River mouth just before Christmas 1903, when all the ex-Shannon plant for the new Prouse and Saunders flaxmill was barged in. They even brought timber for housing, along with all their rewarewa (native honeysuckle, *Knightia excelsa*) tram rails, a mainly North Island timber the locals didn't immediately recognise.

Six men from Levin came as part of the package too. Ivy Walker's father Jacky Rhodes was one of them, who with the others spent the first half of 1904 setting the mill up on the south corner of the river that had access to the stream running down the hillside. A wharf was built at Pah or Melbourne Point in the Inlet, with the tram rails laid out to it so the processed flax could be carted there with the three-horse-team 'trucks'.

A wooden tramway also had to be laid south from Paturau to Sandhills Creek, mostly through steep country with high bluffs, for transporting the green leaf to the mill. Magnolia Richards told how one day the driver made a mistake by putting a grumpy horse in the lead, a position it had not worked before. At the first nasty bluff the horse went berserk, causing the truck loaded with flax to jump off its rails and roll down to a rocky shelf just above the shore. The lead horse was killed, another lay on the upturned truck, and a third was hanging by its harness with its legs in the surf. The driver ran more than a mile to get help, and the two surviving horses were saved.

The mill employed six to eight flax-cutters along with the three teamsters, each with three horses, who all lived at Sandhills Creek, where the shearing shed is situated now. If I had a choice, I would have preferred one of those outside jobs, because inside that mill would have been dreadful and dangerous. Workers had to manually feed the ever-hungry stripper, and there were no Occupational Safety and Health regulations back then. This deafening mechanical monster beat the leaves between a revolving drum and a stationary bar, tearing off the outer skin of the plant and exposing the fibre. Few 'feeders' lasted long with all their fingers intact. Before mechanical methods of collecting the freshly-stripped fibre were developed, a teenaged boy or old man sat beneath the stripper to catch it as it dropped out of the machine. In this position – nicknamed the 'glory hole' – the occupant could not avoid being plastered with a constant rain of slimy leaf material, and emerged bearing more resemblance to a frog than a human.

After stripping, the hanks of fibre were washed and laid out on wire fences for drying and bleaching in the sun. Once dry, the fibre was 'scutched' in another machine with wooden beaters to clean and polish it. But no machine-stripped fibre could ever match the fine, long silky strands made by hand. Mechanical beaters flogged the fibre dreadfully, weakening it and making it suitable only for ropes, twines, bags, sacks and coarse matting.

One of the most memorable photos taken by colonial-era photographer Fred Tyree has to be that of the men who worked at the Paturau mill. Details are long forgotten, but Tyree's journey to Paturau in 1905 could not have been easy. Meticulously, I tried to reconstruct his route using the photographs that he took along the way.

From Collingwood, his buggy laden with bulky photographic gear and two weeks' supplies, he would have headed along the expansive tidal flats of Golden Bay before picking up the muddy track that followed the old trail over Pakawau Saddle and down to Westhaven Inlet. The successful fording of the first deep channel would have been a relief, but there was no time to spare as he spurred his horses, Photo and Lana, into stiff trot. The 12-kilometre slog across the inlet's muddy flats would be a race against the incoming tide, and then there was a final treacherous channel crossing. The recent drowning of two men there was no doubt still fresh in his mind.

Safely through, he unloaded his Thornton-Pickard plate camera and set it up with well-practised precision on its wooden tripod near a makeshift jetty jutting out into the channel. A steam launch carrying flaxmill workers pulled alongside. The men were obliging subjects, doing their best to keep perfectly still while Fred captured their image on a glass plate. Hurrying to make the flaxmilling camp before dark, Fred could not resist unloading his camera one more time, on a shingle shoal in the middle of the Paturau river, to record a packhorse team using the riverbed route to take stores to the nearby Taitapu goldfields.

Fred would go there later as well, but that night he rested at the tiny settlement at the mouth of the Paturau River. Unhitching his weary horses, he joined in the Saturday evening festivities, well pleased he'd made it in time for the workers' day off on Sunday. All were eager subjects, for probably none of the 16 working-class men had ever been photographed before.

He spent Sunday morning setting the scene beside one of the camp huts. A pirate flag was hoisted as a backdrop, bundles of tied flax carefully placed alongside. Fred choreographed every detail before finally crawling under the hood of his camera. Sixteen men, the entire staff of the mill, posed stock-still in various poses: one reading the newspaper *Truth*, another pointing a rifle at a stuffed kiwi (probably one of the many props Fred carried with him into the backblocks). The cook stood proud in his whitest apron while the camp's boozer drained a bottle. Some men held the tools of their trade. There was a clothes-washing demonstration and three musicians posing with their instruments. Fred uncapped his camera lens on the picture-postcard scene. If a picture was worth a thousand words, then a Tyree glass-plate image could say a million.

The mill at Karaka worked until 1911, when it was moved to Mangarakau where Prouse and Saunders concentrated on the Mangarakau Swamp area and expanded into milling. That was when the Paturau River mouth became a popular picnic spot. The swamps of the Horowhenua Plains in the Manawatu may have been the largest producer of flax fibre, but lots of other smaller flaxmills like Karaka played an important part in the economic development of many other parts of the country, notably Southland, Westland, Northland, Bay of Plenty, Marlborough and Nelson.

Many inspired individuals got boosted up the ladder of success. The father of atom-splitting Lord Rutherford of Wakefield owned highly-successful flaxmills in both New Plymouth and Nelson. Profits from these businesses furthered young Ernest's education. Just think: the humble swamp flax plant helped contribute to the splitting of the atom.

CHAPTER 17

FUTURE SWAMP

The year 2000 was billed as a most momentous event. Everything with a silicon chip was going to crash and cause the unhinging of automated civilisation as we knew it. Some people took it very seriously, Golden Bay even saw Y2K bug refugees come to settle, spending their fortunes setting up low-tech 'fail-safe' houses that they thought would render them immune to the savage back-bite of technology.

Those people we could handle, as they were essentially homesteaders, albeit a little late on the job. But it was all the commercial hype about 'The Millennium' that really turned us off, so a group of us organised a 'Stuff the Millennium' party in our huge garden to side-swipe the commercial events. We just put the word out there, and 400 friends and associates, plus a few others, turned up that night to feast and celebrate. Our only stipulation was that no money whatsoever should change hands: it was to be a free event, and everyone got into the spirit of things. Five local bands, sick of being messed around with last-minute New Year bookings, plus a belly-dancing troupe, performed spectacularly under tarpaulins in the rain that got progressively heavier until dawn. When the start of the third millennium dawned over the sea of mud kicked up by the dancing crowd, the world looked much the same to me. And all my gadgets were still working, I noticed. We still had Sky – the real one, even if it was grey.

Our teenagers had all laughed at us 'oldies' organising our own party, which they dubbed 'The Dithering'. They had all opted to attend 'The Gathering' at Canaan Downs, on top of the Takaka Hill, for a three-day New Year celebration. We listened to the news reports about the 'rave' with some anxiety. Torrential cold rain nearly caused a civil-defence evacuation, with many people suffering from hypothermia. But when Nesh came back from it, covered in mud along with all his gear, he declared it had been a 'wicked' time. We had to agree: dancing in sloshy mud was fun, and free.

Summers always brought lots of people to Golden Bay, drawn to its simplicity of spirit and natural wonders. Friends, family, outings for camping, swimming and gathering of kaimoana for the barbeque – including pipi, tuatua, cockles and paua – could always be relied upon to blend into most memorable times. The population in this Nelson sub-region swells fivefold to around 25,000 over the Christmas/New Year holiday period. Even though most of them are Kiwis, we still collectively call these visitors 'loopies', after the earliest tourists to this country who followed a predictably circuitous route around the best attractions, thus heralding the start of our package-tour industry and the peculiar mindset that goes with it.

In summer we lament as our roads go crazy with city-paced drivers racing from one craft-trail driveway to the next. Local parents wisely discourage their kids on bikes and horses from using the road, for fear of being hit. Pulling out of your normally quiet driveway, you sometimes have to wait for a seemingly endless procession of cars to pass.

Shopping becomes the pits, with queues at the supermarket and chemist reminiscent of an Indian railway station. You'd think there was a run on the bank the way the queue stretches out on to the pavement. Absolutely the worse time in Takaka is a rainy day in the Christmas holidays, because everyone who is usually on the beach has nothing to do except come into town. Finding a park or even a coffee would be easier on Lambton Quay or Queen Street – not quite what I came to Golden Bay for. Even Pupu Springs becomes just another tourist trap and break-in carpark.

I recall my cow-cocky neighbour saying to me once, 'That Mussel Inn: I never thought in a million years I'd live next to the busiest liquor outlet in the Bay.' People laughed when Andrew and Jane Dixon built the Mussel Inn out in remote Onekaka, just as people laughed that my idea of a theatre would ever work either. But not only did they survive, they became mainstream institutions. Now there are 'dead-end' cafes at the ends of all Golden Bay's most remote roads – Awaroa, Farewell Spit, Kaituna and Mangarakau.

Golden Bay has earned a reputation as the world's worst whale trap. Whenever we heard about a pilot-whale stranding, which more often than not would occur over the New Year holiday season when the whales were migrating past, we would grab our wetsuits, pile into the car and head out to help re-float the creatures caught on the shallow mudflats, along with every other man and his dog. A century ago strandings of 'blackfish' here were reason for great celebration, reason enough to knock off work, grab a flensing knife or slasher and go to get a year's free supply of the finest lamp oil; and dog food, too.

I covered plenty of whale strandings for various magazines. There was never any shortage of takers for my stories, especially if they were accompanied by heart-wrenching photos like a tiny beached calf lying in a puddle of milk squirted from its dying mother. One Department of Conservation (DOC) worker told me how part of their training was watching for kids wandering off while their parents were too busy 'bonding' with a whale. Many rescuers fell in love with the particular animal they were attending to, pouring buckets of water over them and caressing them in an almost amorous fashion. The London *Sun* ran a great photo showing a rescuer draped over the whale, which was captioned: 'Aoi! We thought you weren't meant to crush 'em!'

It did seem weird to me somehow that the jubilation of killing these beautiful creatures could be turned into delight at saving them. Maybe it's more about the need to come together and celebrate as a societal group, just as all those diggers did in the gold rush. Charged with attending to stranded marine mammals, DOC staff love the PR interface they enjoy with the hundreds of compassionate souls who turn up to help. And let's face it, saving the animals is extremely cost-effective compared to burying the huge carcasses which would take months to decompose if left out in the open.

But it wasn't only washed-up whales that attracted my family's attention. The coastal settlement of Pakawau was always used in Town and Country Planning studies as New Zealand's premier example of ribbon development along a section of highway or coast. Back in June 2001, before a rash of council-approved subdivision made it even longer, its 51 houses all sat in a row with a view of the road behind and the beach out front. One sunny Friday morning a resident looked out to sea and spied a big brown blob lying prone on the shelly mudflats offshore from the river mouth. Probably just another pilot whale, she thought. But closer inspection revealed a more unusual beast; one very large ocean sunfish, dead after stranding on the outgoing tide. The scientific name for this fish (*Mola mola*) comes from the Greek for millstone. Somehow grotesque, this saucer-shaped behemoth measured nearly two metres across and with its two long pointed fins, over three metres high, and weighed maybe two tonnes.

The local DOC office in Takaka asked Solly's Freight to remove the fish. Like whales, bulk marine carrion like sunfish can no longer be left for birds and sea lice to pick over. Commercial cockle gatherers these days would be concerned about the pollution of their harvesting areas. A loader from the local limeworks was sent to collect the sunfish, but only succeeded in tearing through the tough skin. Repositioned to take a better swipe with its bucket, the machine became hopelessly bogged in a shallow channel. The tide turned and was coming in fast.

I came across the scene around the same time as pipe-puffing freight patriarch Trevor Solly, who proclaimed, 'Have you ever seen such a bloody stupid thing? I mean, would *you* send a loader out there?'

The loader driver paced nervously on a crunching pavement of pipi shells. 'I was only doing what I was told.' The tide was now steadily and silently climbing up his boots. He retreated up the ladder into his cab, like a captain preparing to go down with his ship.

More Solly's employees arrived in utes and began laying out chains and wire strops in anticipation of a rescue digger arriving. It brought back so many memories of my early days working for them. Mobile phones rang in unison, answered with strained staccato voices. At the centre of it all, the sunfish lay very still. Brief moments to admire its anatomy: small eyes and gill slits, a remarkably small mouth lined with tiny teeth fused into a sharp-edged plate along each jaw, the inside of which was infested with goose barnacles living alongside giant isopods. Sunfish are typically burdened with heavy parasite infestations, which may account for the tremendous explosive leaps they sometimes make as they propel their huge bulk completely out of the water.

Which right now was rising, causing curious locals to roll their trousers up before turning back for higher ground. Finally, Merv Solly turned up driving an articulated transporter that carried the rescue digger. Traffic along the highway backed up as the rig halted on the centre line. Everyone had to wait: there was a fifty-grand loader at stake here, and insurance companies tend not to approve of getting them stuck in the sea while trying to pick up dead fish.

Merv drummed the digger to a throaty purr and manoeuvred it off with military precision. He hadn't lost his touch one bit. Meanwhile, black exhaust smoke began billowing from the stranded loader as it heaved upwards in one last desperate attempt to escape unaided from its muddy prison. With seawater now up to its greasy hubs, the driver used his fully-tilted bucket to dig in and drag himself forward. He was out!

Bystanders cheered; banked-up traffic and machinery were everywhere. 'God damn, one of those days,' Merv said to me just before he re-loaded his digger. And among all the human commotion, the sunfish lay still, very still. It was finally collected two days later and buried alongside a score of pilot whales near Ferry Point.

How attitudes have changed, about whales, about nets, about stranded sunfish, about hippies – and particularly about swamps. These days government agencies not only try to protect the last remaining big tracts of swampland, but have even started returning them to their natural state. The great North Swamp, inland from Bullock Creek near Punakaiki on the West Coast, is one pilot project, directed by a band of hydrologists and ecologists from NIWA, which will dictate the future feasibility of rehabilitating swamps. By blocking outlets and drains, the water table can be raised easily enough to pre-European levels, but they have found that if this is done too quickly the vegetation that once existed will not recover properly.

In New Zealand, 92 per cent of wetland has been lost since European settlement. Wetland loss in the United States, by contrast, is just 54 per cent. The US's 'no-net-loss' policy will ensure it stays around that figure too, 'Swamp Yankee common sense', some old-timers like Connecticut farmer John Whitman Davis call it: 'You don't upset old mother nature. You work with her. Don't drain the marsh. Don't fill it. Don't dig it up. Don't rut it up. Don't dam it and don't flood it. That's how you do it right.'

Here, because we have so little left, time is of the essence. As one ecologist put it, 'Native forest can no longer be logged, but wetlands, which are under considerably more threat, can still be drained. What gains have we actually made with wetlands in 30 years? Very little.'

Big discrepancies exist between councils too. For example, at the time of writing it's relatively easy to get permission to drain a big swamp in Westland, yet almost impossible in the environmental-regulation-bound Waikato.

One study commissioned for the Tasman District Council (TDC) found that although lowland loss of wetland within the area is still high – 98 per cent for Motueka and Moutere Ecological Districts – overall wetland loss in Tasman is less, around 65 to 70 per cent, because of the high proportion of conservation land. But most of the area's wetlands are small: 92 per cent are less than 10 hectares, with 70 per cent less than one hectare in area.

Disasters still happen too. Two fires at the Mangarakau Swamp, the first in 2004, probably deliberately lit, and the other in early 2006 sparked by a roadside mower, caused combined damage over nearly 200 hectares.

The TDC has copped a lot of flak for its handling of swamp issues over the last few years. In 1998, Peter and Marjorie Miller of Kaihoka went to the Environment Court after they were served an abatement notice by the TDC to stop draining their 19-hectare piece of the sprawling Nguroa Swamp, the same one I had admired as a Solly's driver back in 1978.

The Millers argued 'historical usage': that the former swamp forest had been felled, burnt and grazed back around 1920, then gradually reverted to swamp before a recent flood had opened the outlet again. They also needed it to ensure their economic livelihood (not to mention wanting to get rid of the mosquitoes), and so they were finally granted two resource consents to finish the job.

'We lost count after 72 meetings with bureaucracy,' a fed-up Marjorie Miller told me. The three-year saga cost them around $80,000 and earned them considerable sympathy from local farmers, many of whom had drained much larger areas of swamp to make their farms economic before the days of the Resource Management Act. Despite my swampy sentiments, I felt sorry for the Millers, caught up as they were in so much fickle politics. It's easy to put down farmers. I was grateful that there was no economic pressure on me to 'manage' my swamp, other than leaving it alone to nature. My approach was the easy way out.

I have never regretted choosing the life of a homesteader. Cheap land provided me the pakihi landing-pad for the dream of a lifetime. With youth on my side, I was going against the flow, but it came at a price back then. Many of my old schoolmates became lawyers, accountants and engineers, lavishly watering themselves in high-class bars, building careers and chasing girls around Europe. Compared to them, I was a self-imposed exile in a cold and thorny land. They all seemed to be having fun, and here was I, only 20 years of age, literally holding the baby, and pumping a Tilley lamp every evening so I could permanently damage my eyes straining to read some old faded copy of *The Nelson Evening Mail*. What sort of life was that for a young person?

Much has been written about the social activism of the 1970s, when the air on campus was thick with politics. I am not much qualified to comment on that age of erupting political awareness, because I was just too busy on the land, milking Betsy the cow, trying to figure out by trial and error how to build a house, make compost, grow vegetables and children. Hippy homesteading came as a complete package and did not allow much time for anything else.

Of course I was interested in the shift going on in the cities: *chic* activists leafing through copies of *The Little Red Schoolbook* for revolutionary inspiration, buying condoms from vending machines at the university, proclaiming the manifesto of the new Values Party. Whenever I visited my Wellington Unemployed Workers Union (WUWU) friends who lived at 242 The Terrace, I got an exciting glimpse of what life in an activist flat could be like, with people busy organising collectives, quasi-unions, sit-ins or just working through 'stuff'. Lately these people have even been given a name: 'The Kelburnists', writer Anna Smith dubbed them. Lugging around and hand-turning a Gestetner machine may have been absolutely no different from how you operated a cream separator, but it was a world away from what I had chosen as my life path.

What we all shared though was a desire for change. But whereas the activists wanted to change the world, I suspected my efforts would count for zilch, so I concentrated on changing the sphere I knew intimately, and that sphere was defined measurably in acres: 14 to be exact. Big enough for a family to run around on.

No matter what paths we all chose back in the 1970s, we all eventually saw our courageous dreams and hopes take a tumble towards a more refined and pragmatic wisdom. This may have inspired a whole generation of writers, politicians, artists and poets – there is nothing like experience to bring out maturity, after all – but looking back, I cannot help but feel the changes we sought were all marked by an expedient radicalism. Anything, from drug-taking to idleness to kleptomania, could be justified in one broad sweeping statement: 'Fuck the Establishment.'

However, if there was one thing that becoming a homesteader achieved in an era of cheap land, it was the acquisition of an asset that today is beyond price. Not in any money sense, but more to my mind as a family 'reservation'. A generous piece of land where we could run free, raise stock, plant fruit trees and organic vegetables, ready for when our children left to do their various 'missions' in the world, but be able come back to if required. And not only our children, but extended family as well, such as Melanie's parents who made the choice to build a house on our property and come and live five years ago. It's a family community-village concept that would just not be achievable in any two-bedroom city-flat situation. What grown-up child can afford to buy land in Golden Bay now anyway, with real estate prices close to what you'd expect to pay in Auckland?

Yes, the thought that my children might want to return one day fills me with happiness. Where they could, if required, grow everything to feed themselves, fetch creek water, chop firewood and not be dependent on an electricity supplier with no programme for sustainable maintenance. The old Homesteader Handbook predictions are coming true for cities worldwide – that they would suffer soaring crime rates, clogged motorways, power outages, lowering water standards and unacceptable pollution – even in New Zealand.

Humfrey Newton came to Golden Bay to plant trees. After nearly 30 years his trees are now harvestable, and he has more than enough timber for his rustic-furniture business. Through patience his dream has come true, but not only for himself: his children and their children will have all the timber they could ever want too.

An elderly Fijian man once said to me; 'Even if you never give your kids anything during their lives except land when you die, then everything's "sweet".' When I signed legal documents putting our land into a family trust 15 years ago, it felt such a relief not to own land again, but to hand it over to family. That was everything I ever dreamed of doing. They will never get me off this place unless it's in a box, I tell them: that is one condition clearly laid out. I am a lucky man, and I know it, because I will never have to worry about 'shifting' or scramble for a capital gain.

Every day I give thanks that it turned out how it has. Once I interviewed a senior New Zealand diplomat in Thailand, who told me his dream was to use his life savings from work to buy a place in Golden Bay. I felt so humbled to realise I had so early found what he desired so badly. All this talk about a Waitangi or New Zealand Day: what we lack is a Thanksgiving Day, to celebrate, the way the Maori must have felt when they scored a moa.

At least 400 hippie kids were born in the Bay. Whether they ever liked that term or not is of no consequence, that's just what they got called at school. After thirty-odd years, their hippie parents can stand back and reflect upon their parenting. And despite a good half of those parents once being chronic marijuana smokers, cactus-pulp eaters or grovelling on their knees for mushrooms, even exhibiting the odd kleptomaniac tendency, not only have their kids turned out OK, but they have developed into some of the most creative individuals I have ever met. Better still, their social skills are second to none; maybe the clan effect of their upbringing played a big part in that.

New generations dream new dreams. The second generation of those alternative lifestylers and artists who made Golden Bay their home in the 1970s have already made their mark in wearable arts, graphic and fashion design. David Prebble and Sarah Hornibrooke came to Golden Bay in 1979, their dream to become goat farmers on their land at Kotinga. An amazingly creative sewer, Sarah was soon tutoring TOPS courses in wearable art at the Puramahoi Hall, long before it was anything to wow about. Her daughter Claire joined in most of them, so it was no wonder she would later win the World of WearableArt Supreme Award at age 18, and score a costume designing job at Weta Studios in Wellington.

One long-established artist, Sara Macready, now produces pen-and-watercolour artworks of identifiable Golden Bay subjects in her Commercial Street studio shop. The exterior is the mirror image of the one adjoining, which for two years was occupied by her daughter Hesta Macready, who makes one-off designer clothes as House of Hesta. They are also still tenants-in-common and busy cultivators on their seven hectares of hillside gardens just out of town. Intergenerational creativity is very much nurtured in Golden Bay.

I am more than happy with the way things have worked out for my own children. Joshua is a thriving jazz musician in Wellington, his keyboard and vocalist wife Adrienne making theirs a highly effectual partnership. Young dreamy Catherine, my first daughter, the one whose teacher said I'd ruined her education for ever, attended Victoria University studying anthropology before taking away a Top Achiever doctoral scholarship to Cambridge University in England. Her husband, Matthew Trundle, is a senior lecturer in classics at Victoria. My son Nesh launched his first hip-hop CD a while back, and I was astounded that his production team touted the name Hippy Kids. After being put down for so long as 'hippie kids', they are now acceptable, in fact rather cool, as Hippy Kids, Inc. He works half the year in Queensland and half in Golden Bay, where he continues to plug away making music and films. Nina came back from a year living with a family on Chiloe Island off Chile on an AFS student exchange, while Lucy continues at school – the whole world is her oyster. Earlier than any of the others, my youngest pegged out a hut site for herself. All of them at some time or other have worked at the Mussel Inn, just along the road. Earning their own money can never come too early for kids.

We still keep up with what Nesh's half-sisters are doing too, since they both lived at our place at one time or another. Allannah became for several years a full-time model after winning the Revlon Face of the Year, her gorgeous pouting look earning her big money in countries all around the world. Bethany now strongly identifies with her Ngati Kuri iwi from Northland, and has exhibited her multi-media artwork in Pacific cultural exhibitions as far away as Europe.

We are not exempt from catastrophes: what family is? Cole Chick, who was living with us as Nina's boyfriend for the entire time I was writing this book, was killed in a car accident just before his 20th birthday in June 2006. Close friends of our family have died before; indeed we have celebrated their lives with gatherings at our place, but nothing could have ever matched the shock of losing someone so wonderful yet so young; and without warning. Nearly 300 people turned up for his funeral held in our garden, which culminated in a drum 'n' bass party until dawn the following day. Just what he would have wanted.

A year before, Melanie, with her sister and brother, scattered the ashes of their grandmother on the island in the middle of our pond, on which now grows a graceful kowhai tree. I am convinced that our property, and particularly our garden, has taken on a 'patina', not only from the more formal, sombre events, but also from the celebrations for the weddings and birthdays that seem to happen on a near-continuous basis these days. It is all there just to enjoy. 'Superbarbie', the ferrocement and cast-iron junk barbecue I built alongside the ponds, is supplemented with rustic tables, covered areas, a rustic bar, seats and a stage for performance and bands. Catherine and Matthew's wedding was the last big happy celebration we held. His English relatives descended *en masse*, mixing so naturally in their formal clothes with some of our less-than-formal friends. Catherine's Anthropology lecturer gave me a herd of little plastic cows at the wedding, representing what would be her dowry in another culture. I felt so rich receiving them.

Melanie is content with painting in her studio and tending her vegetable garden these days. But I still often think of the simple Chinese saying, 'House finish, man die.' I know I will never finish all my projects around the place, but I have come to a sense, nearing the exciting age of 50, that the heavy work is over now. After the Millennium, there were two projects I felt some urgency to accomplish though, both of which invoked my Italian heritage. The first was to write a book, *Angelina*, about my Italian grandparents, Angelina and Vincenzo Moleta, who immigrated from Stromboli to a remote farm on D'Urville Island. As I put the book together, I realised it should be told mainly from the viewpoint of Angelina – Nonna, we called her. At the heart of the story was Angelina's high-born Maori friend Wetekia Ruruku Elkington, in whom my grandmother found both solace and mentor. Because the story as told through my mother was so much a part of my childhood, the experience of writing it was hugely cathartic. Not only that, but it was a gamble, approaching the truth via fiction – 'faction', my editor called it. As one reviewer put it, 'Risky technique maybe, but the boat came in.'

The other thing I had dreamt of was to produce our own wine, just enough for our own use. My planting of 140 pinot noir 10/5 variety vines grafted onto Schwarzman rootstocks in July 2002 created the little vineyard I had always wanted. Still a 'rascal digger' at heart, I dug everything by hand: drainage channels along each row, the 48 post and strainer holes, the holes for the vines themselves. The farmer next door had just had a 'drive' for hares, shooting 48 in one night alone, so at least the tender young vines did not have that pest to contend with. I hand-concreted all the posts in with river gravel. Finally I placed a wheelbarrow-load of white rocks around each vine to hold heat and conserve moisture. Everything I did by hand. Establishment costs for a commercial vineyard at the time were something like $48,000 a hectare, land included. My project came in at under $2,000 in total.

It is largely unappreciated that Golden Bay once had a flourishing wine trade. Francis Ellis gave up his struggling goldmining venture in 1868 to plant his first vines at Waiwera, now Clifton, in what must have been one of the country's earliest vineyards. An early English immigrant living next door lamented the cost of imported wines, and so encouraged his neighbour with some financial assistance, it is said. Ellis became a familiar sight along the 6-kilometre track from his 'Broxbourne' winery to the busy little river port at Waitapu – at the reins of his giant spring-cart laden with hogsheads of wine. Government employees in Wellington and Sydney created a steady demand, and F.H.M. Ellis & Sons even won all the top medals for their muscadine wine at the South Seas Exhibition of 1889. However, disaster struck the family business in 1925 when a flash-flood swept away virtually the entire vineyard, including all the maturing wine. For weeks afterwards, passing coastal vessels found barrels bobbing in Golden Bay.

Winemaking stopped here until Dave Heraud planted vines at Clifton in 1989 that produced the first Waiwera Estate vintage in 1993. He was inspired by travelling through the pinot vineyards in Brescia, Italy, that had similar limestone terrain to Golden Bay, just as he in turn inspired me. Pinot noir has proved a good choice for Golden Bay, with its erratic weather, as this variety produces acceptable fruit in all but the most exceptionally poor seasons.

My small planting will never produce the 1,000 bottles that one winegrower advised me be set aside for personal use each year – that's two bottles per day for the household, not so ridiculous if you include party consumption, and two or three hundred left over for gifts and trading – but it was a start to reducing our often hefty wine bill. If we can produce our own wine for our old age, we will be laughing indeed.

What I continue to do in that vineyard in the way of maintenance, pruning and harvesting seems to come entirely naturally to me. Just like the olive trees I put in over 20 years ago, those vines hark straight back to my family roots on the volcanic island of Stromboli. Every family owned at least two acres on the slopes above the village, where they could grow their sweet Malvasia grapes, capers, olives and vegetables. What I do pottering around my small-scale vineyard is exactly what my ancestors have been doing for hundreds of years. Our first crop of pinot in 2005 was only a dozen bottles, but the following was almost a hundred. My daughters trod the grapes in a big barrel, no doubt imparting their pheromones to the family wine. We get some guidance from Ruben, brewer and vintner at the Mussel Inn, but otherwise it's a family affair, and the result is highly drinkable too.

Working in that vineyard I can expect to see strange things, like a wild pig that went running through to my surprise the other day. And I can still call up a fernbird whenever I like. Lately I have not only heard a weka, but seen it, poking its way around the rows. What a blast to see that first one back in years! Reports of their calls and sightings have come in from people around inland fringes of the Bay. Perhaps they have gotten over the disease, or maybe it's been the concerted trapping of stoats and weasels that has finally tipped the balance back in their favour.

But that balance is a fine one. A weka sighting at Onekaka caused a flurry of excitement in that community also, around the same time I heard mine. This one had been spotted crossing the highway near the bridge over the Otere Stream. But just on dusk, a local woman ran over it while driving home from work. When she turned around to check on the bird she could see it was injured and trying to drag itself off the road to safety. But not for long, because around the corner came three cars in quick succession. 'Thump' over the weka went the first car, driven by the chairman of the Onekaka Biodiversity Group. 'Thump' went the second car, driven by a DOC ranger. And 'thump' went the third, a police car driven by the local constable. When the road was clear, the horrified woman went out onto the road to find her 'flatmate' weka reduced to the uniform thickness of thin card.

It's easy to say more will come along. But will they? Some situations, natural or otherwise, get better; others don't. Like the amalgamation of the Golden Bay, Motueka and Richmond county councils into the Tasman District Council in 1989. I personally believe that centralisation of services to Richmond was an expensive backwards step for our remote area. For a start, the Golden Bay County Council had built up an impressive inventory of equipment. Any emergency or road work could be responded to immediately at the discretion of a capable works manager who knew the district like the back of his hand. At his disposal were a fleet of graders, trucks and tractors ready to do the job. These were all removed over The Hill to Richmond, and services then tendered out to big business. Instead of one contractor being responsible for mowing the roadside, we now have four huge tractors plus support vehicles, all with flashing lights, that periodically come over from Nelson to do it in one hugely extravagant circus. Because they all act with standard imprecision, the roadside flax which binds their blades has become their declared enemy. Roadside tailoring techniques as employed by proud locals like Harry Wilson are no longer a requirement for the job.

Our rates go up and up, and the situation we find ourselves in plainly ridiculous. Around four years ago I noticed that a section of culvert that drains my swamp under the highway was collapsing. If it went completely, flooding of the main highway would be inevitable. So I called the TDC in Richmond.

'Sorry, we contract all that sort of thing out now, can you ring Sicon,' the receptionist instructed me. But the man at Sicon said they were only responsible to the Council for bridges and reserves. 'Better ring Transit, they do all the highways,' he advised.

The man at Transit New Zealand told me their highway inspection work was now being done by the consulting civil engineers Montgomery, Watts and Hazard, based in Nelson. 'Better ring them.' So I did, but they told me to ring Opus International Consultants, who had recently been contracted to advise them on impending maintenance. 'We'll be out your way soon, I'll drop in,' the Opus man said. At last I thought, some luck.

Two months later he turned up with a small digital camera, but he didn't seem interested in the culvert at all when I showed him. 'What's its number?' he just kept asking.

'What do you mean?' I said. 'It doesn't have a number. I've lived here for 30 years and it's never had a number.'

'Sorry, mate. It's *gotta* have a number on a peg somewhere,' he said. 'We can't fix it if it doesn't have a number. We're only on contract you know, and we gotta go by the book these days.'

I gave up at that point, deciding to fix it myself, which I did, digging out the offending section with a shovel and re-concreting it before filling in the washed-out section with gravel I carted in from Parapara Inlet.

Just 60 years ago, the 25-kilometre stretch from Takaka to Collingwood had seven roadmen permanently assigned to it, each responsible for a section of the gravel road. Harry Wilson of Onekaka used to be one of them. He told me he knew every culvert along his stretch nearly as well as each one of his kids. Every day he'd walk the full length of his section carrying his shovel, first on one side then back the other, tidying up water tables or re-spreading gravel as he went. Drivers in cars and horse-drawn traffic would more often than not stop to talk to him, keeping him up with the local gossip and road conditions right down to the state of all the big potholes throughout the district. He told me there was nothing he felt prouder of than his bit of road; in fact all the roadmen competed as to who could do the best job. It was a matter of great personal pride among them.

To tell the truth, I'm quite happy to be left alone these days, away from all the bureaucracy and regulations that burden us. When I'm not writing, spending time with my family, shooting out to the coast for some paua, or chopping firewood (the latter still taking me around two months every year), much of my spare time is spent quietly in and around my swamp. There is always something to do down there, keeping tracks clear and boardwalks maintained, cutting out invasive gorse and replanting trees like northern rata and kahikatea that once flourished around here. Encouraging an indigenous ecosystem is my priority, but I believe I am a realist: we'll never eradicate all the 'new' species, so I still am not averse to planting the odd flowering Australian eucalypt around the edges to encourage native birds to feed and deposit their droppings full of native seeds. And in the end there's nothing like the thought of growing your own firewood.

Maintenance has become an obligation, but there is something hugely rewarding about contributing, in a small way, to preserving the diversity and health of life around us. We must ensure that our last swamps never disappear. They must remain a refuge for the unobtrusive, where with patience, an individual – better still, a family – can go to witness the daily dramas of life in a small, fragile world.